W9-AGQ-103

THE MUSICIAN'S DAUGHTER

THE MUSICIAN'S DAUGHTER

SUSANNE
DUNLAP

NEW YORK • BERLIN • LONDON

Published by Bloomsbury U.S.A. Children's Books
175 Fifth Avenue, New York, New York 10010

Library of Congress Cataloging-in-Publication Data
Dunlap, Susanne Emily.
The musician's daughter / by Susanne Dunlap. — 1st U.S. ed.
p. cm.
Summary: In eighteenth century Vienna, Austria, fifteen-year-old Theresa seeks a way to help her mother and brother financially while investigating the murder of her father, a renowned violinist of Haydn's orchestra at the court of Prince Esterhazy, whose body was found near a gypsy camp.
ISBN-13: 978-1-59990-332-3 • ISBN-10: 1-59990-332-6
[1. Musicians—Fiction. 2. Murder—Fiction. 3. Family life—Austria—Fiction. 4. Haydn, Joseph, 1732-1809—Fiction. 5. Romanies—Fiction. 6. Vienna (Austria)—History—18th century—Fiction. 7. Austria—History—1740-1789—Fiction. 8. Mystery and detective stories.] I. Title.
PZ7.D92123Mus 2009 [Fic]—dc22 2008030307

First U.S. Edition 2009
Book design by Donna Mark
Typeset by Westchester Book Composition
Printed in the U.S.A. by Quebecor World Fairfield
2 4 6 8 10 9 7 5 3 1

To sweet Sofia and dearest Charles,
the two youngest people
in my family

THE MUSICIAN'S DAUGHTER

CHAPTER 1

The night it all began, I dreamt that Papa returned from the concert with a new violin for me. I lifted it out of its wooden case, excited to play it, but it slipped from my hands to the floor and smashed into splinters. I still remember how desperately sad I was, holding the one thing I wanted more than anything in the world—my own violin—and before I knew it I'd broken it beyond repair. In the dreams my father's face looked more sad than angry. I reached out to cling to him and ask his forgiveness, but he, too, slipped from my grasp, becoming a column of mist drawn out through my open window by the wind that banged the shutters against the house.

I woke up suddenly with the word "Papa!" in my throat. It took a moment before I realized that the knocking I heard was not the shutter from my dream, but someone at the door. A voice yelled, "*Machen-Sie auf!* Open up!"

At first I was relieved. No treasured violin had been

broken. Then I wondered who would make such a noise in the middle of the night. I pulled back the curtains around my bed, threw off the comforter, and ran in my bare feet to the door, dashing past my mother, who had also been awakened but could only hobble slowly because she was very pregnant.

"Theresa Maria! Get away from there. You'll be seen by God knows who in your shift!"

I didn't pause, not caring how I was dressed. When I reached the door, I drew the bolt and yanked it open. I hoped it was Papa, knocking because he had forgotten his key. We had all stayed up late waiting for him to return from playing the violin at a concert in Prince Esterhazy's winter palace. But he hadn't come, which wasn't so very unusual on a Christmas Eve, when there would be much merrymaking after his work was finished, so at last we had gone to bed. Mama had looked a bit worried, but I was certain Papa had simply gone drinking with his friends. The musicians would have received their annual bonuses from my godfather, Kapellmeister Haydn.

The next few moments were very confusing. Three men wearing cloaks with hoods drawn over their faces pushed into our apartment, struggling with a large, black sack between them. They laid the sack gently on the floor, and then one of them—I still can't remember which—took a small dagger and split it open down its middle.

"Maybe you shouldn't look," said a voice I recognized

as Heinrich's. He spoke with a rich baritone that reminded me of the horn he played.

"No, they will have to see him," said another of them, who I later realized was Jakob, the timpanist.

My mother stood next to me holding the lamp up high with one hand and clutching her shawl closed at her throat with the other. My little brother, Tobias, was still asleep, and Greta, the cook, hadn't stirred—nothing woke them. Mama and I were frozen to our spots like the icicles hanging from the eaves of St. Stephen's Cathedral. Just thinking about them made me shiver.

Or maybe I was shivering because of what the sack contained.

Even though I was several paces away and the light flickered in the wind that whooshed up the stairs through the still-open street door, I could see that it was my father. I recognized his slender face with its high forehead, pronounced cheekbones, and the tiny dent in his chin. But why wasn't he moving? And why was his mouth so dark? I crept closer, fascinated and repelled at the same time, until I could see that the strange color was from the dried blood that had caked on his lips and frozen in a trail out of one corner of his mouth and down his cheek.

My mother had inched forward with me, her hand on my shoulder. I felt her grip loosening and turned, catching hold of the oil lamp just as she crumpled into a heap on the floor. The men, who had stood around breathing heavily after their exertion, sprang into action, two of them rushing over to help Mama. I don't know what made me do it exactly then, but I puked all over the boots of one of them, realizing as I did so that it was poor Heinrich, and noticing vaguely that his boots were covered with sandy mud.

CHAPTER 2

The third man, the one I had not yet identified, approached and spoke to me from deep within his dark hood. "Are you all right, Rezia?"

I didn't look up. I didn't have to. Only Zoltán called me Rezia. Zoltán was one of the young Hungarian musicians Kapellmeister Haydn had engaged to play in the string section of the orchestra. He was good enough at both the violin and the viola to fill in wherever necessary, and sometimes even played the cello. "I'm better now," I answered. "Someone should take care of Mama. She is near her time."

Even before I spoke, Heinrich had scooped my mother up in his arms and Jakob opened the door of her bedchamber. The two of them went through to settle her just as Greta emerged from her sleeping alcove, looking like a mountain of snow in her huge white nightgown and cap.

"Fetch a doctor!" she said.

Zoltán shook his head. "It is too late now."

"No, for Madame Schurman. The shock—it is not good for a lady in her condition."

"I'll go," said Jakob, who had just returned from Mama's room.

Zoltán had his hood off now, revealing his face, still wet from the snow, and still handsome despite the drawn look and the shadows beneath his eyes. I glanced out the window and could see the big flakes coming down in the dark, slapping now and again against the panes. Zoltán would not look directly at me.

I had the most peculiar sensation that I was still in my dream, only my dream had become real and transformed into a nightmare. Every so often a wave of something terrible washed through me, but I was afraid to let it take over, and I willed my heart and mind not to feel anything. There would be time later. As Zoltán spoke, I knelt down by my father's side and picked up his left hand. It was very cold. I knew it was his because I could feel the calluses on the tips of his fingers that had come from years of pressing down and sliding along cat-gut strings on a fingerboard. His calluses were harder than the ones that had just started to form on my own fingertips from playing the viola—not the violin, which was what I really wanted to play.

"You have to tell me," I begged Zoltán. "You have to tell me what happened."

"We don't know. We found him like this."

"Where? Why?" I wanted answers. Right away. I wanted answers or I wouldn't believe it. Papa wasn't really dead.

He would open his eyes and wake up, laughing at the joke he'd played on us all, just like Godfather Haydn, who led the orchestra and was always playing jokes.

Zoltán held a handkerchief out to me. "I can tell you nothing more."

At first I didn't understand what the handkerchief was for, but when I touched my cheeks, I realized they were wet. *I must be crying,* I thought. I took the cloth and buried my face in it.

I had the briefest hope that when I looked up again, I would discover that none of what had happened that evening was real. Of course, it all was. I cast my eyes around the parlor, which somehow felt overcrowded and empty at the same time. I knew that room without ever having really noticed it before. All the familiar landmarks were there: the hooks on the back of the door, the new black stove in the corner, the chairs with their seats worn shiny from years of sitting. Yet something was wrong—missing.

All at once I realized what it was. "Where is Papa's violin?" My father never went anywhere without his violin, and he would have had it after the concert for certain. The violin was as much a part of him as his right arm.

"I cannot say. We found him, that is all, and it was too late."

"Don't *you* know anything?" I asked, turning to look toward Heinrich, who had returned to the parlor.

"Perhaps you and your brother could come and stay with us for a few days," Heinrich said.

I didn't want to stay in Heinrich's noisy household.

He had six children, with a daughter about my age who used to be my friend, and I would no doubt be called on to help change soiled linens and give the older ones their lessons. No. And I needed to stay here with my mother, and if I stayed, so would Toby. He was only eight. I thanked God that he was still asleep. I wanted to be able to explain it all to him when he woke up, before he had time to be confused and frightened. Yet why wouldn't anyone tell me what had really happened? "Where? Where did you find him?" I asked again.

Heinrich was about to answer, but Zoltán stepped forward and cut him off, giving him a fierce look. "By the river, some way out of town."

I thought about this for a moment. "The concert was at the palace."

"We went—," Zoltán began, then passed his hand across his forehead. "We went to the tavern afterward."

Suddenly I felt as if someone had driven nails through my knees and I would never again rise from the floor.

"Did he fall? Was it an accident?" I looked back and forth between Heinrich and Zoltán.

Zoltán shook his head but did not look at me. "No. It was no accident. Someone must have killed him. Perhaps a thief."

This was too much. I could not think about that. Not yet. And I could not stay there, in the middle of our parlor, in the middle of the night. Papa could not stay there. Zoltán and Heinrich and Jakob, when he returned with the apothecary, could not stay there. "What must I do?"

"He should be laid out, soon. Do you know how?" Heinrich asked.

I was about to shake my head "no," but then I realized that I did know how. I had watched the women dress my grandmother's body for burial the year before. They closed her eyes, washed her down, and put her in her favorite clothes before folding her hands across her breast. I remembered that there were three of them, though, and she had been on a table. And they had a casket in which to place her afterward. "I know how it's done but I'll need some help."

At that moment, I heard the sound of a curricle drawing up before the door at the street, and the jingling of harness bells and the squeak of springs complaining as someone got down from it. Hurried but quiet footsteps on the stairs followed. Jakob entered without knocking, leading in the apothecary, Herr Morgen, and his wife. They crossed themselves when they saw my father.

"I'll see to Frau Schurman," Herr Morgen murmured, stepping gingerly around my father's body to pass through to the bedroom, where Greta had remained. I could hear my mother moaning like a dying cat. I wanted her to be quiet so that Toby would stay asleep, so that I could have until morning to think of what to say to him. "Oh Papa," I whispered.

"What's to do, what's to do," Frau Morgen muttered, getting right to work around me. I didn't move.

I heard the three musicians who had brought my father's body home all shuffle out of the apartment at once. I'd like to think it was Zoltán who rested his hand on my head for a moment before he left.

My mind was racing and numb at the same time. What could have happened? Father was well liked, and always with his friends. Who would have murdered him? And his violin—where was it? Had it been stolen or just lost?

"Hold that, my dear," Frau Morgen said. I took the bit of sacking in my fingers, not looking. "Now, you wash his face and I'll take care of the rest."

I took the damp cloth Frau Morgen gave me and wiped at the blood on my father's mouth, but I had to turn away.

"That's all right, dear," she said, taking back the cloth. "Tomorrow we'll see about a funeral. Do you have any money?"

I couldn't answer. Papa was supposed to bring the money that night. Just once a year, I felt as if we were rich. Last year the gift from the prince had paid for our new stove. This year it was to be for Toby, to purchase his apprenticeship to a violin maker.

"That's odd," Frau Morgen said, more to herself than to me.

"What?" I asked, still unwilling to look.

"Well, just that you'd think they'd have stolen this. It looks valuable."

She extended her hand toward me. Lying in her palm, coiled up like a tiny, sleeping snake, was a medallion on a chain. It appeared to be made of gold. I turned my palm upward, and she let the chain and the medallion fall from her hand to mine. It felt heavy and cold. Perhaps it really was gold.

"A family piece?" she asked.

I shrugged. "I suppose." The medallion had some writing on one side in an odd language, and on the other the head of a hawk or an eagle. In truth I had never seen it before and could not imagine what it was doing in my father's possession. But I didn't want to get into a long discussion with Frau Morgen, so I slipped it into the pocket of my shift.

"Now let's move your dear papa. The table in the dining room will do." Greta and Herr Morgen came out just in time to help us.

I believe that was the moment at which I began to laugh. Not just a stifled giggle, but helpless, tears-in-the-eyes guffawing. All at once the image of us seated around the table together, plates empty and knives at the ready with the esteemed Herr Antonius Schurman, violinist in His Highness Prince Esterhazy's orchestra stretched out like a centerpiece, was too hilarious. And now that he was all tidy and his eyes had been closed, my father looked as though he were just taking a quiet nap and would awaken, refreshed, at any moment, and enjoy the joke with us. There was something different about him, though. The man I knew who had taught me his love for music along with the skill to play, despite my mother's complaints that a viola was no fit instrument for a lady to master, had never been in the house that evening. He was somewhere else. Looking down from above, perhaps, for I had no doubt that, faults and all, he had gone straight to heaven.

So, shaking with unseemly laughter, I helped Frau Morgen, Herr Morgen, and Greta shift the stiff body from its place on the floor to a state approaching dignity on the table, where we most certainly would not break our fast the next morning.

CHAPTER 3

I thought a lot, at the beginning, about my father playing the violin. I still remember the first time I ever saw a concert. I was very small, and we had just come to Esterhaza, a magnificent palace in Sopron, Hungary, when the prince's household moved there from his winter palace, at Eisenstadt, near Vienna. I think it may have been the first concert Papa took part in there. I had a new dress for the occasion, and Mama looked beautiful. I don't think Toby was born yet, or if he was, he was a small baby and stayed in our rooms with a nurse.

The palace at Esterhaza was so new that it still smelled of raw wood and paint. The rooms were very grand. I had never seen so many candles in one place before. And they were expensive wax candles, not foul-smelling tallow. We stood to the side to watch the fine ladies enter. I thought they looked like dolls, their faces were so perfect. Later my mother told me that they painted them with white lead to make their skin artificially smooth and pale, and then rubbed rouge into their cheeks and lips, and drew lines of charcoal around their eyes so they would appear larger. And the headdresses—in those days the fashion was to have hair that towered up, stuck into place with diamond combs, with ribbons and pearls festooned around. And no matter what color it was naturally, ladies powdered their hair to snowy whiteness, so that the light of the candles was magnified by the glow from the people themselves.

And the men, too, were powdered and patched. Their gold buttons and lace were almost as gaudy as the ladies' finery. But the enormous panniers that held the ladies' skirts out to the side so far that they had to move sideways through doorways fascinated me most of all. I could barely be persuaded to turn my eyes to the orchestra when the concert started.

We were not seated with the guests. In fact, I think we were tucked away in an anteroom. The door was open so we could see through, and everyone pushed me forward to let me watch my father, who looked up now and again from the music and gave me a quick smile. The candlelight danced over the rich wood of his violin, the beautiful Italian instrument, an old Amati, that my grandfather had given him. Kapellmeister Haydn—who was also my godfather—sat at the harpsichord, smiling broadly all the time, waving one hand in the air to direct, then putting it back on the keys and instead using his head, bobbing and nodding to bring the winds in, or to indicate the entrance for the cellos. He looked like the music, I remember thinking. I wish I could bring that particular sound to my mind, but it has since blended with countless other concerts. I'll always remember what it looked like, though. The light. The shimmering glow of everything and everyone.

⁂

That morning, the day after the bleakest Christmas I had ever spent, I had to deal with the awful reality of getting my father buried. He became a macabre object, now that his soul was gone. I tried to remember everything I could about him. Already some of his expressions seemed to have faded from my memory. The sound of his voice was very clear, though. I kept it in my mind as I watched the gravediggers dump his wrapped-up body into a large pit with a dozen other poor souls who lacked the money for a private grave.

It's not really Papa.

I clung to that thought. His spirit would never be buried. His body was only the useless shell of flesh and bone that descended into the earth.

Yet when I thought about it, I had so little of him except insubstantial snatches of memory—memories, and the medallion Frau Morgen had found in my father's pocket. I had put it on as soon as I had a private moment and worn it ever since. The medallion was not very large—barely as big as my thumbnail—and I had tucked it inside my bodice, thinking I might find an opportunity to ask Zoltán if he had ever seen my father with it before. I hadn't shown it to Toby. Its unaccustomed weight around my neck, the tickling of it against my skin, kept reminding me of everything I didn't know.

When the gravediggers had finished letting the different-sized parcels of the dead tumble from the cart and into the ground, everyone in the small, ragged group of mourners assembled outside the cemetery gates began to trudge off in different directions. The day before, Zoltán had told me that he wanted to bring more of the members of the orchestra to the burial, but I was ashamed. It was not right that Papa should be interred with so little ceremony. If my mother could have said anything, I believed she would not have wanted more witnesses than strictly necessary, either. On the other hand, if my mother were able to say anything, she might have been able to tell us where we could find money to pay for a better funeral. But the funeral was not the most important thing. Better to wait until everything was clearer; then I could pay for a special Mass for Papa. Perhaps Godfather Haydn would compose the music, and no one need ever know we had sent my father to a pauper's grave.

Toby, Zoltán, and I were by far the most respectable-looking people there. The others were little better than beggars. I was suddenly furious. How could this have happened? How could my father, who had promised he would teach me to play the viola no matter what Mama said and one day buy me a violin; who promised he would earn enough money so that I could have a silk gown and attend one of the public balls in a year or two, when I was old enough; who told us stories and laughed, who scooped us up in his arms with joy—how could he have been so careless as to go drinking and end up murdered, leaving me with so many unanswered questions?

I knew it was unreasonable to be angry, but I turned away from the sight of that horrid burial and started walking back toward the city gate, not caring whether Zoltán and Tobias came along or not. They did, of course.

It had been awful, telling Toby what had happened while he slept. He had never seemed smaller to me than when his impish face crumpled into confused tears at the sight of Papa stretched out on the table. Since then, he had not let me out of his sight. And Zoltán had been hovering like a great sheepdog, too, showing up at dawn on Christmas morning, the day after he had found my father, and staying as long as was decent, then helping me by finding two or three vagrants who would shoulder my father's body to the burial cart for the price of a few Kreutzer.

There were no formalities, no papers to sign for someone so poor.

But we weren't that poor! The skirts that caught between my legs and made it impossible for me to run were of fine, soft wool. And unlike a really poor girl, I could afford the pocket hoops and petticoats required to make them hang properly, even if they were of coarse linen and had no lace or ruffles. My feet were well shod in good leather boots. My hands, clenched in tight fists that made them colder instead of warmer, were hidden inside a muff of softest rabbit fur.

The musical instruments in their cases at our apartment—which we owned, thanks to a rare moment of generosity on the part of my late grandfather—could be sold for enough money to support two families.

I stopped so abruptly that Toby, who had practically been on my heels, crashed right into me.

"Watch where you're going!" I snapped.

"It's not my fault."

Those were the first words Toby had spoken since the morning before. He only came up to my shoulder, and had to lift his chin to look into my eyes. I noticed then that his best coat wasn't buttoned correctly. I took off my muff and let it dangle on its cord while I unbuttoned and rebuttoned his coat and made sure his cloak was fastened at the neck. He continued to stare at my face, as if he was still waiting for me to explain myself.

"The question is, where is Papa's violin?" I asked, not really expecting an answer from my brother, but suddenly realizing no one had even attempted to answer the same question the other night. I turned from the gaze of Toby's round, brown eyes to face Zoltán. Even though I wasn't in the mood to notice them at that moment, I had always found Zoltán's eyes unsettling. They were that indistinct color that sometimes looks green and sometimes blue, but the color didn't seem to matter. It was something deeper inside them that made them extraordinary. I could never look into them for long without beginning to feel warm.

"I don't know," Zoltán said.

What use was he if he knew so little? I found myself growing cross at him, too. "It must have been stolen." Stolen, I prayed, not destroyed. That was something to think about later, when everything was clearer.

"Yes, perhaps it was. It was a valuable instrument."

Zoltán was right, but it still felt wrong. But then, everything felt wrong. In one night I had become the only person in the household capable of making decisions. Mama was incoherent, attended every few hours by the apothecary whom we could not afford, and fussed over by Greta, who left her side only to ensure that Toby and I were still alive. Toby was seven years younger than I was, and that was too young to become the head of a household. He needed my father even more than I did. I stole another glance at him. He was still looking at me, and he reached out his hand to take hold of my arm, but I turned and continued tromping back toward the center of the city, which meant crossing the cold, sluggish Danube by the city bridge and passing through one of the gates that pierced the Bastei, the thick wall that ringed the city. There was no mother present to yell at me for taking strides that were too big. And it helped me think, to walk so fast.

I kept going, not even noticing the cold or the fact that my shoes were wet through. But poor Toby! He was so small he had to run to keep up. Instead of entering the crowded streets, once the sentry had let us pass through the gate I mounted the stone steps to reach the top of the Bastei. It was cold and gray, so no one promenaded around it to take the air and enjoy the view over the city and the countryside. That suited me. I could stride as fast as I wanted to and not bump into a soul. I think we circled the city about five times. Only then did I calm down enough to realize that nothing would be accomplished by storming around in anger at our dead papa. When I finally stopped, Toby positively rattled with cold, and a light snow had begun to fall.

"Let's have something hot to drink," Zoltán said. He held his arm out in the direction of the steps down, and led us to a nearby café. Its small windows were completely steamed up. It would be warm inside, and crowded. I looked up at the sign. It was Biber's, a favorite place of the musicians in the prince's orchestra. I shot a questioning look at Zoltán, but he wouldn't meet my eyes. I wondered if somehow he had managed to steer us here, even though I was the one leading the way.

⁂

We entered, and suddenly the normality of the world that no longer contained my father hit me hard. People were talking loudly and laughing. Smoke from the men's pipes collected in a cloud near the ceiling. Someone plunked out a popular melody on the spinet in the corner. It was the day after Christmas, and everyone looked happy. A few heads turned as we entered, but mostly no one paid us any heed. Zoltán moved me gently aside and led the way to a table at the back.

"Drei Schokoladen," he said to the fellow hovering nearby, and I realized I had no money in my purse to pay for tea, let alone hot chocolate. I didn't remove my cloak or my gloves.

None of us said a thing until the three steaming glasses were set on the table that was barely big enough to hold them. Toby was first to break the silence, with "Thank you" as he wrapped his hands around his glass and brought it to his lips. I had knitted the mitts he wore and given them to him for Christmas. What a strange Christmas it was, with no ceremony. The stockings we had carefully arranged at the ends of our beds on Christmas Eve were not filled with sweets when we awoke on Christmas morning to a world that would never be the same for us.

I watched Toby drink his chocolate with deep concentration, as if it were the most important thing in the world to him right then. I knew I should thank Zoltán as well and drink my own cup of cocoa, but I was still so full of bitterness and anger that I didn't think I would ever be thankful for anything again.

"I spoke to Kapellmeister Haydn," said Zoltan. "He would have come, you know."

I twisted my gloves in my hands. Zoltán knew my reasons for keeping our group of mourners small. "Later. When Mama has recovered . . ." I couldn't summon the strength to finish the thought.

"Well, in any case he still wishes to see you," Zoltán said.

I nodded to let him know that I had heard what he said. I had been dreading this. We lived on Papa's stipend from the prince. No Papa, no income. Herr Haydn was my godfather, so he probably just wanted to tell me this grim news himself.

"He is here." Zoltán turned in his chair, and only then did I notice the familiar, wiry figure of Kapellmeister Haydn. He did not wear the blue-and-gold livery he was normally required to wear as a household officer of the prince. Instead he was dressed just like the other men in the tavern: a brown, cutaway coat with lace ruffles sticking out from the shirt underneath at the wrists and the neck. He had on black silk breeches with buckles, and white hose. As soon as he turned our way, though, I recognized his profile, and the kind light in his blue eyes.

"I was sorry to hear about Antonius," he said. "He was a fine violinist." Herr Haydn reached out and took my hand. His was warm and large. He placed something in my palm when he did so, and at first I thought he was playing one of his jokes on me. When we were little, he often made bits of paper appear from behind our ears, or pretended to find his pocket watch in our bowls of soup. But this was no joke. I could feel the coins through the soft leather of a bag. I looked up at him, puzzled.

"Your papa forgot to take his bonus away with him. I don't know why. He was in such good spirits after the concert."

I could not look at Godfather Haydn's face, or I knew all my efforts to be strong would be destroyed.

"If there is anything you need—anything at all—you must come to me. We stay in Vienna until Easter. Although without your father . . ." His tone made me raise my eyes. A shadow had passed across his face, but it vanished in a moment. He stood and patted Toby on the head. "Anything at all. Remember."

I watched him thread his way through the revelers and noticed then that his shoulders sagged and his chin sank down toward his chest. I had never seen him sad before. *He must be thinking about my father,* I thought.

"Finish your chocolate. You should be home," Zoltán said.

I had hardly tasted my treat, and in truth I didn't want it. But Zoltán stared at me. Perhaps I should pay, with the money Kapellmeister Haydn had given me? I started to open the pouch. Before I could tease apart the first knot in the cord, Zoltán's hand clamped down around mine. "Not here," he whispered. He reached into the pouch dangling from his own belt and tossed a copper Kreutzer on the table. I sipped the cocoa. It was bitter and sweet, and although I didn't think I would be able to finish it, I drank until the last drop was gone. "That's better," he said, and smiled. We all stood and left the café.

The gnawing anger I felt had abated somewhat, and I began to emerge from the fog that had prevented me from noticing my surroundings very much. "Was that why you brought us here? To meet with Kapellmeister Haydn?" I asked.

"Yes," Zoltán said. I expected him to elaborate, but he said nothing more.

"Do you rehearse tomorrow?" I asked again.

"Yes," he again replied.

Now that Papa was buried and Haydn had discharged more than his duty to us, I expected Zoltán, too, would return to his own life and not come around anymore. There was really nothing to bind us to anyone in the prince's court. Yet the idea of being so completely alone with my very pregnant mother and Toby, with only morose Greta as company, suddenly filled me with panic. I wanted to see Zoltán again, I wanted to keep some tie with my father's life, and thought quickly for what I could say that would allow that to happen without making an outright request. Besides, how else was I to find out any more information about the thief who had attacked my father?

"I want to go to the place where you found him." The words just leapt out of my mouth before I understood what I was asking. I immediately wished them unsaid.

"Tomorrow then, after rehearsal."

I was a little surprised that Zoltán didn't argue, or even refuse. Perhaps he had wanted me to ask. The last two days he had certainly seemed at times on the verge of telling me something, and then stopped himself. Perhaps he didn't know how much to say.

We continued in silence until we arrived at our apartment. Zoltán left us at the street. I watched him walk away. He was not bowed like Haydn, but straight, and there was music in his gait. “Come, Toby,” I said, and pulled my brother upstairs. I hoped Greta had thought about dinner. If not, it would be up to me to see what we had.

CHAPTER 4

Cold ham and boiled potatoes. And a bit of blood sausage and cheese. That was all there was. Toby and I sat in the parlor eating with our hands. I couldn't bear the thought of putting the food on the dining table just yet, even though Greta had scrubbed it thoroughly.

"Who will teach me my letters?" Toby asked. A bit of food dropped out of his mouth onto his lap.

I noticed that his knees looked bony through his breeches, and he had not buckled his shoes. His feet were already too big for his little body, just like Prince Nicholas's wolfhound puppies. Toby was going to be tall, like Papa. "I will," I answered. I couldn't think of anything else to say, and was too tired to scold him for being so messy.

The corners of his mouth puckered slightly, as they did when he used to cry as a baby. "Will Mama get up tomorrow?"

"She'll get up when she's well. Soon." I knew I wasn't

doing a very good job of reassuring him. I truly did not want him to cry. Usually I could stop him by making a funny face or taking his attention away from whatever it was—a bee sting, once, in the country, or the time he had worked for weeks building a tiny, wooden table and chairs and Greta had stepped on them when he arranged them on the floor to show me.

"I think I'll go fix that sailboat," he said.

I nodded. It was our secret signal, or at least, his half of it. "I'm going to fix the sailboat" meant that he wanted to be alone for a while. If I said, "I'm going to write to cousin Regina," then he knew not to disturb me. We had devised the system when he'd walked in on me nearly naked in the room we shared in Esterhaza, about a year before. I don't know which of us had been more embarrassed. Toby wasn't much like other boys I knew who were his age. The sons of the prince's cooks were always sneaking around trying to pull the laces that held my skirts on. Toby played with the boys, but reluctantly. He usually ended up bruised and crying. Sometimes I wished he was a little more like them so that he would just run off and play and leave me to myself. But now, I was glad he was there, even when we didn't say anything.

Toby turned before he left the room, his small child's hand on the doorjamb. "You're going to try to find out what happened to Papa, aren't you," he said, a statement instead of a question.

I didn't say anything. How could I? He turned away and closed the door behind him.

Right now, I had to make sure we could survive, at least until I figured out something else to do. I braced myself to go in to see my mother, who as far as I knew had not uttered a coherent sentence from the moment she had collapsed the night they brought my father's body home. Greta could do little else but tend to her. Mama was due to have the baby any day. I remembered her losing two other babies not long after calling us together to inform us that we would have a new sister or brother. Papa tried to tell us that we wouldn't after all, but he couldn't. Mama was stronger that way. She had wept and wept, but managed to squeeze out the words. It happened all the time, she said. God didn't always want his little ones to suffer on earth, and took them directly to heaven instead.

I didn't really mind so much, and I think Toby cried mainly because Mama was crying. It was hard to imagine a baby before it was born, and our apartment is small and I could not see how we would all fit anyway. Now, the thought of a baby that might look more like my father than Toby does, to remind me of him—I wasn't sure whether that made me happy or sad.

I ate what I could, then knocked on Mama's bedroom door.

⁂

"Come," Greta called.

"I'll sit with her," I said, leaving the door open behind me. "See if you can persuade Toby to eat some more. He's gone to his room." Greta clearly didn't want to leave Mama, but I was beginning to build up a mountain of questions, and some of them I wanted only my mother to hear. If she could hear them, that is.

My mother's face was pale, but her eyes were open and she stared at the ceiling. On the table by her bed Herr Morgen had left a beaker of greenish liquid and a packet of powder. The black-letter script on it said *laudanum*. I didn't know much about doctoring, but I knew that laudanum made people sleepy. I was surprised she was not fast asleep. *"Mutter,"* I said, perching on a stool next to her and whispering close to her ear. "Have we got any money?"

I know she heard me because she turned her head in my direction and smiled. I waited a bit, thinking she would answer, but she did not open her mouth.

"I need to know, Mama. Toby is to start his apprenticeship after Epiphany, and I must pay Herr Goldschmidt, the luthier."

Without the slightest indication that she understood what I had said, Mama turned her head slowly back so that she once more stared up at the ceiling. I found myself looking up to see what she was watching there, but it was nothing more unusual than a tiny spider hard at work on a web.

"Mama, have you ever seen this before?" I drew the medallion out of its hiding place inside my bodice and dangled it before her. This time she did not look in my direction. I picked up her hand, which was smooth and cool. It lay in mine like something inanimate, a glove, there for ornament rather than use. I placed the medallion in her palm. She did not close her hand around it. Clearly there was no point in talking to her now. She had gone somewhere else. Her face looked serene. The faint lines that had begun to show had smoothed out and she appeared younger. Although she had passed her first youth, Mama was still very pretty, with large blue eyes and long lashes. And when she smiled, her whole face glowed. She had not gotten fat, just a little plump, and looked very elegant when she was all dressed to attend one of Papa's concerts. Now, though, her big belly raised the blankets, and as I watched, I saw the lump shift slightly. The baby was still alive at least. If Mama did not eat, that state of affairs might not last long.

I placed her hand back on top of the coverlet and crept out of the room. Toby's plate was cleared away, so I assumed Greta had taken it down to the kitchen we shared with the other people in the building. Although Greta cooked our simplest meals on the stove in the dining room and we had our own pantry, the kitchen was where the water pump was located. And the cooks and kitchen maids from the other apartments spent many hours there peeling potatoes and turnips and gossiping. I could only imagine what they were saying about Papa. Perhaps I should ask them if they knew something—anything—that might explain why someone had murdered one of the kindest men in Vienna, who had never harmed anyone, as far as I knew.

I took a candle and passed through the dining room to

my own small nook. Normally I was happy to be in Vienna instead of at the prince's court in Esterhaza. In Vienna we had this apartment, a real home with furniture that belonged to us. In the prince's palace, we had two rooms, with an extra little alcove for Greta. Toby and I had to sleep in the same bed there. It wasn't so bad when he was small, but now that he was older, he flailed his arms and took up all the space. He had nightmares, too, and sometimes woke up crying. And just this past summer I had started to bleed. Papa had said he would make Toby his own cot. I did not want to be sharing a bed with my brother when I was already a woman.

In Esterhaza, we ate in the servants' hall. It was grand enough, and the food was much better than Greta's stews. Sometimes we had parties, at holidays and on the prince's birthday, and would be served boar's head and pheasant and everything the fine folks ate. Afterward, there was always music. I liked it best when we were allowed to sit in the corner of the private music room, while Haydn, my father, Zoltán, and the principal cellist, Herr Schnabl, played string quartets. There were usually only a few guests, and the playing would go on until very late at night. Toby sometimes fell asleep. I'd have to half carry, half drag him back to bed while my father was still playing. I'd go to sleep with the beautiful music ringing in my ears, and often I would dream about it all night. But still I preferred home.

My room was small—Papa had carved two spaces out of a single one when we first moved in, so that there could at least be a thin wall between me and Toby. My part was just big enough for the bed with a chest for my clothes at its foot, and a table and stool so I could write. On the table lay the plain, wooden case that held my viola. Mr. Goldschmidt had made the viola for Papa many years ago, when he had to double up during a lean time for the prince. He was paid extra for playing both instruments, and I remember how happy Mama was. Now the court was wealthy, so he earned—or rather he used to earn—just the violinist's stipend. He preferred to play the violin. I, too, would have preferred the violin, but the viola was better than nothing, and it was my own. I was determined one day to make music as my father did.

I knew I was a good student. I had planned to continue being one. I practiced whenever I could, which was whenever I had no other chores and when Mama was either not at home or too busy to notice and complain. "Playing the viola will not get her a husband, and she cannot work for her keep," she said so often I could hear her voice repeating it now. "At least, no daughter of mine will ever work. There is her dowry, you know. Her uncle Theobald will see that she gets it when the time comes."

I thought about Uncle Theobald as I unlaced my gown and let my skirt with its bone hoops drop to the floor. He lived in a grand house in the Graben, near Stephansplatz. I didn't remember ever being inside it, but in the evening whenever we happened to pass by it, I could tell that the rooms were very large because the windows were tall and wide.

I shivered. My chamber was too small for a stove, and in any case the one in the parlor had been left to go out by now. I pulled a shawl off my bed and tied it around my waist, then took another and tied it across my shoulders. I wanted to think a little before I went to sleep, and I was afraid if I lay down, fatigue would claim me instantly.

Just a year ago I had started to wear stays. Mama noticed that my breasts had begun to bulge. Now, I felt naked without the boning that held me tight. My breasts weren't much—still not enough to mound out over the top of my bodice—but like this, in my chemise, I could see them quite clearly. Standing in the near dark wearing loose clothes, I felt as free as one of the Gypsies who wandered the countryside near Esterhaza.

I had once heard a Gypsy man play the violin. It was at carnival, when traveling players sometimes came to court. Puppeteers and acrobats, clowns and dancers all gathered to try to get a bit of money from the prince. There was a masked ball, and Toby and I and the other musicians' children had been allowed to creep into the stairwell and see the grand ladies and gentlemen in their costumes.

Some of the costumes were magnificent, all covered with jewels that caught the light of thousands of candles. Others were just funny. Two nobles had dressed like bears, clearly having used the same tailor to make their garments.

They walked up to each other as if approaching a mirror, then turned with the same shrug and walked away, which only made the impression that they had stopped at an invisible looking glass all the more vivid.

But everyone stepped back and cleared a path for a scruffy, dirty man in bare feet, wearing a bright yellow waistcoat trimmed in bits of lace that had been salvaged from other garments and carrying a violin, who had somehow managed to gain access to the ballroom. He walked right down the middle of the floor toward the prince with his head held high, a proud smile on his face. His teeth were beautiful and white in his dark skin. He made a low, courtly bow to Prince Paul Anton (the father of the one Papa had worked for), then without asking permission, began to play.

The violin he put to his shoulder was very fine. I could see that even from where I stood. And the music he drew from it sounded like angels weeping. He played a simple folk melody, but with such passion that everyone in the ballroom attended to him. When he finished, the prince begged to hear more, but the Gypsy shook his head, bowed, and left. I could not take my eyes away from him, wondering if his face was dark because it was dirty or because his skin was naturally that color. He would have walked right away without even one Gulden had the prince's steward not rushed up to him with a velvet bag of coins.

I was tired from the events of the last few days, but

thoughts and memories kept flooding my mind. I approached my viola and rested both my hands lightly atop the rough wooden case. I had not opened it since the day before Papa died. I let my fingers trail over the now splitting edges to the latches that held it closed. I opened first one, then the other, and lifted the lid. The viola was wrapped in linen cloths, hidden out of sight, but the bow lay temptingly on top. I picked it up, turning the screw on the end to tighten the horsehairs. From there it was natural to take the crumbling block of resin, hold the bow with the frog toward me, and run the resin up and down until the hairs were evenly covered. It had taken me a while to learn how much to use. Without it, the hairs would not grip the strings and the sound would be faint. Once I had finished, I replaced the resin and teased the protective cloths away from the viola so that it was exposed, like a baby in a cradle.

At first I did not want to lift it. Instead I crooked my finger under the D string above the bridge and plucked it. Not quite a D, of course. It needed tuning. But it was late, and I would disturb my mother if I took up the viola to tune and then play.

Then I realized that Mama was in a state where nothing would disturb her, and Toby was deep in his sound sleep. Before I could change my mind, I grasped the instrument by the neck and raised it out of its cloth nest, settling it in the crook of my left arm, just below my shoulder. The viola was almost too big for me, and my arm was close to straight when I reached for the tuning pins. I started with the lowest, the C string, the one the violin didn't have, and worked my way up to the sweet A. I longed to have that higher string, the E, to play the most pungent notes, but the viola has a melancholy quality of its own that the violin cannot match. Papa used to say that a violist has to be stronger and gentler than a violinist, and that once you master the viola, the violin is easy. But I think he just said that so I wouldn't yearn so for a violin.

Violin or viola, playing is not easy. But I love to do it more than anything in the world. I cannot imagine my life without the sensation of holding a delicate, living piece of hollowed-out wood strung with catgut in one hand, and drawing a perfectly balanced bow across the strings with the other. The viola, resting just below my throat and against my upper arm, becomes my other, deeper voice.

I closed my eyes, at first only thinking the sounds, but soon I knew my hands and arms had taken up the melody inside me and made it spill out to fill the room. When I play, everything except the music disappears. That night, until the candle started to sputter, there was no Papa in his grave, no Mama so sick she was insensible, no money lacking—and no missing violin.

But playing the viola forever would be like diving under water and never coming up again. I was not ready to bid the world farewell, and so when my left arm became tired, I laid the viola down, wrapped it up well, placed the bow on top of it, and latched the case closed. Whether I wanted to or not, I had to think, or what was left of our world would crash around our ears.

Before I took off my shawls and climbed between the sheets, I opened the pouch Godfather Haydn had given me in the café. Five silver Thaler spilled out into my hand. It was a great deal of money, perhaps more than my father had received from the prince as a Christmas gift. Why did Haydn make this gesture? How would I ever repay him? For I was certain that Papa had received his bonus along with everyone else, and that his murderer had stolen it—or if not his murderer, then some waiting vagrant, a scavenger. Yet if the money had been stolen, and the violin as well, why not the gold medallion, which now hung around my neck like a burden?

Someone must know something. There was nothing to be done about it that night, though. I turned my thoughts to what I should do in the morning to begin finding out what had really happened on Christmas Eve. All Zoltán had said was that Papa had left his friends in the tavern, a little drunk but still in possession of his wits. He had said he was going home—or so Zoltán told me. He didn't look in my eyes when he said it. Maybe Zoltán was lying. But why would he? It did not make sense.

And then there was the matter of our daily life. I would have to talk to Greta and ask her to tell me what credit we had with the grocer and the butcher. I would visit Uncle Theobald and beg him for my dowry early. I did not care if I never married. After that, I would go to the prince's palace and wait for Zoltán to finish his rehearsal, so that he would take me to the place where they had discovered Papa. Once I'd done all that, I couldn't begin to imagine what would happen next.

CHAPTER 5

Persuading Greta to give me any information about our household accounts felt like trying to pry the secret to a magic trick from a magician.

"Your mama is in charge."

"But Mama is not speaking, and we must have money to buy food."

Greta had laid half a loaf of yesterday's bread and some cold sausage on the table. Toby was clearly ravenous, and did not blink at the idea of what had occupied the table only the day before, which surprised me. Usually he was so sensitive about things. In truth, I knew I had to overcome my own revulsion and let life return to normal, but I could not take a seat in my usual chair. Instead I clutched a crust and walked up and down as I ate.

Greta folded her stout arms across her bosom and clamped her lips together.

"If you will not tell me exactly our state of affairs, I shall simply go to the butcher myself and ask. Then everyone will know our difficulties and we will all be turned out on the street." The Viennese merchants were not known for their compassion. They would go to the magistrates without delay and force us to sell our possessions to pay them what they were owed. I needed exact information before I could make a plan.

I saw the fear in Greta's eyes, which she shifted in Toby's direction.

"Toby, there's a good fellow, take a plate into the parlor so Greta and I can clear things up." I didn't expect him not to hear or at least to guess what we were saying—he was too smart for that—but I thought that making him leave might give Greta an excuse to be honest with me.

Toby scooped up what was left of the bread and skittered off to the next room—leaving the door slightly ajar. Greta reached into her pocket and pulled out her key ring, then opened the strongbox that contained the family plate and a few pieces of silver jewelry, as well as whatever currency we had in the house. Since we were not completely destitute, I did not tell her about the money from Kapellmeister Haydn or the gold medallion. Something told me I would need my own resources for other things.

Aside from a few paper *Banco-Zettel*, which I knew the local merchants preferred not to take, we possessed only twelve Gulden and twenty Kreutzer—enough to purchase bread for a few weeks, a ham, and two dozen eggs, and perhaps some poultry. The money I had from Herr Haydn would last a month if we were very careful. "What have we in the larder?" I asked.

Without a word, Greta led me down to the kitchen below, unlocked our larder door, and showed me a dressed fowl, twenty sausage links, eight eggs, a tun of beer, and a sack each of potatoes and turnips. We would not starve—yet. Upstairs we had a box of tallow candles and a gallon of lamp oil, and I knew Papa had got in wood for the stoves that should last the winter. I hoped that he had paid the rent for January at least. That would give me a month to figure out how to get fifteen Gulden to pay the next month's rent. If only we had father's violin to sell, we could buy Toby's apprenticeship and live for a year at least, which would give me time to figure out how to gain a more secure income.

I thanked Greta, put on my cap and cloak, and walked out into the cold streets. I thought at first I might visit the grocer. The idea that we could possibly have an unsettled account there disturbed my peace about my reckoning with Greta, and I longed to know that we were out of debt. But if I went, and the account was very much past due, I could be forced to pay him and deplete our supply of emergency cash. Better to see if other sources of funds could be secured first. I turned my steps toward Uncle Theobald's grand house.

The day was cold but sunny. The brightness cheered everyone, and shopkeepers nodded to me as I passed by their windows, still decorated with fir branches and holly boughs for the Christmas season. I loved the way the city smelled at that time of year. The scent of pine and wood smoke created a fragrance that I forever associated with holidays.

The door of Uncle Theobald's mansion was garlanded with fir branches, and candles illuminated all twelve of the street-facing windows—an incomparable luxury at that time of day. Surely someone who could afford such a display of wealth could spare something for his ill, widowed sister and her children?

I lifted the brass knocker and let it fall from my hand against the shiny plate. My breath puffed out in white clouds while I waited. I didn't realize I had been walking so fast, and now I was a little winded. After what seemed like a long time I heard footsteps approaching on the other side of the door. Three bolts were drawn, and the door opened just a crack. I saw a young face—a serving girl perhaps my age—peek out through the opening. I suppose if I had been a liveried attendant announcing the arrival of a carriage she would have thrown the door wide to welcome my masters. But instead she kept it nearly closed.

"Who are you?"

"I am Fräulein Theresa Maria Schurman," I said, "come to visit my uncle Theobald Wolkenstein."

She stared at me blankly. We had not visited Uncle Theobald since I was a babe in my mother's arms. Mama's family was distressed that she had married only a poor musician, and to punish her had turned their backs on her completely. It was Papa who told me about her visit to them to inform them of her husband's prestigious court appointment, proudly carrying me, thinking they would regret their harsh treatment of her and welcome us as family. But the only result was that Uncle Theobald had agreed to furnish me a dowry—so long as we never darkened their door again. Mother only ever mentioned the dowry part of the story, but I knew the complete truth. Standing there returning the maid's puzzled look made me wonder what could have possessed me to think I should come to Uncle Theobald for help when it was obvious that he wished we did not exist. I was getting cold. "He's expecting me," I lied, and stepped forward. The maid, whose eyes were set deep in her head and whose chin jutted unattractively, had no choice but to let me in.

She ushered me into a large front parlor, then hurried off to find someone else, I hoped my uncle. I had seen him only from a distance, and although I thought I would recognize him because he must resemble my mother in some way, I was not confident that I would know to greet him if he came upon me by surprise.

I was too nervous to sit, so I wandered around the room, picking up knick-knacks and looking at them without really seeing what they were. The room was much bigger than our parlor, but so full of upholstered furniture, porcelain figurines, and pictures that it felt smaller. Somewhere a clock ticked. I tried to follow the sound to see where it came from, but the surfaces of the room bounced it around. Eventually, I spotted a small brass timepiece on the mantel, almost hidden between two plaster lions. I could not imagine what it would be like to live among so many unnecessary possessions.

Just as I was beginning to give up hope of seeing my uncle, the door to the room opened to admit a distinguished gentleman wearing a powdered bob wig and a green velvet coat. His dress was rather formal for midmorning, but I simply assumed that, like Kapellmeister Haydn, Uncle Theobald had some court position—perhaps even worked for the empress herself—that required a uniform. Although I did not see much resemblance to my mother in his features, I decided that I had to impress upon him immediately the dire nature of our circumstances. I put the back of my hand to my forehead and uttered a cry of distress, just as I had seen the opera singers in Esterhaza do, then ran forward and threw myself at my uncle's feet.

To my immense surprise, he did nothing. I tried hard to cry tears, but I could not. I had so effectively dammed them up after that first night that I was unable to pretend to be weeping with any conviction. Soon I just stopped and lifted my face.

"Herr Wolkenstein is not presently at home."

What had I done? I saw the smile playing around the fellow's lips. He must have been no more than a valet, and I had made a fool of myself in front of him. He did not reach down to help me up, and my toe caught in the hem of my underskirt so that I nearly fell over again. Once I was upright, I lifted my chin and stared him down.

"The parlor maid said you claim to be Herr Wolkenstein's niece?" he said.

"No, I do not *claim* to be. I *am* his niece, and am in need of his—" If I said "money," I might well be tossed out on my ear. Running through the possible reasons for my unexpected visit, I landed on "Advice."

This response did not impress the valet. "Many people seek the councilor's advice. I suggest you petition him in his office at the Hofburg." He held the door open as if he expected me to walk through it.

Instead I spoke again. "But how many of them are his niece?" *There, I've caught you*, I thought.

He sighed. "A great many, I fear."

I opened my mouth to speak, but nothing came out. His words caught me completely by surprise, and so I walked past him into the vestibule and waited for him to open the main door for me. I refused to behave like a servant when Herr—apparently Councilor—Wolkenstein was in truth my relative. He waited, I assumed to see if I would be stubborn, then walked in three long steps to the door and opened it. I stopped in the doorway so that he could not shut it. "Please be so good as to tell my uncle Theobald that Theresa Maria called. I wish to discuss a matter of business."

I whirled around and walked calmly away. Truth be told, I felt like running home as fast as I could, but I forced myself to keep my chin level and my pace sedate. The morning's adventure had been completely unsatisfactory. I heard the bells in the Stephansdom chime eleven times, and my stomach rumbled angrily. I had not eaten more than a few bites since Christmas Eve.

The fine morning began to cloud over, and the air had that icy dampness that foretold snow. I slowed my pace. I did not want to return home with no progress made in any direction.

It was a little too early to go to Prince Esterhazy's winter palace to meet Zoltán. Yet if I went right away to the *Wallnerstrasse*, where it rose in all its splendor from the other buildings around it, I would have time to seek out Kapellmeister Haydn before rehearsals started. Perhaps my father had said something to him that would indicate that someone bore him a grudge, or someone coveted his violin, if that had been the cause of the attack. I still could not imagine anyone wanting to harm Papa. He was all goodness and music, treating everyone kindly and always giving a few spare *Pfennigs* to the beggars most people simply ignored.

I turned my steps toward the north. I felt anxious, but I decided there was no sense delaying an interview with the man who had already been very kind to me, and whom Papa had respected more than anyone else in the world.

CHAPTER 6

I knew my way around Prince Nicholas's Vienna residence from years of being allowed to play hide-and-seek there with other children of the officers and upper servants in his household. It was not quite as large as the palace at Esterhaza, but just as grand. Not bothering to enter through the formal front door, I made my way around to the kitchen entrance. The prince's cooks always had treats for the younger children and never minded having the older ones help peel potatoes or apples by the warm kitchen hearth.

"Ach! Theresa!"

Before I knew what was happening I was engulfed in mounds of flesh and getting flour up my nose. Elsa, the prince's baker, had known us all our lives. She could always be counted on for sweets, but we had to submit to her suffocating embraces before making off with tiny cherry tarts or slices of torte. Today, I did not mind. There was warmth in her meaty grasp, and I had been feeling so alone ever since the night of my father's death that contact with anyone felt reassuring.

Elsa's eyes shed fat, round tears that she wiped away with her apron, smearing yet more flour over her already decorated face. "I was so sad when I heard. He did not deserve such a thing. There are criminals everywhere! But you look so thin. Are you ill? What about your mama? Is the baby safe? And Toby—don't leave without a basket of his favorite bon-bons."

She went on and on so that I thought I would be stuck in the kitchen forever, but I did not want to hurt her feelings by telling her I had business elsewhere in the palace. I barely attended to her words until she said, "Heinrich's daughter was here earlier, young Marie. Isn't she your particular friend?"

Marie and I had grown up together around the court, but we couldn't be more different. She never had much interest in music, and lately had become so obsessed with the latest fashions that she could talk of nothing else. No, she was not the person I needed by me just then. She would never want to talk about the one thing that obsessed me: what had happened to my father. I hoped she was not in the palace. I smiled noncommittally at Elsa in response.

It was Zoltán who rescued me in the end. He had come to request a glass of tea for Herr Haydn, who had just finished rehearsing the quartet.

"I'm here to see Kapellmeister Haydn," I said quickly, suddenly embarrassed about being there so early, and not wanting Zoltán to think I was hovering around just waiting for him to be finished so that he could show me where Papa had been found. His last rehearsal might not be over until later that afternoon, after which Haydn would direct only the singers in a small service of prayer before supper.

"He will be delighted. Come with me."

I kissed Elsa and gave her assurances that I would come by as often as I could so that she could fatten me up, then followed Zoltán through the maze of corridors in Prince Nicholas's winter home.

⁂

When we found Godfather Haydn, he was in an anteroom off the ballroom, his informal office, resting in an armchair with a damp cloth over his eyes.

"Maestro," Zoltán said, his voice full of gentle respect.

Quickly, the Kapellmeister sat upright, pulling the cloth away from his face as if he'd been caught stealing something.

"Ah, little Theresa!" he said. "Although now that I see you standing, you are not so little anymore. Quite a lady, tall like your papa and pretty like your mama. Your papa would not have wanted to see you still so sad." He rose and kissed the top of my head. "Sit, child," he said, motioning me to the chair opposite his.

"Shall I rearrange the chairs for the symphony?" Zoltán said.

"What? Oh, of course. Off you go."

I said a silent thank-you to Zoltán for having the discretion to leave us alone. I was beginning to notice that he had a way of understanding what I wanted before I even understood it myself.

"Now, dear one, what is it that troubles you?"

I didn't quite know where to start. What did I want from Haydn? He had already given me money. I knew he wasn't a wealthy man, however much the prince respected him and however much it looked as though he belonged with the nobility. He worked as hard as any laborer. "I suppose," I started, "I suppose what troubles me most is wondering what became of my father's violin. I mean, if robbers attacked him and took the fiddle to sell, surely it can be traced."

Haydn leaned back in his chair. "Do you care so much more about the violin than about Antonius?"

I felt ashamed. My question had not come out at all as I thought it might. "No, of course not. Only the violin—the music—it was him, wasn't it? And if the violin was destroyed too . . ." I couldn't go on. The thought was too horrible. It would be like having my father die twice.

"Are you still playing the viola?" Haydn asked.

I nodded. A large knot had suddenly lodged in my throat, making it impossible for me to speak.

"I thought you should know that I have told Prince Nicholas that I replaced your father immediately with another musician."

It seemed odd that Maestro Haydn would tell me this, especially when the pain of my loss was so new and raw.

"I neglected to give him the name of this fine new *artist*, but he trusts me and will continue to allow me to pay a stipend—not as large as your father's, you understand, but that of a young musician starting out, twenty Gulden a month."

All at once what he was saying became clear. He had lied to the prince, pretending to have hired someone new, so that we could continue to receive some money. And it was enough to pay our rent, at least, with a little left over for food.

I could hardly speak I was so moved. I wanted to tell Haydn what he had done for me, granted me the time I needed to try to discover what had really happened, to retrace the steps Papa took that last night, piece together the events, dig back into the past if need be. How could I not? Only the answers would make me able to go on. Nothing could be worse than not knowing. "Thank you, Godfather," I finally managed to say. "You will have helped me discover the truth."

Haydn had a distant expression on his face, as if he was thinking of things far away from us at that moment. "It's not always best to know the truth."

Not good to know the truth? The truth was all that was left to me. "Whatever it is, I shall find it out before long."

"Well, my dear, if verity is what you seek, perhaps I should start by telling you that my gesture—the stipend—is not really a gift. I'm afraid I have rather a large favor to ask of you in return for having told a small untruth to the prince."

A favor? What could I do for the most eminent musician in Austria and Hungary? He turned away from me, rubbing his eyes and pinching the bridge of his nose, then fumbled in his pocket for something. I expected him to pull out a handkerchief, but instead, he held a pair of spectacles between his thumb and first finger.

"I have been wearing these for some time. The demands on my eyes, as I get older—you understand."

I nodded, but still couldn't see what his spectacles had to do with the task he said he wanted to give me.

"Last month, I composed a mass—it was just a routine work, in fulfillment of my regular duties. I wrote out the score initially by myself as is my custom, and then gave it to one of the copyists. But when we came to rehearse, there were sour notes all over the place, and I thought my own musicians were making a joke at my expense."

The maestro walked over to the desk where his paper, quills, and the special five-nibbed pen he used to make staves on the paper lay. He picked up a sheet that was partly filled with notes. "I quizzed the copyist, at first insisting that he was being malicious, but he swore to me he simply wrote out my sketches, filling in some of the parts as usual. He showed me. I have since destroyed that manuscript, but here is another one."

He held out a score and I took it from his hands. It was the beginning of a string quartet, with the main parts for the two violins, viola, and cello written out, gaps left for the accompanying sections, where notes simply needed to be repeated. It looked just as it should to me. "It's a quartet," I said.

"Yes, but look more closely!"

I started humming the lines to myself, and then I began to understand the difficulty. Several of the notes were misplaced, in the spaces when they were clearly meant to be on the lines and the other way around.

"You see, it's my eyes. Even with the spectacles, the lines of the staff wave and I can't seem to get the notes down anymore. Your father knew. He more than knew."

It seemed that Maestro Haydn was trying to tell me that my father had helped him somehow. "What did he do?"

"He is—was—acting as my hands. He had an exceptionally good ear. Never made a mistake."

"Why don't you ask someone else in the orchestra to help you?"

"At this time of year there is simply no time. Everyone has to rehearse. Besides, your father had an interest that went beyond the music . . ." He paused again. "But even more than that, I need someone who is very fast. If I do not meet my contractual obligations, which call for new compositions every week, I will lose my position. And . . ."

His voice trailed off. I knew how much the Kapellmeister accomplished. The more I learned about music as I increased in ability myself, the more astounded I was at all the new symphonies, divertimenti, chamber music, masses, and even whole operas he wrote every season. When it came to music, Prince Nicholas was insatiable. But surely, if he knew Haydn was having difficulties, he would find some way to help him. "What more is there, Maestro?"

He shook his head. "You are so young. I don't want to burden you with my sorrows. But I must beg your assistance—if you will trust me."

"Of course I will do whatever you ask of me, if I am able." It was a rash promise. Not the sort of thing I should be saying to anyone, when I hardly knew what would happen day to day.

"No one must know. It is apparent that you have much of your father's talent. Let us hope you share his excellent hand and keen ear. Meet me at my apartment every morning at ten of the clock." He scribbled the address on a scrap of paper and gave it to me.

"But my mother—" I began to say that she would object, since that was the normal hour of my needlework lessons, but in her present state I doubted she would even notice. "No, I suppose it will not be a problem. But Maestro," I continued, "what of my father? Can you not tell me anything that might help me find out what happened?"

Haydn's expression was difficult to read. He was holding something back from me, I could tell, and I desperately wanted to know what.

"Your papa was a good man. He cared a great deal about many things. And he loved you very much, and your mama and Tobias."

I knew all that about Papa! Why must he be so mysterious? "Can't you just tell me what happened after the concert on Christmas Eve?" I cried, too frustrated to be polite.

He paused again before answering. When he did, he looked straight into my eyes with an expression that pierced through me. "Your papa did not play in the Christmas Eve concert."

CHAPTER 7

Zoltán returned just at that moment, before I could collect myself enough to ask the maestro anything else.

"Are you prepared?" Zoltán asked me. "Kapellmeister, I have an engagement with Fräulein Schurman, if you would excuse me from the symphony rehearsal?"

"Of course, of course," my godfather replied.

At first my thoughts were so confused by my godfather's revelation that I wondered, *prepared for what?* Then I remembered that Zoltán had said he would take me to the place where they had found Papa. I gathered up my cloak and gloves. I supposed I was as ready as I could be. I nodded.

"I will see you tomorrow then, as arranged?" Haydn's tone held something desperate in it. I still couldn't quite understand why weak eyesight could not easily be overcome with a little assistance. But I was happy enough to help him, after all he had done for us, and hoping that spending time with him would give me an opportunity to ask him everything he knew about my father.

Zoltán did not speak to me until we reached the kitchen courtyard of the palace when he gave me a black mask to hold over my face. No one in our class of society ever wore masks in public—they were mainly for the well-born who wished to disguise themselves while meeting a lover, or to avoid the anger of the populace after the passing of an unfair tax that benefited the nobles. "What's this for?"

"It would be best if you were not recognized where we are going," he said.

"Who would recognize me?"

"It is for the best." Zoltán turned away from me and strode off, clearly not wanting me to ask any more questions at the moment.

An icy wind had come up. I pulled my cloak around me more tightly as I followed him to a carriage stand. He spoke to one driver, who responded by shaking his head emphatically. Before I caught up with Zoltán so that I could hear what he said, he had moved on to the next driver. This fellow gave a more halfhearted refusal, and I saw with dismay that Zoltán fished a silver coin out of his bag and gave it to him. Surely we could not be going anywhere so far as to require such handsome payment. But whatever our destination, the second driver agreed to take us there, and Zoltán handed me into the carriage as though I were a fine lady.

I found myself inside a small space that smelled of old

sweat, despite the cracks in the leather hood that let in the wind and would certainly not provide shelter from a driving rain. Fortunately it was too cold for that. And the close space meant that we had to squash together to fit. I was both grateful that I could take a little of Zoltán's warmth from his nearness, and afraid that it was somehow unseemly to do so. I wondered what he was thinking. I glanced quickly toward him, hoping he would not notice.

I caught him looking away from me, scanning the houses and farms we passed. His expression was not kind and gentle. Instead the lines of a frown creased his forehead, and the corners of his lips were drawn down. I began to feel distressed that I had asked him to perform this service for me, especially if it was going to cost him money and cause him pain.

We took a direction that led us out through one of the city gates. Very soon we were crossing open country. The roads, well packed and cleared closer to Vienna, became rutted, and the cold weather had frozen the ruts so that we were jostled severely from one side to the other, even though we went at a walking pace. My hood fell back and my cap was pushed askew. I tried my best to adjust it, but as I was doing so, another jolt tossed me into Zoltán's side. He took hold of me and steadied me. His touch was comforting, but as soon as the road became less rough, he let go, and I felt cold.

We entered a forest glade, mostly tall pines. The darkness around us created a false nighttime. I peered out the unglazed window and thought I saw a group of men through the trees, watching us pass with casual interest. "Where are we going?"

Zoltán reached across me and lowered the shade. "I think now would be a good time for you to put on your mask."

Between the mask and the lowered shade, my sense of where we were became confused. From quiet countryside we passed into some kind of settled area, a village perhaps, or a small market town. I heard the ringing of a blacksmith's hammer on an anvil, and voices calling out their wares in a mix of a coarse Austrian dialect and some other language. By the light I figured that we had emerged from the forest. I had no clear idea of how much time had passed before I heard the coachman call, "Hold up there!" to his horse.

We climbed down from the carriage and approached the settlement. As we neared it, Zoltán pulled my arm through his and kept me tightly at his side. He, too, wore a mask and drew his hood down so that it hid his face. The cold afforded us ample excuse for covering ourselves. Through the tunneled vision of the piece of velvet-covered stiff paper I could see that I had guessed correctly about coming to a village of sorts. But the sight of the Danube stretching away like a gray satin ribbon through the hoary landscape took me by surprise. And I saw that not far down was the island of the Prater, the pleasure ground where people went for picnics in the summertime. I had pictured us winding deep into the countryside, not circling back toward the busy trade route—which at this time of year was considerably quieter because of the ice patches here and there that could damage the smaller boats.

"The place I want to show you is just down there, but we need a reason to pass that way at this time of day. Give me your muff."

I could not imagine why Zoltán would deliberately take my warmest item of clothing away from me, but I complied, not enough possessed of my wits to ask a question just then.

To my complete amazement, he glanced around quickly and, seeing that no one paid us any heed, tossed my only fur muff down an embankment onto the sandy edge of the river. It landed but a pace away from the icy water. "What have you done!" I exclaimed, and before he could stop me, I picked up my skirt and petticoats and scrambled as best I could down to retrieve it. Zoltán was close behind me.

"Why did you do that?" I whispered. He put his fingers to his lips.

"Here it is, *Liebchen.* Quite undamaged," he said aloud, clearly more for the benefit of the curious onlookers who had gathered to see the commotion than for mine.

His words had the desired effect, and the odd assortment of people, clustered near to what I now saw were crumbling piers, went back to their business. I had not had the opportunity to fully understand where we were until that moment. The huts and lean-tos that made up this village by the banks of the Danube were of the flimsiest construction, some no more than heavy canvas stretched over wooden supports, and in many cases attached to wagons. Despite this, they were decorated with brightly colored silk banners and had chains of shiny metal discs draped upon them, so that I imagined the wagons would make a cheerful sound when they were driven across the countryside. Horses and goats wandered freely through the makeshift lanes—only an ill-tempered-looking hog was penned apart from the people, who numbered something above a hundred. Among them were children, their feet wrapped in cloths against the cold ground, wearing short cloaks pieced together of colorful patches of wool, silk, cotton—any scrap of this or that. Not a single brick house was to be seen, and there were no smartly clothed ladies wearing high headdresses and Brunswick capes.

"We are among the Romany people," Zoltán whispered into my ear.

Gypsies! Had it been they who fell upon my father and robbed him? I began to tremble.

"They will not harm us," Zoltán continued. "Fine folk come here all the time to stare at their foreign ways. They are splendid musicians. Your father knew them, and on Christmas Eve bid us meet him here for some spirited music-making after the concert."

"But Maestro Haydn said he did not play in the concert."

"Nor did he. I'm afraid I was not entirely candid with you the other night. I'm sorry. There was no arrangement to meet at the tavern, either, but I couldn't explain it all then. We—Heinrich, Jakob, and I—were concerned when Antonius failed to take his place in the orchestra that night. We decided we had best come to look for him here as arranged, thinking perhaps he had prepared some surprise."

We strolled as though admiring the river view, but stayed close to that one spot. "Did my godfather know about the arrangement to visit this camp?" I asked.

"I do not know what your father may have told the maestro. In any case, when we arrived, the Gypsies were in a festive mood, celebrating midwinter. Torches blazed, and everyone was wearing their finest costumes. They welcomed us and gave us wine when they discovered we were musicians. But your papa was not among them."

"Then what happened?"

"The time grew late. Heinrich had had a skinful and then some. He staggered off to—you know—and tumbled over the edge of the embankment in the dark. We went looking for him, and that's when we found Antonius. Here."

He stopped by the carcass of a skiff, now more a loose collection of blackened boards than something that had once plied the river bearing people across to the Prater. I could see no evidence that a body had lain there, but the ground had been frozen for some weeks, and would not have yielded easily to his weight. I turned and slowly took in the embankment. It would have been difficult to scramble up quickly if one were being pursued. Some way down, boulders had been set into the earth to act as steps, but in the dark, without knowing they were there, Papa would never have found them.

"And then?" I asked. I needed to know more. With every word, every fact I discovered, a picture was beginning to take shape. As yet it made no sense, but I believed that if I could get enough of it, it would soon point me in some direction.

"We raised the alarm. The Roma men came down. It was their black blanket we used to wrap him, and their leader's son, Danior, drove us in his cart back to your house in Vienna."

"Where is this Danior?"

Zoltán looked up toward a wagon a small way off from the center of the village. I thought I saw someone vanish inside. "We promised we would not bring soldiers to the camp, vowing that we would try to avoid any implication of the Romany in your father's death."

"Do you believe they did not do it?" I could not imagine what else might have happened. It was clear: Papa had come to take part in their music and been killed for his bonus—and his violin. I wondered if a search of this Danior's hut would lead us to the Amati.

"I am certain they did not. What would have been their reason?"

"Surely the money . . ." Though it suddenly occurred to me that if Papa had not been at the prince's palace on Christmas Eve, perhaps he had not received his bonus after all. "When were the musicians given their Christmas pay?"

"Immediately after the concert."

Zoltán led me toward the stone steps, keeping his hands on my waist as he pushed me up ahead of him. He had large hands for a violinist, but then I remembered he played the viola and cello, too. My mind was swirling. The sensation of Zoltán's hands confused me, and I could not focus on the matter of my father. I wanted the climb up the bank to last forever, but it didn't. And when we reached the top, he let go of me, and I was able to concentrate again. If Papa did not have his bonus money with him, why would he have been attacked?

Our hired coach was where we'd left it, at the edge of the village. Zoltán bought me some roasted chestnuts from a vendor. I could tell everyone was staring at me and I began to feel a little frightened. A toothless old woman approached, coming quite close to me, and pointed at my breasts. She gabbled something in a language that was neither German nor French nor Italian, the languages I understood. I looked down, and noticed that the gold medallion lay outside my dress, just visible where my cloak hung slightly open. I tucked it away quickly.

"How very odd," he said. "She called you *chey*, 'daughter.' "

How did he know? Zoltán was Hungarian. As far as I knew, he did not speak the peculiar language of the Gypsies. And what was it about the medallion that would make her call me "daughter"?

Despite the many questions I still had, we barely spoke all the way back to Vienna. I went over and over the events of the day. My head hurt with the effort to comprehend what they all meant. But I couldn't help returning to one instant in particular. *Liebchen,* Zoltán had said. Beloved. I knew he'd done it so that it would appear that we were a young couple on a jaunt for the thrill of saying they had visited the Gypsy camp, but in the desolate landscape of my present life, I held that word in my heart and vowed I would never forget it.

CHAPTER 8

Where have you been! Your mother is so worried!"

Greta's bulk blocked my way into the apartment. All I wanted to do was lie down on my bed, close my eyes, and think, but clearly this would be impossible.

"Theresa Maria! Is that you? *Mach Schnell!* Come here this instant!"

Ever since I understood that I had been named after the empress of Austria, I had felt as if I carried a burden, as though I was expected somehow to be a humble version of the virtuous Maria Theresa, with her widow's weeds and sixteen children. My full name called out from anywhere was a certain sign that punishment was to come because I had done something wrong—not completed my chores, been unkind to my brother, spent too many hours practicing the viola when I should have been sewing—something that made me unworthy of that name, and so the sound of it filled me with dread.

Yet hearing my mother call for me now was a relief.

Never again would I be annoyed about it. Mama was sensible again. She had recovered. She would be her same, dear self, with all her worrying and fretting over nothing. I ran directly in to see her, desperate to talk to her about everything I'd been through in the past few days.

Toby sat in the corner of her bedroom with his slate on his knee. I saw that he had been working on a sum for a while—the edges of the slate were filled with doodlings of trees and flowers. Our mother sat up in bed, her eyes open wide and shining. Her pretty face was pale and she seemed thinner. I could see hollows below her cheekbones instead of the plump, rosy cheeks I remembered. When I kissed her, she still felt a trifle feverish.

"Why did you behave so badly? You know Uncle Theobald will not give you your dowry unless you are a good girl. And where is the money from your papa? He should have brought home his Christmas present from the prince. But Greta has solved that, and Toby will go to Herr Goldschmidt in a week."

I couldn't tell whether she expected me to answer her questions or not. I decided I'd best just try to calm her first. "Mama, I'm so glad you're well now. As is Toby. You know about Papa, of course, but he is safe with the angels now."

I instantly regretted mentioning Papa. A line appeared on Mama's forehead between her deep blue eyes, and she looked at me with such yearning I had to turn away. "Yes," she said, "Greta told me, but I didn't want to believe it. What shall we do?"

She understands. I was so relieved. "Kapellmeister Haydn is helping us. We won't starve."

"What can the maestro do? It was your papa who worked for him. I always told him he must take some measures to secure our future, get the prince to grant him an annuity, or a widow's jointure for me. Otherwise we would be helpless without him. We must get you married. Your dowry is our only hope."

I forced myself not to sound as cross as I felt. She could not know everything I did. "My godfather has every intention of being as helpful as he is able. And I don't think that getting me married would solve our difficulties. Anyway, I went to visit Uncle Theobald." I took hold of her hands. "I did not see him, but I saw enough to believe he will not take kindly to being asked for money. He's a very great man now."

A little of the fire of shrewdness she always possessed lit my mother's eyes. "All the more reason for him to help us. He is still my brother. What's necessary is simply that we find someone suitable for you. Greta has asked the matchmaker to come to visit me. I expect her tomorrow morning."

"But, Mama—"

"Greta said you'd been willful while I have been ill. It's unbecoming." She reached out her hand to stroke the side of my face. She smiled, softening the reproach in her words. "You must return to your needlework and be a good girl. No man wants a wife who cannot keep house and is disobedient."

I knew my mother did not mean what she said unkindly. We were her principal concern in life, and she'd never done anything to harm us. But I seethed at Greta's treachery. How could she tell my mother such tales! If it were not for me, we might be unable to continue as we were, even for a little while. I was about to inform Mama of everything, of Haydn's agreement to hire me as an assistant so that we could still receive our money from the prince, when Greta walked in.

"Herr Goldschmidt sent his lad with this."

She handed Mama a piece of paper, folded but not sealed. Mama opened it and read. "Thank you, Greta," Mama said, nodding in a way that sent the cook reluctantly out of the room. "You see, *Liebchen*, all is arranged. You must not take it too badly. I only did it because I knew it was for the best." She gave the paper to me.

I read it through three times before I allowed myself to believe what it said. Mama had sold him my viola! "How could you?" I asked. "The viola belonged to me!"

"It was your father's, and he wanted Toby to have this apprenticeship. Herr Goldschmidt must be paid, or your brother will have no future. We owned nothing else of enough value."

I tried to pull away, but she grabbed my hand and held onto it with strength that surprised me. "It is for the best. The viola will not help you get a husband. And we must all make sacrifices." She squeezed my hand before letting it go and resting both of hers on her bulging belly. She looked down with a soft smile. The infant inside seemed to sense her attention and shifted beneath her hands. When she looked up again, there was just a hint of happy tears in her eyes.

Mama was right. It was selfish of me to stand in the way of Toby's advancement. Toby, who would need a lucrative trade if he ever hoped to marry and have a family of his own. Toby, who was still so young I could not imagine him living somewhere else, let alone working long hours each day.

Yet I knew I would never quite forgive her for it. Because no matter what she said, practical as it was and effective at solving our most immediate difficulties, it proved to me that she did not understand how I felt about playing the viola. She had never understood that, and therefore she could have no knowledge of who I truly was. Only Papa knew how important it was to me to make music, and Papa was gone.

Although at first I felt only anger, I soon realized that her actions, insensitive as they were, freed me in a way. I need no longer feel guilty about pursuing my own plans, no matter how much they interfered with whatever schemes she concocted for me.

"Yes, of course, Mama," I forced myself to say, putting on my most submissive expression. "Perhaps Godfather Haydn will have an instrument I can practice on when I go to assist him each morning after breakfast, to earn money for our keep." My words were calculated to achieve the greatest effect. It was cruel of me to anger her; her health was still delicate despite her improvement since yesterday. But at that moment, I didn't care.

"You will do nothing of the kind! I expect the matchmaker tomorrow. You must stay here so that she can examine you and make a judgment about whom you should marry."

"I cannot disappoint the Kapellmeister," I said as I kissed Mama. She could not rise from her bed and come to fetch me, and I avoided her for the rest of the evening.

My stomach growled as I prepared for bed that night. I was too angry to eat the supper Greta had placed in front of me. I realized that now, with Papa's violin gone and my viola sold, we had no musical instruments in the house. I didn't remember a time when that was true. Toby had followed me into my room, his eyes dark with shared sadness. "I'll make you a viola as soon as I am able," he whispered. I hugged him close and felt him return the embrace before squirming away. No doubt he would cry himself to sleep as he had every night since Christmas.

Once I was alone again, all I could think of was that day when Papa first helped me draw a bow across a string. I don't know how old I was, maybe five. At first, all I could do was make a scratchy, squeaky noise. I couldn't understand how he could coax such a glorious sound from the violin. Haydn had lent him a half-size fiddle that he had had made, thinking he would have his own children to teach, so Papa said, but the children never came. At the time, I remember wondering how his children could stay away from him when he was such a kind man, not understanding that Papa meant he had none.

"Gently, gently—let the string do the work. Don't press down." I could hear his voice, feel his comforting arms supporting mine. And eventually, I did it. I felt the vibration all down my hands and arms, and it tickled and made me laugh. After that, we spent time every day, and gradually I was able to make the sound on my own. And he taught me how to read music, too.

Mama was a little jealous, I think, although she claimed only to be concerned that I was learning to play an instrument generally considered unsuitable for girls.

"Let her be. She has talent. Who knows, by the time she is grown, perhaps she could give lessons," my father would say.

How well I remembered her response. "No mother would allow her son to be taught by a girl! At least, not taught a trade." That's all it ever was to Mama—a trade—although I knew it wasn't her fault that she had no real appreciation. She smiled and tapped her foot when she listened because that's what she thought was expected, but the tapping was never in time. Yet she was able to dance and move her head and hands prettily in a minuet, and everyone admired her. I remember once thinking as I watched her at some holiday festivity, when the servants and musicians were allowed to have their own ball with a small orchestra made up of Gypsies and apprentices, that she was the most beautiful lady I had ever seen. Even more beautiful than the nobles who danced stiffly in their tight stays and panniers.

There was no use thinking about times gone by. It would not help me find out what had really happened to Papa. I was beginning to realize that the task I had undertaken would be even more difficult than I thought, especially with Mama so bent on finding me a husband.

I lay awake in the dark and reviewed my circumstances. Clearly I would have to adjust my plans. First, I must not let Mama settle my marriage too quickly. Aside from the fact that it would make it hard for me to wander about the city on my own or with Zoltán piecing together my father's movements on the night he died, I was not ready to marry. I had no doubt that I could run a household as well as the next girl, but to do only that, and have babies until it was one childbirth too many and I died from it—surely life held more for me. I could not have been born with the ear and the hands I possessed only to use them to listen for an infant's cry and to knit stockings.

I looked with longing at the empty table in my room. Only Papa would understand how I felt, the emptiness that engulfed me when I realized I no longer had an instrument to act as my voice. "Oh, Papa!" I said aloud to my room. "What happened? Why did you leave us?"

I soaked my pillow with tears that night, and dreamt of my father, smiling and playing in an orchestra that poured out glorious music. But the music was not in Prince Nicholas's palace; it was outdoors, in the countryside. And the orchestra was not the one in which he occupied the first chair. All the musicians looked dark and wore tattered clothes, like the Gypsies, and all of them wore gold medallions around their necks, similar to the one the apothecary's wife had found on my father's body. The concert was magnificent, and the brilliant green leaves and bright flowers rustled and nodded in time to the music. I could smell the sweet fragrance of the country in my sleep. I awoke feeling cleansed, and more determined than ever. What could my mother do, after all? I had money from Haydn so I would not starve even if she refused to feed me, which I knew she would not. She could talk to the matchmaker, and once I had satisfied myself concerning what had befallen my father, I would sit with her and go over the list of candidates, no doubt old widowers who wanted a young bride to keep them company and nurse them in their dotage. For no one else would take me without a dowry. Even though I had not met him, I knew that Uncle Theobald would never come through and fulfill his promise.

Still, I wondered about my wealthy uncle. His actions did not seem very honorable to me. Just because my mother's family could claim ties generations back with minor nobility seemed no reason to cut off a sister who married beneath her. She could see what her brother could not, that a musician who entered the right circles with a wife who was capable of looking and acting the part might rise and achieve more than any other tradesman, the fashion for music being such a craze among the nobility and royalty. Mama was an impressive sight when she dressed in her finest open gown and ribbon-trimmed petticoat, put on her one miniver-trimmed mantelet, and had her hair piled high into a sugar-water-stiffened mountain with bits of lace and velvet ribbon. We were none of us as good as Mama at appearances. I wondered how long it would be until she rose from her bed and made her own dignified way to the house in the Graben where her important brother lived. I hoped I could see it. I feared that she would be unable to manage it until after the baby was born, and I did not know how long it would take her to recover from the birth.

I tried to imagine myself turning my back on Toby because he had chosen a bride I did not approve of. Apart from the fact that the idea of little Toby married was so absurd it made me smile, I could never see it. If he needed something from me, he would have it no matter whom he married.

After devouring two fresh rolls Greta had baked because Mama was eating again, I put on my long wool cloak and mitts, readying myself for the long walk to my godfather's apartment in the Marienhilf suburb, outside the city wall. That morning it snowed halfheartedly; heavy, wet flakes that soaked into my cloak and chilled me through. By the time I arrived, my teeth chattered.

"Come, come, come!" Haydn said, leading me into a small parlor with a blazing fire in the grate. His housekeeper took my cloak and spread it over two chairs to dry. "Please forgive my wife for not being here to greet you. She could not delay a previous appointment."

I had heard rumors in the kitchens of the Esterhazy palaces about Haydn's bitter and unfaithful wife. It was said they never slept in the same bed, and that she visited an old witch who gave her an elixir that prevented pregnancy. Everyone felt sorry for Haydn, and never criticized him when he had occasional trysts with kitchen maids, or for the affair he was said to have had with the widow of one of his musicians.

"Forgive me for not giving you time to settle properly, but I must be at the palace in an hour." He pulled a silver pocket watch out of his waistcoat and shook his head at it. I knew that watch well. It was the one he used to let us listen to ticking away, and that he would produce from the oddest places to make us laugh—a flowerpot, our ears, his own mouth. "Do you prefer to sit or stand when you write?"

I saw that the desk was a high one, like those used by clerks in offices, and although I was not accustomed to standing up and writing, I told him that was what I preferred. When I took my place, I noticed that six or seven sheets of paper had already been lined, and the clefs for a string quartet had been mapped out. I still couldn't quite see what I would have to do. I had no trouble hearing—my pitch was perfect—but I had never actually tried to write down notes as I heard them. The maestro must have sensed my doubt, because he spoke to me quietly and reassuringly.

"Your papa used to dash in just the heads of the notes first as I sang, then go back later and add the stems. I still seem able to fix the rhythm. The flags don't jump around as much as the staves and the dots for me."

He started with the lowest line, the cello. He did not sing it all, but more often simply called out the harmonies. My father had schooled me in figures, so I knew how to sketch in the bass that would hold the upper parts together and give them depth. The first movement was a lively allegro, and as we continued with the first-violin part, I could anticipate what was coming. Or at least, I thought I could. Every once in a while Haydn sang a note or a phrase that took me by surprise. I would look up questioningly, and he would say, "Yes, yes, that's just what I mean, there's a good girl."

When we got to the upper parts, the ones in the range where he could sing, I sometimes thought the maestro simply forgot I was there. He wandered around the room, swaying to the music he heard in his head and singing so fast at times that I could hardly keep up. Although I had to glue my eyes to the page most of the time, every once in a while he would pause and I could look up. Then I would see him gazing off into the distance, eyes sometimes misting over as though the idea of music was too powerful to bear, and then they would brighten and he would start to sing again, and I would have to focus on the lines and spaces and write as fast as I could.

By the time the mantel clock chimed the next hour, my hand was in a cramp and I realized I had bitten the inside of my lip and could taste the salty blood. Haydn approached to look at my handiwork. I trembled with fear that he would find it unsatisfactory.

He picked up the sheets, scanned the lines, brought them close to his eyes, and held them at arm's length and sighed. "In truth, I will not know how well you have done until after the rehearsal. But in general it looks as though you have written everything down. Accuracy is the issue."

"Will you refine the movement tomorrow?" I asked.

"Oh dear me, no, there isn't time for that. It's first time or nothing, you see, at this time of year. You may as well come tomorrow for the other movements, which won't be as long as this one."

I wanted to ask him if he had the notes all in his head already, or if they simply came to him as he paced around the room, but in spite of his kindness and consideration, I was a little afraid of my godfather. He could end the stipend at any moment, tell my mother to keep me at home where I belonged, and put a stop to my inquiries to discover what had happened to my father. I didn't really think he would, but decided that the fewer questions I asked him the better it would be for everyone.

"Your cloak is dry, I see!" He held it out to me. "Stop in the kitchen for some cakes to take to your mama."

He put on his own cloak, a splendid, blue-satin-lined

affair that went with his court uniform, bowed to me, and left. I had no idea where the kitchen was, but the maid who had showed me in soon appeared with a basket full of treats. “The master said to give you these.”

I thanked her and began the long walk home.

CHAPTER 9

I spent the rest of the day listening to my mother talk incessantly about Frau Zimmer, the matchmaker, who had left before I returned. I kept trying to find an excuse to run an errand, but she continued to create little tasks that would keep me busy until the curfew bells rang and it would be foolish to go out by myself.

Toby and I had our dinner at the table in the dining parlor, and Mama took hers on a tray. She was under strictest orders from the apothecary not to rise from her bed, which obliged either me or Greta to empty her chamber pot into the water closet. Although ours was not as advanced an apartment as some, it was equipped with a pan that would send the waste down to the sewers beneath the city—built only in the last ten years—and refill it again from a cistern placed on the roof. It was a luxury not to have to go outside to visit the privy, which we had to do when we resided in the country at Esterhaza.

"Here is a list of your chores for tomorrow. There will

be no time for you to wander off. I wish I could rise myself and help with some of the work. Activity can be so soothing."

I looked at the long list Mama handed me. It included washing her linens, mending all the stockings, counting the silver and other valuables to inventory for the matchmaker so that she would know exactly the state of our wealth, and writing a begging letter to Uncle Theobald, requesting a meeting with him at his home with our lawyer. "Do we have a lawyer?" I asked.

"We'll get someone to pretend to be one. He won't know. The point is, it probably will not come to that, because he will immediately recall his obligation and make over the funds for your dowry." Mama's mind was back to its old self with these plottings and plannings of hers. I also noted that she had regained her appetite and had a bloom in her cheeks. Perhaps she had suffered such a severe shock upon seeing my father dead that all her mourning had been concentrated in a few days of inertia and madness. I did not know. Or perhaps the need to provide for the infant she carried made her postpone her sorrow, as I had mine. Whatever it was, I was not a little apprehensive about how matters would develop, and what changes I might see from one day's end to the next. I was rather glad she'd been insensible when I showed her the medallion, or it might well have gone the way of the viola and been converted to cash. I did not want to relinquish it until I found out exactly what it meant. I must continue with my own plans, no matter what.

"Toby will need new clothes to start his apprenticeship next week," I reminded Mama, suddenly struck with an inspiration. "I shall take him to the tailor tomorrow. I think that's much more urgent than anything else at the moment."

"Yes, I suppose you are right." She could not argue. Only a few days before Christmas she herself had commented that Toby's breeches barely covered his knees anymore. And now I had engineered a way to leave the apartment for an indefinite period of time. Which was essential. In addition to meeting with Haydn (Toby would just have to wait patiently for me), I had awakened that morning with the conviction that I must find my own way back to the Gypsy camp and look for the violin. Where else could it be? Even if they had not killed him, the Gypsies would be more likely to understand the value of a fine instrument than some desperate robber, who was probably looking for coins. It gave me some satisfaction to think that Papa had not yet received his bonus, and would have had little beyond the few Kreutzer he carried for daily expenses. I could leave Toby with the tailor for the price of enough sweets and promise of more, find the same driver at the stand, and use some of the precious money my godfather had given me as bribes if necessary.

⁂

The next day started out exactly as I had planned. Toby was happy enough to get away from Mama's constant prodding and quizzing him about his letters and sums, and I was so determined to follow the course I had laid out for myself that I didn't even mind his skipping forward and running back, stopping at vegetable stands and peering into shop windows. Despite growing all in a rush recently, Toby was still small. I couldn't imagine him working twelve hours a day learning a trade. His delicate hands that did such fine work on the miniature wooden toys he carved would soon be rough and calloused. I had seen the boys in Herr Goldschmidt's workshop. They all had pale, dirty faces and wheezed a little when they spoke. I expected the wood dust settled in their lungs. If they could make it through, though, they would have a craft that would assure them a decent living. The apprenticeship lasted nine long years. Toby would be a man by the time he was finished. No harm in letting him remain a child for a while longer.

By the time we had walked out Marienhilferstrasse to Haydn's apartment, thinking about what lay ahead for Toby had thoroughly chastened me. How could I be so unhappy at the prospect of marrying and keeping a house when my young brother would soon be little better than a slave to the exacting Herr Goldschmidt and suffer beatings if he made mistakes?

These worries were soon overtaken by others. I walked into the parlor of Haydn's apartment with a great deal of trepidation. Had my notation the day before been correct? I didn't have to wait long to find out.

"My dear, my dear, my dear!" Godfather Haydn said. "You are quite as talented as your father. I thought as much. There wasn't a wrong note to be found anywhere."

I was relieved. But now I would have to work even harder to make sure my accuracy wasn't just the luck of inexperience. We got right to it, and in an hour I had put down the next two movements of the quartet. The maestro thanked me again, gathered up his cloak, and left just as quickly as he had the day before. I collected Toby from the kitchen. We raced back into town, both breathless by the time we stopped at the tailor's. I gave Herr Machen the instructions for the clothing that Toby would need, mostly practical coats and shirts and breeches with reinforced knees. I used one of the silver Thaler Haydn had given me to pay for the clothes, and asked if he could get the cobbler to stop in. When the tailor left us alone in his stuffy workshop for a moment while he went to get Herr Schober, the cobbler, I took Toby by the shoulders and made him attend to me.

"There is something I must do, and no one—least of all Mama—must know about it. I have to leave you here. Do you know the way home?"

"Yes. It's not far from here, and I'm not a baby, you know."

"Tell me."

He sighed impatiently. "I head toward the Hofburg."

"That's right. And mind you don't take shortcuts down any deserted alleys. When the cobbler finishes measuring your feet, you're to go straight back. I don't want you being kidnapped and sold to the Gypsies!" I said. "Here is a Kreutzer in case you need it. Tell Mama that I had to run an errand for Kapellmeister Haydn."

"She won't like it," he said, crossing his arms and frowning.

"She won't, but I have to do this. You can either make trouble for me, or you can help me. It's important." I stared him down. He was stubborn, but I was more so.

"All right."

"Promise me?"

"I promise."

I knew I was taking a risk by leaving him to find his own way home, but he was a smart lad, it was not even midday yet, and the weather was fine. He wore his warmest cloak and new stockings that I had knitted for him just before Christmas.

⁂

I had taken care to dress as drably and modestly as I could, but I still felt as if I drew stares from everyone I passed. Some men who were laying bricks for a wall called out rude things to me, like "There's a ripe one!" and "Come on over and give us a kiss!" I knew they were just doing it for a laugh, but I wanted to spit at them. I wasn't trying to attract their attention. Why couldn't they just ignore me? I checked several times to be sure the medallion and its gold chain were well hidden, and I pulled my cloak around me to hide myself as much as possible. Groups of men had frightened me ever since Marie whispered to me that one of the servants' daughters had been brutally raped when she took a shortcut down a deserted alley on her way home from the market. Her parents were so ashamed they sent her off to be a menial in a convent. I never understood why they blamed her, and no one made much of an effort to find the men who attacked her.

By the time I reached the carriage stand, I was beginning to have serious doubts that I could get back to the Gypsy camp without creating so much of a fuss that the entire world would know I had gone. But I'd come this far. Now I just had to find the driver who would take me. I didn't recognize any of them from the day before. It was entirely possible that the one we'd had was out with another passenger.

"Excuse me, sir," I said to the first fellow I came upon, leaning one elbow against the flank of one of his horses. He was older than the others, so I thought it would seem less odd for me to approach him. He stared at me as if to say, "*Get out of my way, little girl, I'm waiting for business.*" "Excuse me," I repeated, not to be put off, "but I'm looking to engage a carriage."

"Oh, you are? And where might you want this carriage to take you?"

"I—" I couldn't continue. Where did I want him to go? I hadn't been able to watch the direction. All I had was the vaguest description. "There's a camp, of the Romany people, by the river," I whispered.

The driver almost sent me tumbling back on the ground with the force of his laughter. "You want to go to the Gypsy camp, alone? Don't you have a mother to tell you such things are dangerous, Fräulein?"

By now all the drivers were looking in our direction.

Some had even drawn closer to hear the dispute. "I can pay good money," I said, keeping my voice low.

"Nein," he said. "There's no money good enough to make me take such a risk." He turned to his mates. "Here, lads, she wants to go run off to the Gypsies! Maybe she thinks she can swallow fire, or tell fortunes."

Right at that moment, I just wanted to run away, to find Zoltán and ask him to come with me. I looked down at the ground. The drivers all went back to their carriages, laughing and joking at my expense. I turned and started to walk away. Someone tapped me on the shoulder. I looked around to see that one of the younger carriage drivers had followed me.

"I know where the camp is, Fräulein."

"And will you take me there?"

"Cost ye," he said quietly.

"How much?" I whispered.

"Five Gulden."

I almost exclaimed aloud. That was half the money I had left. "That is too much! I shall give you one Thaler."

"In advance."

I paused for a moment, then remembered that Zoltán had paid the driver first yesterday, and so I fished out the coin from my reticule. He examined it carefully, tucked it in his pocket, then walked off in the direction of the carriage stand. I assumed I was to follow him.

His was the most dilapidated-looking vehicle of all. One of the wheels was missing a spoke, and as I climbed in, it creaked so that I feared a deep rut would shatter the entire thing to pieces. I crossed myself and said a quick prayer to St. Christopher. As we drew away from the main street and into the countryside, my heart began to pound. How did I know this fellow would take me where I wanted to go? He could simply drive me out to the deepest part of the woods, rob me, and leave me to starve or be eaten by wolves or wild boar. Why had I been so foolish! Why could I not have trusted Zoltán to help me? Because he did not believe, as I did, that the Gypsies had killed and robbed my father. If not for money, then for his violin. And how exactly would I find it? Would I walk up to that Danior fellow and demand to search his wagon?

By the time my driver reined in his horse, I had worked myself into quite a state, and was trying to figure out how to tell him just to turn around and take us back to Vienna.

"We've arrived, Fräulein," he called down, making no move to get off the box. Clearly he was not going to hand me out of the carriage. *I'm here*, I thought. This was what I wanted, to look for answers. I couldn't just back away at the first sign of difficulty. I opened the door and climbed down. There was the camp, a few hundred paces away. Although he'd stopped under cover of the woods, he had brought me where I'd asked him to. I started to walk toward the huts and wagons when I heard the driver say, "Get up now!" and turned around to see him starting up at a brisk trot, heading away from me.

"Where are you going?" I yelled. "How shall I get back?"

"Half the money, half the trip!" he called back. I swore he was laughing.

Now what was I to do? A look at the sky told me that I had only a couple of hours before the short winter day would end. I thought about abandoning my quest and simply walking eastward down the river until I reached Vienna. But I had taken such a risk already, and would not be likely to dare such a thing again. I didn't have enough money to squander another Thaler, for one thing. And it would be a shame to leave without at least trying to find out something, see if any of the Romany had heard or seen anything that night. I smoothed my cloak and wrapped it around me tightly, then walked with determination toward the Gypsy camp.

CHAPTER 10

At first only a few children looked up at me. Although they were fully clothed, the way their garments were distributed among them gave the effect that they had shared a single outfit. One had scarlet breeches, patched at the knees with blue. Another wore a waistcoat of the same deep red with multicolored buttons. An older girl who looked to be about my age wore a black dress, but had tied an apron of the scarlet material around her waist and wrapped a scarf of bright red silk around her neck. They paused in their game that amounted to tossing stones into piles and ran toward some women who were clustered around an open fire roasting what looked like squirrels. The women looked up at me with expressions that held more curiosity than suspicion. One of them walked over to a group of five men. The men's eyes turned to me one by one as she spoke, and then, as if by some silent signal, in a group they started to walk toward me. I continued in their direction with my chin held high. My stomach was flipping over inside of me, and I could feel sweat trickle down my sides from under my arms, although my hands, face, and feet were icy cold. *What was it I wanted to say?* I thought to myself, my mind suddenly a complete blank. *Oh, yes. The violin. My father.*

We stopped a few paces apart from one another. They said nothing, obviously waiting for some explanation from me. I dipped a quick curtsy. Perhaps politeness was called for. "I humbly beg your pardon," I said in a voice that sounded pinched and shaky to me, and that I hoped did not sound too fearful to them, "but I am looking for something of my father's that was lost."

The largest of the men folded his arms emphatically and flared his nostrils at me. Still no word from any of them, but I could hear the children whispering behind me.

"He was found here—murdered, I'm afraid . . ." *Murdered.* I had thought the word so many times in the last few days, but this was the first time I had allowed it to pass my lips. And here I was, standing alone in front of this group of hostile Roma men, each of whom appeared strong enough to strangle me with one hand. I felt my eyes fill with tears. I tried to say something more, but my throat was squeezed and I could not draw breath without making a great, raw scraping that sounded like the sob of a wild animal. I doubled over.

All at once I felt myself lifted off my feet. For a moment, I flailed my arms and kicked. But then a deep voice said, "Hush." I don't know why, but the voice calmed me and I started to cry. The man carried me and placed me on an animal skin inside a hut or a wagon, I did not know which. By then, I was giving full vent to my despair, not caring who saw or heard me. I had forced myself to be strong until now, locking my grief inside me as long as I was within my own world and trying to be brave for Toby and Mama. I don't know why the curious, blank faces of strangers had made me suddenly crumble.

⁂

"Here. Taste this."

The woman's voice was gentle but insistent. When I took the cup of fragrant tea that she thrust under my nose, I noticed that the skin on her hands was dark, and that she had long fingernails that had been filed to sharp points at their ends and painted bright red.

"It won't hurt you, *kushti*."

I sipped. The tea was hot. I sipped again. Something in the tea soothed me. I sat up and looked around.

I had been brought inside a hut made of stout sticks with heavy cloth stretched over them. A fire burned in the middle, its smoke drawn out a small hole that had been left directly above it. The floor of the hut was covered in brightly colored blankets and animal skins, and a silver samovar sat in the corner, gleaming and ready for use. Despite its apparent impermanence, the atmosphere inside the hut was warm and welcoming.

"You had better tell me what it is you want," said the woman.

"I'm so sorry. You must think me foolish and weak."

"A young Viennese girl finds her own way out to the wicked Gypsy camp and addresses all the elders—without even carrying a weapon. Foolish, yes. Weak, no."

I smiled in spite of myself. "I came because my father's body was found here, by the river. He was a musician. I don't understand why he was murdered—he did no harm to anyone. I need to find his violin. It disappeared the night he was killed."

"A fiddler, you say?" Her eyes grew distant, as if she was thinking of something. "Yes, I think I remember."

"Our friend—Zoltán—brought me here the other day. He said my father knew of this place and came here to listen to the music."

"Your father. What was his name?"

"Antonius Schurman. Violinist at Prince Nicholas Esterhazy's court."

She opened her mouth as if to say something, then thought better of it.

"Do you—did you know him?" I asked.

She shook her head. "No. Never."

I didn't believe her, but I didn't know how to ask again without insulting her. I drew in a long, shuddering breath and let it out in a sigh. "I just want to know what happened to him, and why someone would take his violin."

"This violin—it is important to you?"

"Yes. It could be," I said. I was beginning to hope that some of my questions might actually be answered.

"Danior will know something. Wait here." The woman stood. She lifted the flap of carpet that served as a door and vanished through it, letting in a short shock of cold air. I pulled my cloak around me more tightly.

Danior! I thought. The very person I had hoped to see. At least one part of this strange adventure was going as planned. I didn't have to wait long. The woman returned almost immediately with a young man whom I presumed was the fellow Zoltán had mentioned the day before. The flap opened again, and behind the man and the woman I thought I saw the older girl I had noticed before, peering in to try to get a look at me.

"Kon se rani?" the man said as soon as he caught sight of me. I had no idea what he meant, but his voice held a challenge in it.

"This is Danior," the woman said to me. Then, turning to him, she said, "She is the daughter of a musician, a violinist, she says, in the court of Prince Nicholas Esterhazy."

"What brings you here?" Danior asked, fixing me with his penetrating gaze.

I tried to meet his eyes, but I could not. I don't recall noticing their color. I had the impression of deep darkness then, but it was dim inside the hut.

"She says her father came here. And that his body was found by the river."

Until that point, Danior had stood staring down at me where I sat on the ground, feeling small and vulnerable in my quilted petticoat and my plain, fustian dress. But after the lady spoke, he crouched down, squatting quite comfortably next to me as he examined my face. "Yes. I have seen her. She resembles her father."

He knew my father! But where had he seen me? He must have noticed me with Zoltán the day before. I had removed my mask while we were down at the river's edge. The idea of being observed unknowingly by this fellow with his dark skin and deep eyes disturbed me.

I summoned up my courage and spoke. "I once heard a Gypsy violinist, and I know my father was fascinated by the music. If he came here from time to time to hear you play perhaps you might know why someone would have—harmed him?"

Immediately I regretted the implication of my words. Both the lady and Danior drew back visibly. "You believe that, because we roam the world, no land to call our own, we must therefore be thieves and murderers?" Danior said.

Yes, I thought, *that was precisely what I had permitted myself to think.* It was what everyone said, everyone who was fearful of the Roma ways. "Forgive me," I said. "Zoltán said no one here was involved, but I am at such a loss to understand how it could have happened. My father was well liked. We were a respected family. He was only a musician."

"Zoltán?" Danior said, picking out the one name I had uttered.

"He is also a musician, and my friend."

"He brought you here. I saw him, too. What did he say to you?"

"He told me where they had found my father's body. And he said you would not have the violin. Yet why else was my papa murdered? Who can have wanted to harm him, unless it was someone who wanted his beautiful violin?"

Danior rubbed his chin thoughtfully. "Are you certain theft is the only possible reason for his murder? Perhaps you did not know your father so well as you thought."

I gave him a skeptical look. My father did not seem the sort to have mysteries. Then again, I would not have expected him to make a habit of coming to a Gypsy camp for entertainment, nor to own a gold medallion I had never seen before. Least of all would I have expected him to suffer a violent death.

The idea that he might have secrets gave me a horrible thought. I looked up at the Gypsy woman, who stared back at me with not unfriendly eyes. These Roma women were said to be fascinating to men, with their smoldering looks and wild ways. Could my father have taken a mistress from among them? Perhaps the medallion was a love token. My mind leapt to the idea of revenge as a possible motive for murder. A father, perhaps, or a brother. Or a spurned lover. Were there children? I immediately formed the idea that my father could have had an entire family I did not know about. He spent much time away from home, performing.

But a moment's reflection made me realize that my father's busy life would make such a thing difficult if not impossible. And we moved like Gypsies ourselves every year, to Esterhaza from Vienna and back again. Yet the Roma wandered, too, and this band of Gypsies could be the same as the one that spent its summers not far from Esterhaza, and whose members the prince's cook would blame for every little thing that went wrong on the estate.

"You should stay and break bread with us," the lady said.

"I'm not hungry, but thank you."

"It is not polite to refuse food when you are a guest of the Romany," Danior said sternly.

All at once I realized that, however well I'd been treated so far, I was entirely at the mercy of my hosts. I surreptitiously felt my reticule. It still contained coins—I had not been unwittingly robbed. Then I blushed again that I would have expected to be. "Thank you, of course. You are very generous."

Danior stood and reached his hand down to me. I took it and he pulled me to my feet. His grip was wiry. He had calluses on his fingertips. "You are a fiddler!" I said.

At that moment, a wide smile lit his face, revealing two rows of small, straight teeth. I noticed only then that he was quite a young man, and that his features had that balance that make expressions look alive, his nose straight until its end, where delicately flared nostrils softened the slight downward hook. He was clean shaven except for a thin mustache, revealing the perfect symmetry of his face. He wasn't quite as handsome as Zoltán, but there was something fascinating about his looks.

∻ ∻

When we emerged, I saw with dismay that the twilight had already started to draw in. How would I get back to Vienna now? Mother would be worried. And Toby? Had he found his way home all right? Would he be punished for my actions?

We sat with the others on mats of carpet woven with fanciful pictures of animals and flowers, positioned around a large fire with a cauldron hung over it on a makeshift frame. No sooner had I settled in my place than the girl, the one who seemed to be my age and who I had seen peering in when the flap of the hut opened, came and sat down next to me.

"I am Mirela," she said. "You are Theresa. I know. I speak German. I can tell you what they say." She swept her arm to indicate the entire camp. At that moment, everyone chattered noisily in that odd language I had heard before. Mirela spoke with a strong accent, but I could understand her. And the accent had a kind of music in it.

"Thank you," I said, and asked about the woman whose hut I had been in.

"That's Maya, and Danior is her cousin."

A toothless woman with skin so wrinkled and tanned it looked like tough leather ladled out portions of stew into wooden bowls and broke hunks of brown bread off the loaves on a table at her side. A very small girl child brought me the first bowl. I thanked her. There were no spoons, I observed. Once all had been served, they stared at me.

Mirela whispered in my ear. "They will not eat until you do. It's polite." I turned to her, and she made a gesture as of lifting a bowl to her lips.

I did as she indicated and drank the broth. It seemed to be what was required, because immediately after I finished, everyone else did the same and the assembled crowd resumed chattering in their language with a few words of German sprinkled in.

Mirela proved a useful source of information about everyone in the camp. She pointed out the elders, the ones who resolved all disputes and dispensed justice, and then she arranged the assorted children into family groupings. These numbered around five.

"Where are your mother and father?" I asked.

"Oh," she said, shrugging, "they have died, so long ago I hardly remember them. Maya took care of me, with Danior."

I thought about asking her how it was not to have a father, wondering if she could understand what I felt. She seemed just like any other girl to me, aside from her clothes. "See that boy there? That's Omar. He teases me." She put on a pout, but I could tell the teasing pleased her. Omar smiled in our direction.

"How shall I get back to Vienna?" I asked, interrupting her constant prattle. Everyone around us appeared to have settled in for a long, social evening.

"Back? Oh, I don't know. I'm sure you must not worry." When I thought back later, I could have sworn her eyes flicked to the area around my neck. But I was so distracted at the idea of not being able to get home that I soon forgot the impression.

As it grew darker, my heart sank. The liveliness of the conversation and the music of laughter swelled into the night. Mirela offered me a cup of wine and I willingly accepted, hoping to numb my growing sense of panic. The wine was stronger than I thought it would be. It warmed my throat, and soon I fell into a drowsy state. The fire crackled and danced, and Mirela's voice lulled me. I was at the center of several rows of people who had gradually filled in the space behind me. When the meal ended, the talking died down, and here and there men and women stood. Some wandered off into the bushes, I thought probably to relieve themselves. I felt the need, too, but I didn't want to venture alone away from the group.

When those who had left returned, some carried instruments—tambourines and drums, a recorder of sorts, and a couple of mandolins. They did not start to play right away, only strumming the occasional soft chord or riffling a tune full of strange intervals. They were waiting for something it seemed.

"This is my favorite part of the night," Mirela whispered. "I forget all my troubles."

I wondered what she was referring to, but there was no time to ask. Everyone quieted and turned toward the woods, where a torch had been planted in the ground. I watched as Danior emerged from the shelter of the trees with a violin at his shoulder. In the dusk he looked like a ghost, the torchlight flickering across his face, as he lifted his bow high and brought it down across the strings. The sound silenced everyone and locked them in whatever position they happened to be, sitting, standing, crouching, bent over to pat an infant on the head. Even Mirela was still. And me? I entered heaven—or hell—as I always did at the sound of a beautifully played violin. I thought then that it was my too-lively imagination, but I felt as if I had heard those Gypsy melodies before. Not exactly those, perhaps, but others like them, as if it were me and not my father who had made a habit of sneaking away to hear the Gypsies in the dead of night. I could not place the scraps of tunes, so after a bit I stopped trying. I stopped thinking altogether and surrendered myself to the power of the music. It was warm there, by the fire. Mirela slipped her arm around my waist and rested her head against mine. The companionship comforted me. I could have remained where I was until the end of time. I did not care if I ever returned to Vienna.

CHAPTER 11

If I gained no specific information about my father's death during the hours I spent at the Roma camp, I grew to understand why he came there. Music was part of everything and everyone.

After Danior's first, long solo finished, he stepped into the group and the other musicians clustered around him. They played music for dancing, and this was the signal for everyone except the very old to rise to their feet and begin to move. Mirela took my hand and drew me into a circle of children who clapped and stepped. The men formed their own figure, snaking around in a line through the camp, lifting their feet and slapping them with their hands, stopping now and again for one of them to perform an acrobatic leap or turn. These became more and more difficult as time went on, and the children and women gradually stilled to watch their antics. One fellow rested one hand on the ground, tipped himself up so that all his weight was on it, then danced his legs in the air for what seemed like a very long time, until sweat poured off his face and onto the ground. Mirela and I stopped dancing and stood to the side with some other women to whoop and cheer him on, until with a catlike spring, he pushed upward and landed on his feet, a smile stretched across his face.

I entered into the spirit of the music and dancing as much as anyone. When the men's dance finished, I thought the entertainment was over, and was about to ask Mirela again how I was to return to Vienna so that my mother would not be worried, when the plaintive sound of Danior's violin once again silenced the crowd. This time, though, he was not the focus of the performance. Several of the men lit torches in the fire and stood in two lines leading from the tent I had been taken to when I first arrived, forming a sort of grand entranceway.

"It's Maya! She will dance. It must be in your honor, Theresa," Mirela said, and she took me to a spot near the center of the crowd to sit. After Danior's sinewy, twisting introduction ended on a long trill, Maya, the woman who had given me tea in her humble hut, stepped out of it, dressed not in the plain clothes she had worn earlier, but in a skirt edged in bright ruffles, with filmy scarves hanging from her head and draped in her fingers. I could not take my eyes away from her hands and arms. She moved them as though there were no bones in them, in perfect time to the music Danior played.

How different was this dancing, with its movements that seemed to rise from the soul of the music itself, from the formal minuets and contredanses at court balls. I remembered watching from a balcony once, admiring the symmetry of the figures below me, the controlled movements that let a toe point here, a head angle there, the arms held just so for the entire dance. The ladies' stiff gowns hardly moved, only the sparkle of their diamond earbobs catching the light as they turned to whisper something to their partners when they stepped through a close figure. How shocked those dancers would be to see the Gypsies!

As the music gradually became faster, Maya changed her movements to match. At one point, every part of her body seemed to be in motion, from the ends of her long, dark hair to the tips of her toes. She slowed, and a child took two wooden bowls and upended them on the ground. A man brought a long, curved sword. In time to the music, Maya stepped up on the bowls and placed the flat of the sword on her head. As she continued to dance on the tiny platform of the bowls, she let go of the sword and balanced it on her head. I held my breath. I had never seen anything so thrilling in all my life.

In those hours that I stayed and listened and watched, I believed I had found the soul of music. I understood, as my father must have, that it did not live only in the opulent courts of princes, nor could it be fixed to a page with ink and quill. It came from within, from the place where one's spirit lived. Directly from God, perhaps. Or from something beyond God.

Maya's dance ended, and the band was about to begin another lively tune, but one of the older men raised his hand high and a sudden hush descended on the company.

Everyone stopped their noise and revelry and listened intently. Mirela grasped my wrist so hard I could feel her fingernails begin to dig into the soft flesh on the inside. I heard nothing except the rustling of the wind in the evergreen trees behind us. I opened my mouth to ask a question, but Maya put her finger to her lips and gave me a look that would frighten a Turk.

With hardly any warning, a group of about five men burst out of the forest and ran, crouched low to the ground. In hoarse whispers they said something in their language that started everyone scrambling to pick up their belongings and douse the fire. I stood in the middle of a whirlwind, while around me huts were broken down, belongings packed onto wagons, and livestock herded onto carts or shooed off into the forest, no doubt to reclaim at a later time. Mirela wrapped her arms around me in a brief, fierce embrace, then skittered off to join the frantic activity. Even the children behaved as if they had been rehearsed in a ballet, no one in the wrong place at the wrong time, until horses were harnessed to carts and everyone was ready to move on—except for me.

One of the men who had entered the camp, a lighter-skinned fellow with sandy hair, barked something toward Danior, who now sat on his wagon seat with the reins in his hands. Danior answered. I thought I heard the word "*Geiger*," and assumed he was explaining that I had come in search of my father's violin. I didn't have much time to wonder what would happen next, because the fellow grabbed me by the waist and slung me over his shoulder like a sack of turnips. I opened my mouth to scream, but another man stuffed a rag into it to stop me up like a wine bottle. They tossed me with little ceremony onto the back of Danior's cart. I landed amid some pots that jabbed into my side. I heard the crack of a whip, and the cart lurched off over the rough ground. My heart pounded. From being soothed by music and dancing, I had been thrown once again into a state of fear. What would they do with me?

∴ ∴

Danior turned the horses sharply and I was thrown into the pile of his possessions. That was when I must have hit my head, because I do not remember what happened next. Everything was a blank until I awoke in a strange apartment, lying on a cot with a vinegar-soaked cloth on my forehead. "What?" I could not even form a question. My head hurt where it had been bruised.

"So, you are back with us."

I tried to sit up. That was Zoltán's voice. A woman's hand pressed me back into the soft pillow. I turned my head to look at her. She was very beautiful, with soft, curling blond hair peeking out from under her cap, and blue eyes that seemed almost too large for their sockets brimming with concern. "There," she said, "lie still." She removed the cloth and soaked it in a basin, then pressed it on my forehead again.

"Where am I?" I managed to ask.

Zoltán said, "Danior broke away from the caravan and

brought you here to my apartment. He took a terrible risk. Why the—"

"Hush, my dear, do not trouble her now. Can't you see she is hurt? And I daresay there will be time enough for Fräulein Schurman to regret what happened."

The lady's voice was melodious and kind. She had called him "my dear." Was Zoltán married? Why did I not know? And why did that knowledge suddenly make me feel like weeping, even more than understanding how close I had been to mortal danger? I heard footsteps—Zoltán's, I imagined—stride across the room, and a door open and close. I did not want to look. I couldn't face the idea of him. He must think me such a fool, not to have trusted what he'd said and to go storming into the Gypsy camp as though I could do no wrong. I reached instinctively for the medallion around my neck.

It was gone. I sat up quickly. My head swam. "Where is it?"

"I think it would be good if you could take some broth," said the lady. "Where is what?"

"I was wearing a gold pendant. A medal, on a chain."

"You did not have it on when you came here."

It must have been stolen, I thought. But when? While I was unconscious? Or before? Was that why the Gypsies had gagged me and tossed me into Danior's cart? I could not understand why they would treat me so roughly after having been so kind. And why did everyone disperse like that? What threatened them, that they would have to pick up everything they owned and move so quickly in the middle of the night? My head was too full of questions, and I was still too groggy, to fix on any one thing to say to this gentle lady.

The lady's back was turned. I saw her rinsing something in a basin. When she came back, she had a damp cloth with her, and she patted my face with it. *I must look a mess,* I thought.

"We sent word to your mother," the lady said. "We told her you had been detained at the prince's with your godfather, and that Zoltán brought you here to meet me."

Of course, I realized how my mother must have worried, and that should have been my first concern. "Thank you. The medallion—I don't think it was valuable, at least, that's not why I wore it. My father had it, when he . . . died." I felt ashamed again, and I noted that she had said *we* sent word. Why did that make me so sad? Why did it suddenly feel as though I might as well not bother to rise from that comfortable bed ever again? I had betrayed Zoltán's trust. And he was *married.* I watched the lady I assumed to be Madame Varga move around the room, hoping to find some fault with her. I tried to discern some lack of grace in her movements. I looked for something less than perfect symmetry in her features. I searched to uncover some evidence that she was not worthy of my friend's love. I wanted to ask her name. I couldn't bear the idea of calling her Madame Varga aloud. I did not even think of Zoltán as Herr Varga. He was too young, really only a few years older than myself. I remembered him when he was still a youth and I a small child. I considered him more a friend of mine than my father's, my only ally who did not consider me a pointless little girl and pay attention to me out of pity. "To whom do I owe . . ."

"I am Alida. My brother tells me you recently lost your father in a terrible manner."

Her *brother*? Could I have misunderstood everything so completely? It was all too confusing. "You are Zoltán's sister?"

"Yes. I was living in Buda until recently. I have come to be a maid of honor to Archduchess Maria Elizabeth."

"But—" A maid of honor? They were not really maids, not like the scuttling creatures who empty chamber pots and sweep up ashes. They were more like companions. To attend the empress's family members, one had to be high born at least, and most likely noble. And normally one lived in the palace; that I knew from stories I had overheard my mother telling Greta of intrigues and scandal. "Why aren't you at the Hofburg?"

"My mistress is very lenient. She lets me come and keep my brother's house for him once a week while he is in Vienna. Otherwise we would never see each other." She paused to ladle some broth into a bowl and bring it to my side. "Zoltán tells me you are a musician, too. I might be able to arrange for you to attend a concert at the Hofburg sometime."

I smiled. I was beginning to think Alida the kindest, most beautiful person I had ever met. How could I have harbored even the smallest amount of ill will for her? "I wouldn't dare hope." The idea of the concert almost made up for my disappointment about losing the medallion. I thought perhaps I deserved to lose it. It was stupid of me to wear something that might be valuable out on the streets, let alone to the Gypsy camp. And I had neglected to show it to Haydn or to Zoltán, who could have helped me figure out what it was and where it had come from. Now it was too late.

"Drink this." Alida gave me the broth. "You'll be all right here until morning, then we'll get you home."

I tried to say more, but she shushed me and drew the curtains around the bed. The fizzling sound of a candle being doused and the dimming light when she turned the oil lamp low were the only evidence that Alida was still in the room. I wondered how she could move so silently. I barely heard the dry crunch of horsehair stuffing when she stretched out on the divan.

I felt a little guilty that I had been given the more comfortable place to sleep. *I must be in Zoltán's bed*, I thought. I imagined the imprint of his head on the pillow and buried my nose in the bedclothes, wondering if I could smell him. But the sheets were clean, exuding only the scent of soap and winter wind. There was something a little dangerous and thrilling nonetheless about being there, Alida acting as unconscious chaperone to keep my thoughts from straying too far in a forbidden direction. I allowed myself for only a moment to imagine what it would be like if Zoltán lay next to me, cradling me in his arms. I would be older, of course. And we would be—no, I couldn't think about that.

I shook my head to clear it of these disturbing thoughts. By the time I subsided into sleep, the other events of the day had asserted their claim. My mind was a confused jumble of music and dancing. I saw Danior and Maya and Mirela smiling and laughing, and soon I was so overcome with fatigue that I could no longer keep my eyelids raised. *What if it was Mirela who stole my medallion?* I thought. I hoped it wasn't. I liked Mirela. She was an orphan. Like me, in a way. That was my last thought before I drifted into an exhausted, dreamless slumber.

⁂

I harbored a small hope I would see Zoltán the next morning, but he had clearly gone elsewhere to pass the night so as not to expose me to any gossip.

"We are but a short distance from your home," Alida said. I had risen and dressed, and we shared our breakfast of chocolate and bread like comfortable old crones by a cheerful fire. When I took my leave of Zoltán's sister, she promised me that she would find a way to invite me to a concert. "The emperor has been petitioned by an extraordinary young musician from Salzburg who seeks employment at court. A Herr Mozart, who made a sensation when he was a little child, when he and his sister played the harpsichord and the violin for the emperor and empress. If he comes, perhaps I could arrange it."

Nothing could have been more exciting to me than that. To hear the newest genius, and at court! I felt a little disloyal to my godfather, Haydn, but he was already settled in as prestigious a position as one could ask for—next to the imperial court itself. As I walked quickly home through the cold morning, I almost forgot that I should be ashamed of the worry I had caused my family, and that I had managed to lose something that might be important and that I suspected might yield a clue to what had happened to my father.

I was reminded of my responsibilities, however, as soon as I passed through the door of our own apartment. Toby rushed up to me before Greta could make her way from Mama's chamber and whispered, "You're in trouble. I thought Mama would burst with worry, and then when she found out you were not dead, she was so angry."

I knew he didn't mean it the way it sounded, but I didn't have time to explain anything to him, because the door of Mama's room flew open in the next moment as if by the sheer force of her voice. I soon realized it was only Greta marching through, carrying a breakfast tray. I found myself grateful that Mama had been confined to her bed.

"Theresa Maria! I command you to come before me this instant! How could you be so foolish. Where have you been? Uncle Theobald himself came here yesterday, and now I fear he believes you are disobedient as well as bold!"

Uncle Theobald? Here? I looked at Greta for confirmation. It seemed more likely that my mother would fabricate such an event to chasten me than that the great man would actually deign to visit our humble residence. But Greta lifted her eyebrows and smiled slightly. So it was true. "What did he want? Why did he come?"

"What did he want? Such a question! He wanted to meet you so that he could determine your worth. He said he had some ideas for a match for you, that his valet had described you to him when you came the day after your father's—" She could not speak of it. Despite her anger at me, I knew my mother was still distraught about Papa. "He brought a basket of delicacies. I'm afraid that because you weren't here, you have missed the sweets."

It struck me as comical to have my mother hold the denial of sweets over my head as punishment, as if she did not realize that in the last few days I had lost everything that remained to me of childishness. I walked forward and sat on her bed. What had I been fearful of? This lady, with her pretty face and pregnant belly, really could do nothing to harm me but scold. I was overcome with affection for her, recalling that unlike many of the friends I had had over the years, I never suffered beatings at her hands. Once she spanked me when I ran off with the cook's daughter to play without asking permission. But I had always been too occupied with music to get up to much mischief.

I embraced her, interrupting her torrent of angry words. "I'm sorry I worried you, Mama. I'm well now. Shall I bring you some tea?"

Her complaining sputtered out until she was quiet. All at once I was aware of how vulnerable she was, lying there in her bed, unable to do anything for her family at that moment besides worry and harangue. I would not like to be in her position.

She sighed before responding at last. "I had my tea, thank you, Theresa."

Only one name. I was on safe ground again.

"There is mending left from yesterday, but before that you must tidy yourself and put on your best gown. I promised my brother that you would attend him at his house this noon, when he returned to take his second breakfast, so that he might see if he could help you—and thereby help us."

It was not yet nine of the clock. If I hurried, I might be able to keep my appointment with Haydn and still reach the house in the Graben on time. I took my mother's hands in mine.

She gasped. "What happened to you!"

I looked down and realized that sometime during the flight from the Gypsy camp, I had gotten a bad bruise on my arm.

"It is nothing, Mama," I said, rapidly trying to think of something to explain the bruises. "Only that I tied my sleeves too tight against the cold yesterday. But did I tell you that I am now acquainted with a maid of honor at court?" Alida and I had formulated the excuse that morning, so that my mother would be spared too much distress about what I had been through. I had planned to explain that we had been chatting together and lost track of the time, until it was too late for me to go home without disturbing the family, and that that was when Alida sent a lad to assure them I was safe.

The words "maid of honor" acted like balm to soothe

my mother's troubled spirit. "Ah, my dear, you see? There are compensations in life that go far beyond music. Even your father would have admitted that."

She turned her head away from me. Tears collected along her lower eyelid and then spilled out over her cheeks. I stood and curtsied to her, then left her to her grief.

CHAPTER 12

My plan for the morning worked almost perfectly, except that in hurrying to complete the work for Kapellmeister Haydn, I tipped over an ink bottle that was nearly empty and now had blotches of black on my best day gown, a sprigged muslin caught up at the sides to reveal a petticoat with a row of lace near the hem. I knew I looked like a maid wearing her mistress's spoiled castoffs, but there was nothing I could do about it. I knew also that running the final stretch to my uncle's house would cause me to arrive breathless and disheveled, but it seemed the lesser of two evils when compared with being late.

The same young maid opened the door to me. This time rather than attempt to shut it in my face, she surveyed the disordered state of my clothing and gave a disdainful sniff before ushering me in. I untied my cloak and held it out to her. She was forced to take it and drape it over the hall chair before showing me into the same room I had entered before.

I did not have to wait as long that morning for the valet to arrive. And now he made no disrespectful inquiry of me, but maintained a bland expression as he asked me to follow him into the dining room. I was not a little curious to have a chance to examine my uncle at close quarters. He had formed such a part of the myths of my childhood that I imagined him alternately a prince and an ogre.

At first I did not see him in the grand room. A long table occupied the center of a space that was lit by tall windows looking out over a wintering garden. The smell of fried meats made my stomach growl. In fact, one end of the table was so covered with food that until my uncle lifted his head up from scooping sweetbreads into his mouth, I would have thought it had been set for a banquet that would take place later.

"Ah, Theresa Maria. Come closer where I can see you properly." His mouth was still full of food and I watched in disgust as a trickle of saliva-laced fat traced a path down his chin. He took up a large linen napkin from his lap and wiped his entire face with it as if performing his morning ablutions, then leaned back in his chair, his double chin shuddering as he did so. I searched for some trace of resemblance to my mother and could find it only in the color of his eyes, a clear, watery blue. Although there were empty seats all around, he did not invite me to sit. I curtsied, a little belatedly. "*Guten Tag,* Uncle Theobald."

"Turn around. Slowly."

I flushed. He did not even bother to return my greeting!

"The figure is good," he muttered, as though he were

assessing a horse for purchase. "And she has inherited her mother's beauty."

Did he think I was a deaf-mute? Why speak of me that way, and in my presence? I recalled something my father had once said when Mama raised the promise of Uncle Theobald's dowry. *She'll have to earn it first, I'll wager, and that, my dear, is no profession for a lady*. I wasn't certain what he had meant, but his words had silenced my mother, who did not speak of Uncle Theobald again for some months.

"So, Theresa, your mama wants me to find you a husband. What are your accomplishments?"

"I—I—" What exactly did he mean, my accomplishments? "I play the viola and the violin tolerably well, Uncle."

"That won't do. What about the harpsichord, or the guitar—perhaps the harp?"

"The harpsichord, when I have to. I have never learned any other instruments."

"Do you sing?"

"Not well."

"Draw?"

"I never saw the need."

"Your needlework—surely your mother has at least schooled you in *that*?"

Now I began to fume. He held my dearest achievements as lightly as a spaniel's ability to fetch a stick. Perhaps less so. "I assure you, I am an accomplished seamstress, as it has long been my task to mend all the family's clothing."

"My dear!" I thought he would leap from his seat, but he merely appeared to rise by the degree to which he pulled himself upright. "*That* is not what I mean by needlework. If you marry well, a maid shall do all *that.* I mean fancy needlework, to occupy your idle hours in the evening when you've no company."

"I prefer to occupy my idle hours by reading, Uncle. I have been schooled in German, Italian, and French, and can make my way slowly through Virgil if given a little assistance."

"I see my task is even more difficult than I had supposed. We shall have to trust to your physical charms, which are—admittedly—considerable." He licked his lips, although I did not see any crumbs there, and let his eyes take the measure of me from my indoor cap to my stout walking boots. "I would be willing to undertake this important role, but I must have something from you in exchange."

At that moment, I wanted nothing more to do with this uncle, the one who was supposed to have my interests at heart. What should I have expected? He had found it perfectly easy to turn his back on his only sister, despite some times of true want before my father had his post in the prince's household. And he apparently remained unmarried, keeping the entire disposal of his fortune to himself and his own comforts. "If I have displeased you, Uncle, perhaps it would be best if we simply said our good-byes and thought no more about it." I dipped a quick curtsy and turned to go. To my dismay, the stern valet stood blocking the doorway that would lead me back out to the hall.

"Not so fast. I see you are offended. I did not mean to wound your pride, but you must be aware that you have hardly been groomed for the position of a great man's wife."

Since I had no choice, I remained where I was, waiting for him to speak again.

"And this task I have for you—it's nothing, really. I would only like you to attend a small ball I am hosting in the assembly rooms for a few close friends—no more than a hundred or so—and to be kind to a certain gentleman whom I will point out to you. Just to listen to what he says, and tell me about it afterward. In exchange, you shall have unlimited credit at the most fashionable dressmaker in Vienna—for one week, so that you may be appropriately clothed. In fact, I had better come with you to ensure that you do not forget some detail of your costume."

Again he looked at me in a way that made me feel like a prize cow, and I imagined myself draped on a platter in front of him as he prepared to sink his teeth into my tender flesh. I shivered.

I wanted to run from the grand house and never enter it again. But what would I tell my mother? She had the highest hopes of great benefit resulting from this meeting, and after the worry I had put her through the previous night, I decided I had better make an effort to be agreeable. Let it be Uncle Theobald who gave up on me, and then she would have less cause for complaint.

When at last I departed, after promising to meet my uncle at the dressmaker's that same evening before curfew,

I wandered out not really thinking where I was going, and nearly collided with a man about to knock on the door.

"I beg your—" I stopped in midsentence. "Herr Schnabl!" I exclaimed. It was the first cellist from the Esterhazy orchestra, the one who often played in quartets with my father. He was getting quite old, and Papa had said that he drank too much and was always in danger of being fired. Apparently Haydn had defended him on several occasions, and it was only through the maestro's kindness that he remained. "What are you doing here?"

"Oh," he said, after nodding to me in greeting, "just an errand."

He had a portfolio tucked beneath his arm. I tried not to make it obvious I was glancing at it, but it appeared to contain sheets of music paper. I did not know my uncle was musical. I was glad if he was. Perhaps he was not as entirely bad as I was inclined to think from my recent experience with him.

"Well, good day to you, Fräulein," he said, and waited until I had walked a little away before knocking on my uncle's door.

I soon forgot the odd coincidence as I continued on my way, I didn't think where. My mother would assume my interview with her brother had gone well and that I had spent the afternoon at his house, so I did not feel it necessary to rush home. Instead I let my steps take me where they would, as long as I could withstand the cold. I felt very free, knowing that for a short while, at least, no one expected anything of me. It was my first opportunity to think about the previous day's adventures, and after very little time, I realized that most of all I owed Zoltán an explanation—if he could ever bear to speak to me again—and that I really ought to tell him about the medallion in case he knew of it from before, even if I could not show it to him. After a few turns around Stephansplatz I went toward Schwedenplatz, where Zoltán lived. I hoped that Alida might still be there.

I walked in through the double street doors and started up the large wooden staircase. Aside from knowing it was on the third floor I couldn't really remember which apartment was Zoltán's, but I thought as I looked around that I would at least recognize the door.

Fortunately, I didn't have to risk knocking at the wrong place. As I mounted the steps, a door opened and slammed shut on the floor above me, and somehow I knew that the footsteps hurtling down toward me were Zoltán's. He stopped abruptly when he saw me, his momentum almost continuing to carry him headlong.

"I'm sorry! I had hoped to be able to thank Alida—and you—for your hospitality last night." My words sounded hollow and unnecessary.

Zoltán bowed frostily. "I shall convey your thanks to my sister, who has had to return to her position at court until next week."

He was about to continue on his way. It was obvious he was still furious with me. "Zoltán, please." I put my hand on his arm. "I need to speak with you, and . . . beg your pardon."

His determined frown relaxed a bit, but lacked the open friendliness I was accustomed to. "I must hurry to a rehearsal with Kapellmeister Haydn. You may walk with me if you wish."

Permission was better than outright dismissal, not as satisfactory as an invitation would have been. Still, I chose to swallow my pride and walk with him. His strides were long, and I scurried to keep up, so that my explanation sounded breathless. "It wasn't that I didn't believe you. I just had to see. And I'm glad I spoke to them. Danior and Maya were very kind, and I met a girl, Mirela. Why didn't you tell me Danior could play the violin like that? And Maya danced so beautifully. I'm beginning to understand why my father visited there. It was for the music, wasn't it? I mean, it must have been wonderful to be able to escape the formality of court for a little while." I stopped speaking and paused to catch my breath. "But there is"—I panted—"something else." I waited for Zoltán to notice that I no longer followed him. He hadn't said a word, but he only took two more paces before turning to me, not saying anything, but with a question in his eyes. "Frau Morgen found something on my father's body when she was laying him out and gave it to me," I said. "A gold medallion, on a chain."

He came toward me and took my elbow in his hand, steering me on in the direction of the Esterhazy palace, slowing his pace a little so that I could keep up. "A medallion, you say? Can you show it to me?"

Here was the difficult part. "I'm afraid I have lost it. I wore it yesterday, to the Gypsy camp."

He said nothing.

"I know it was foolish, but I did not want to leave it at home where Greta might have found it."

"Did you show it to anyone?"

I shook my head, then described it to him as best I could.

"Which way did the eagle face?"

I thought for a moment, then realized what had been odd about the eagle. "It had two heads, one facing in either direction, with a crown above it."

Zoltán stopped walking altogether and rubbed his forehead. "She could not have known," he muttered, then turned to me. "I think it is best that I give you some more information, so that you will not take any further risks. You must leave the investigations to others more qualified than yourself."

Something about his tone angered me. How dare he treat me that way, as if I were a nuisance who had interfered! I didn't see him doing much of anything to solve the mystery of my father's death. But then, perhaps he was doing something but was simply not telling me. Why should he, after all? "I'm not afraid. I need to understand. It's all that really matters to me."

"To understand," Zoltán said, "you must be made acquainted with matters that would put you in almost as much danger as your father faced, every day."

"Danger? As a violinist? What do you mean?"

"Your father was not merely a violinist. Nor am I merely a musician. Once you know these things, you will no longer be merely a girl."

A tingling sensation started somewhere in my middle and flowed quickly down to my fingertips and toes. What could he be saying? I had lied to him before when I said I wasn't afraid. I was.

"Your father met my father among the Roma in Hungary, before he began to work for the prince."

"Did he go to listen to music even then?"

"It started as that, but soon he became interested in our people, our difficulties."

Our people? What was he saying?

"I am part Gypsy. My sister is only my half-sister. Her mother died shortly after she was born. Our father met my mother when her tribe was camped near our village. She was beautiful."

Zoltán—part Gypsy, and an orphan, too. I never knew, or thought about it. I never asked, I supposed.

"We are a baronial family, but when my father took a Gypsy wife, he was banished from court and his lands were confiscated. Only through the good offices of an uncle who is a bishop was he able to secure a position at court for Alida."

With every word, Zoltán shocked me more and more deeply. Compared with his difficulties, my life seemed very safe and calm. I still didn't see, though, how all this related to some danger to my father.

"When your father was hired by Kapellmeister Haydn, the maestro became more than his employer, he became a friend. They spoke about many things, including our family. Your father brought Haydn out to hear the musicians in their camp, and then Haydn acted as intermediary, hiring some of the Gypsy musicians to go with the prince's guards when they marched to keep order. Others he engaged to entertain during carnival. These small gestures saved the entire community from starvation. They had been expelled from a place where they had made their camp and raised their livestock for generations."

"Expelled? Why?"

"Someone falsely accused them of stealing."

He did not need to say another word for me to feel the full force of the damage my actions might have done if I had shared my suspicions about the Gypsies with anyone else. Yet it appeared that they may well have stolen from my family after all, if someone took the medallion when I was at the camp the day before. I was afraid to mention my suspicion to Zoltán.

Instead, I changed the subject. "Why did my father never tell us any of this? He always did his best to be liberal with us, to give us a broad view of things—I was even permitted to read Voltaire." Although I remember how horrified my mother had been. The English colonies were in a state of open revolt, and she was convinced that the world as we knew it would come to an end because of the radical teachings of such men.

"There was another side to his championing the Romany,

and through them my family. Not long ago, the Hungarian nobles retained the right to treat their serfs as slaves, in direct contradiction to the reforms of the empress and Archduke Joseph II, now the Holy Roman Emperor and supposedly able to command such obedience from them. But the Hungarians called together all the noble families and the wealthy merchants for a meeting, and because they had standing armies that could have disrupted the peace of the region, they were not forced to comply with the new laws."

"But still, we are Austrian, not Hungarian. And my father was neither a Gypsy nor a serf."

By now our brisk walking had brought us to the Esterhazy palace. I wondered where the prince, whose title was Hungarian, stood with regard to reforms in favor of the serfs. He was very wealthy because of them. It was said he personally owned millions of souls. Yet who could own a soul? Wasn't it God who had the rights to a soul?

"My father had compounded his so-called crimes by being on the side of reform and had intended to free his serfs, but his domain was taken from him before he had the chance. Out of friendship for him, I believe, your good father worked tirelessly to bring about these reforms in Hungary."

That was the last thing Zoltán was able to say to me before we had to walk inside and thread our way through the corridors of the magnificent palace. I followed him without asking if it was all right for me to do so, believing that my godfather would not mind my attending the rehearsal.

When we arrived in the music room, all the other musicians in the orchestra were assembled, but Haydn was not there. Zoltán asked the concertmaster, Signore Torelli—who had recently taken over the first desk now that my father was no more—where he was.

"He will not come, Signor Varga. We cannot make him unlock the door of his study and bring the parts so that we may rehearse."

In my preoccupation with matters concerning my father I had forgotten about Haydn's difficulties with his eyes. Yet I had left him in a decent state of preparedness that morning, and no more than usually agitated about his immense workload. "I'll go to him," I said, and ran toward the anteroom where I knew I would find the maestro.

CHAPTER 13

Please, Godfather, let me in!" At first I only knocked, but then I started to pound on the door. I was about to give up when I heard footsteps approach on the other side, and after that a bolt slid back with a clunk. The door opened a crack and I pushed it open just far enough so that I could squeeze through. My body was thin, but the quilted winter petticoats I wore to stay warm made the operation more difficult than it should have been. As soon as I passed through, Haydn shut the door and bolted it again.

"What in heaven . . ." I looked around at the normally tidy room, where I had seen manuscripts carefully organized and filed in cubbyholes with labels, where a desk that looked hardly used was the main furniture, and where it was clear that the Kapellmeister didn't really do much of his creative work. Today, there was not a square of floor visible beneath the piles of disordered music. Sheets were mixed together haphazardly—I picked up two lying one on top of the other, and found a violin part from a symphony in one hand and a soprano aria from an opera in the other. "How did this happen?" I asked.

Haydn himself mirrored the chaos in the room. His bob wig was on crooked, the lace of his cuffs was tucked partly into his sleeves, and he had misbuttoned the row of buttons on his cutaway coat so that not only were the tails of uneven lengths, but the coat was so tight on him I could see the seams straining to burst.

"I did it, all myself. You see, I cannot find them. I prayed first, which has always worked before, but the parts I need are nowhere to be found."

And now not likely to be found by anyone else, either. "Did I not write them down for you this morning?"

"Yes indeed," he said, "and I brought them here in a folio. But I left the room to go to the water closet, and when I returned, the folio had vanished."

"Had the maids been in to clean?"

"They never come during the day. The prince has directed them not to, so that I would not accidentally be disturbed."

"Could you not have asked for help to find them?"

He did not answer, but stopped his frantic, half-blind searching for a moment. "I cannot. No one must know of my difficulties. It will destroy everything I have worked toward."

I did not know whether it was pride or stubbornness that made the maestro so unwilling to seek help—other than from me, with my limited ability to notate his work for him. It seemed an altogether inadequate solution for his failing eyesight. "Why can you not seek a physician? The prince must know the finest men in Vienna."

"It is not the prince I am worried about. It's Artaria."

"Who is Artaria?" I was beginning to think my godfather was losing his mind as well as his eyesight.

"He is a publisher. Most recently he has branched into the realm of music, and my dear prince has finally permitted me to lay before the public some of the works I have composed for him in recent years. Artaria will publish them." As he spoke, Haydn wandered around kicking scores here and there, picking up pages randomly, holding them close to his face to inspect them and then dropping them on the floor again.

I began collecting the music and reassembling it in piles, beginning with types of compositions—chamber music here, arias there, symphonies in another place. "But that is wonderful news, is it not?"

"It would be, were it not for the precise terms of the contract." He stopped his aimless picking up and putting down and flopped into a chair, watching me as I tried to put some order into the reams of music he had scattered around the room. "I did not realize when I read it that my eyes were so poor, and thought I had agreed only to give him new works. But it seems I committed myself to letting him publish everything I have produced in the last five years. If I do not surrender all such manuscripts to him by the fifteenth of January this coming year, I shall owe him all the money he paid me at the start of the contract."

The fifteenth was less than three weeks away. "Would it not be worth the purchase price of some time so that you could decide for yourself what you wish to give him?"

He sighed. "The money is long gone on gowns and gloves for my wife."

I had never met Frau Haydn, only seeing her occasionally from a distance. She came to court as little as possible and refused to be friendly with the musicians and their families. She was quite beautiful, but aloof. I wondered how such a warm, affectionate person like my godfather could ever have chosen to marry her. "There must be a way to remedy the situation. But what will you perform for the prince tonight, if you cannot find the parts for the symphony?"

I worked in silence for a while, and soon succeeded in placing most of the scattered music into neat stacks. Haydn stood from his chair and approached, I thought to examine my handiwork. As I watched, an impish smile spread over his face. He picked up the orchestral music and shuffled through the pages. "My dear, do you think you could find all the ones in the key of G for me? I'll look, too. I think I can see the signature well enough."

He handed me about half the pile. By now the musicians waiting in the other room to rehearse must have been truly puzzled, wondering what could be keeping their director. But none of them would be more so than I was at that moment. I commenced sorting, with no idea of what the eventual purpose would be.

"Rezia? Maestro?" Zoltán called to us from the

other side of the door and knocked politely every now and then.

"I'll be there directly!" Haydn shouted. "Quickly!" he whispered to me.

Soon we had amassed a respectable mound, about enough for a complete symphony. "Now, you find all the allegro sheets in those we've just sorted, and I'll look for the slow movements."

This process took a little less time. When we had finished, he turned to me with his mouth pressed in a smirk of glee. "Kindly go and tell the members of the orchestra that I will be with them in a moment. Just a little more sorting will do the trick."

He took hold of my elbow and steered me determinedly toward the door, unbolting it and opening it just far enough and long enough to thrust me out and directly into Zoltán, who caught hold of me. I righted myself as quickly as I could. I knew I was blushing, even as I knew that he must hate me now for going to the Gypsy camp. "The maestro says he will come as soon as he has refreshed himself. The orchestra is to wait."

"They could hardly do otherwise."

∴ ∾

I walked with Zoltán back to the music room. The musicians waited, indeed, but not impatiently. They talked and laughed, and I saw more than one deck of cards spread out on the floor to play, with copper coins changing hands quickly. Heinrich, whom I had not seen since Christmas

Eve when he helped to bring Papa's body to us, waved to me and smiled from his place among the brass at the back. Zoltán frowned and cleared his throat. Everyone looked up at him but hardly paused in their conversations and games. "The maestro is coming," he said, not loudly enough so that it would cut through the general turmoil. I think he did it purposely. One or two violinists nearby sat back in their seats and started retuning their strings. This got the attention of a few others, and by the time Haydn made his stately way in, his wig righted and coat rebuttoned, all but the percussionists had reassumed their respectful poses.

"Good evening, gentlemen," Haydn said.

There was a horrible crash as the cymbals fell off their stand when Jakob, the timpanist who had helped Heinrich and Zoltán a week ago, tried to scoop the playing cards off the floor too quickly. Everyone started to laugh, but Haydn's serious face brought a quick stop to any merriment. I stood over to the side, and from where I was could see just the faintest twitch of amusement in my godfather's cheek. What game was he playing?

"Herr Varga, would you please distribute these parts?"

He handed the pile of music we'd assembled from bits and pieces to Zoltán, who separated it into smaller piles and gave them to the men sitting in the first positions of each section. It was not long before the players were peering at the music on their desks and scratching their heads, looking at each other with puzzled expressions.

"I have decided to make an experiment with a new

kind of music. Since we are still in the Christmas season, I thought a bit of originality was called for."

"But Maestro," said the youngest flute player, a pimple-faced fellow from Salzburg who had just joined the orchestra, "this is simply the Menuet from the symphony we played last week."

A cellist stood. "No, you are mistaken. We have the allegro of the serenade from last night."

Soon everyone was talking and disputing.

"Gentlemen!" Haydn's voice rang out. I couldn't wait to see what he had in mind. "I shall set the tempo. We are all in the same key. I'll give you one measure, and then you are to play what is before you."

They started as he said, and I didn't know whether to be more surprised that there weren't more violent clashes or more desperate to hold in the convulsive laughter that such absurd music provoked. Haydn maintained his composure—he was notorious at playing straight-faced jokes on any unsuspecting victim—but it took about sixteen measures for the wind players to lose complete control of their mouths, and once they started laughing, the entire orchestra was soon reduced to fits.

"Gut, Freunden!" Haydn beamed. "Now get it out of your system so you can perform it as if you are serious about it this evening. What a joke that will be for His Highness!"

I heard a distant clock chime the hour of five. *I'm to meet my uncle at the dressmaker's before vespers!* I thought with a panic. The rehearsal was now well under way and I could not interrupt it. I tried to catch Zoltán's eye, but he was concentrating too hard on playing without laughing and did not look up from the sheet of music before him. I crept out of the palace into the dark, running as best I could among the evening crowds to reach Mademoiselle Helene's before the gentry would retire to dress for dinner and the shops close for the evening. I had almost forgotten to notice whether or not Schnabl had been at the rehearsal, but my impression was that he was absent. I made a mental note to tell Zoltán about it another time. I had no proof, since I could not look at the music he had taken to my uncle, but I did wonder if the folio Schnabl had been carrying was the one Haydn was missing.

CHAPTER 14

I had never been in Mademoiselle Helene's shop before in my life. Whenever my mother and I passed it on our way to go to market, she would point it out to me and say, "If your uncle Theobald decides to take an interest in your future, I daresay we could afford a gown from Mademoiselle Helene's." We were well off enough to pay someone else to make most of our clothing, but our tailor was the one a little way out of the center, where I had left Toby while I went to the Gypsy camp, not a fashionable dressmaker. Herr Groschen was a pleasant fellow who did his best to keep up with the fashions, and we always looked respectable and as much à la mode as necessary for a musician's family. His shop was a pleasantly chaotic hovel filled with fabrics and ribbons and laces. He had one elderly assistant whom he never introduced but I thought was probably his mother, and children were always given sweets to stand still to be measured. I looked forward to going there. He always seemed to have the latest gossip about the people we knew, the tradesmen and their families, which of them had just had babies, which others had received government appointments, and so on.

I could see right away that Mademoiselle Helene's establishment was much more formal and less friendly. A stiff, powdered footman greeted me as I entered a loge that had four doors leading off it in different directions, and a staircase directly ahead. The footman showed me into one of the rooms, much as one might in the private home of a wealthy person.

There I found my uncle apparently at his ease, drinking tea with a woman who was painted, powdered, and patched to the point that no single surface of her skin remained uncovered. She was squeezed into stays so tight that I wondered how she ever fit any food inside her belly, and her overskirt was caught up with ribbons so that she appeared to be seated on a silk cloud. Above her delicately shod feet her scrawny ankles could not be disguised by the finest silk stockings that must have taken weeks to knit but bagged in unattractive folds.

When I entered, she rose and gave me a tiny curtsy—I wasn't important enough for more than that. "We are to get you up for a ball, I hear. Will this be your first? Yes, yes, of course. So young, so pretty. It is time to make the most of what God has seen fit to give you."

She clapped, and three maids entered while she continued to chatter. They led me to a little platform and began removing my outer garments. I expected them to stop, but to my surprise they continued to unlace me until I stood in only my under shift and my quilted winter petticoat. When one of the girls began to untie my petticoat—which would leave me in my stockings and shift—I shouted out, "No!"

Everyone stopped and stared at me, but it was my uncle's expression that was most disturbing. His eyelids were half closed and his nostrils slightly flared. He wasn't exactly smiling, but his expression made me feel as if I were already completely naked. I folded my arms across my breasts, now starkly obvious without the stays to hold them flat against my chest.

"Come, Mademoiselle, we cannot measure you properly, and we have but one day to make your gown."

"Kindly leave the room, Uncle," I said, ignoring the dressmaker.

"Nonsense, my dear! I know more of fashion than you do and must exercise my superior judgment. And we are family, so there is nothing improper."

I could have sworn I saw him wink at Mademoiselle Helene. I wanted to run from the room, but to move at that moment would expose even more of myself to the rude eyes of my uncle, so I just gripped my arms tightly and glared at him.

"The girl is modest. She is not of the world yet, you understand, Monsieur. Perhaps you would look away while we take our measurements, then when she is properly draped we can again use your practiced eye?"

Although I had been disposed to dislike the dressmaker, I could have kissed her then. My uncle could not argue with her reasonable request and so, taking one last look at me, he swiveled around in his chair and pretended to stare out of a window that had been painted over so that no one on the street could look in.

By the time we finished, my uncle had laid down a great deal of money to purchase a rushed order of three petticoats, a white silk overgown embroidered with tiny blue flowers and three rows of ruffles at the hem, new stays, a lace tucker, a pair of soft kid gloves, silk stockings, silk evening slippers, a fan with ivory sticks and embroidered silk leaves, several yards of ribbon to wind into my coiffure, a velvet mantelet lined with silk and trimmed with fur, a matching muff, and a black silk necklace. The finishing touch was a wide-brimmed hat with a large, blue ribbon on it to match the flowers on my skirt. I liked the hat best of all.

The maids had redressed me and fixed my hair so that I looked somehow a little smarter and neater than when I had arrived. As I stepped out to the street with my uncle, I noted that the lamps had already been lit and were casting a lurid light over people now dressed for their evening entertainments. My stomach growled. I wondered if I had missed dinner at home. He put out his arm for me to take but I pretended not to see it and walked a little ahead of him.

"It is customary for a girl to thank a gentleman who furnishes her with expensive new clothing," he said.

I turned and faced him. "Thank you, Uncle, for fulfilling your promise to my mother so completely. I know she will be most grateful for the dowry at such time when I marry. Where shall I meet you to attend this ball?"

"We could have supper at my house before and then I could take you in my carriage," he said, that look coming into his eyes again.

"I would not want to leave my mother alone for such a long time. It would be better if we met at the assembly rooms." I would not give way in this. It was becoming clearer and clearer to me what he was about, and I didn't like it in the slightest. I knew my father would never have let things get even this far. I doubted my mother really understood what she had agreed to on my behalf. And if she were well, she would have come with me.

My uncle struck his forehead with the heel of his hand. "How stupid of me! I am afraid you must come to the Graben to dress. I have asked Mademoiselle to deliver your garments there." He shrugged and smiled. I felt like slapping him.

"Very well," I said, trying to keep the anger out of my voice. "I shall bring my own maid to help me. Tomorrow then? At six?" I smiled inwardly at the thought of Greta's presence to prevent any unseemly conduct on the part of my uncle. When we parted, I expected he thought he had arranged things completely to his satisfaction.

∴ ∴

Far from being cross with me, my mother was so pleased with how things had gone with my uncle (who had sent word to her about the appointment at the dressmaker's so that she would not worry) that she had asked Greta to keep some dinner warm for me and bring it on a tray to her room. She wanted to hear all about my new finery and the coming ball.

"I shall need Greta to help me dress," I said, leaving out the details about my uncle's behavior. I wanted only to secure my own peace of mind, not worry her.

"Greta? But she cannot leave me. I am as yet unable to rise from my bed. No, you had better make do with one of my brother's maids."

I had not expected this response. "But, Mama, do you think it's entirely proper for me to go without my own maid?"

"If your uncle were not your uncle, then yes, I would agree. But as he is family, there can hardly be any question of impropriety."

If only you knew, I thought. Yet I dared not say more. She was still in a delicate state of health. I would have to trust to my own wits to see me through. If I could survive wandering alone into a Gypsy camp, then what was one unpleasant uncle?

I was not at all at ease as I tried to close my eyes to rest for the next day. I had had to leave Zoltán without hearing the end of his explanation about my father, the Romany, and the Hungarian nobles. He had implied that somehow Papa had gotten involved in a cause that may have earned him powerful enemies. I still didn't understand exactly how or why, and whether there was anything other than friendship for Zoltán's father that would have made him do it. I needed to know everything. I determined that I would try to see Zoltán again the next morning. Perhaps he could also give me some advice about my uncle and the ball. Surely his sister had found herself in difficult situations with gentlemen. She was too beautiful not to have been an object of conquest many times. Somewhat comforted, I closed my eyes and tried to rest so that I could be prepared for whatever the coming day would bring.

CHAPTER 15

When I awoke the next morning, all the bells in the city were ringing to announce the new year. I felt as if I hadn't slept at all. I had had such vivid dreams I thought they were real. Zoltán stared down my uncle, who backed off and fell into the river. My mother rose from her bed looking well and had a healthy, rosy baby in her arms. Haydn sat at the keyboard directing his orchestra with confidence, a huge smile lighting up his face. I felt I had not rested much, but somehow my dreams had made me less anxious and worried. There had been a lot of snow overnight. The world outside my window had been transformed, and the light that reflected off the new snow even under a cloudy sky shed a soft, pure glow that always raised my spirits. Whatever difficulties lay ahead with my uncle, that night I would attend my first ball, wearing clothes I never dreamed I would own. For one night, I would feel like a lady.

I sprang from my bed and dressed, emerging before Greta had even finished laying out the rolls and cheese for breakfast. I ate a little, but my stomach was too unsettled and nervous to take much in the way of food. As I was tying on my cloak, Toby wandered in still looking as though he were deep in slumber. "Come Monday," I said, "you will be awakened at dawn to work. You had better get used to it."

He shot me a hurt look, and indeed I wondered why I was being so unkind to him. So far he had done nothing but help me, keeping his promise to be quiet about leaving him for so long at the tailor's and letting him walk home by himself. I know he felt just as wretched as I did about Papa. I could hear him through the thin wall that separated our rooms crying softly as he fell to sleep at night. Although he did not have the same feeling for music as I did, he loved to make things, and Papa had already taught him a great deal about the construction of a violin. His room was littered with all the bits of wood he had carved into whistles and toys with his skillful fingers. He would make an excellent luthier, I had no doubt. But that would be many years in the future. The time of apprenticeship stretched cruelly ahead. I knew he was clever enough, but I wondered if he would be strong enough to withstand the long hours of backbreaking labor.

I was suddenly struck with an idea. "Toby, would you like to come with me today? I'm going to see Godfather Haydn, and then there are some errands I must run. I will take you to a café for some chocolate and a cake."

His face brightened immediately. "May we play in the snow on the way?"

I mussed up his hair in response. "Eat quickly and then go and dress. I'll wait for you."

Within the hour we were skipping merrily through the fluffy, new snow. I had almost forgotten the joy of scooping up handfuls of the stuff and forming them into balls to throw at my impish brother's back. He flung one at me that hit my hair and undid what little of a coiffure I had made for myself. I was not worried. I could tidy up at Haydn's house, and in any case would have my hair completely rearranged for the ball that evening. I wondered if I would be the only young lady there who had spent the earlier part of her day hurling lumps of snow at her brother.

Our games made the walk pass quickly, and soon we arrived at my godfather's apartment. Just as I was going to knock at the door, it opened to permit a lady all dressed in the latest fashions to emerge. She took one look at our unkempt state and turned away with a frown on her face. The maid behind her stifled a laugh. "Come in, Fräulein Schurman," she said, leaving the door open wide for Toby and me. I glanced quickly and noted that the lady, whom I knew to be Haydn's wife although I had never seen her up close before, was climbing into a crested carriage stopped a little way down. My mother had told me that she carried on affairs so publicly that it was a disgrace. No doubt this was some lover's equipage, come to take her to a rendezvous. I seethed for my kind godfather.

I sent Toby off to the kitchen for treats, shed my snowy cloak, and rushed directly into the parlor to get to work before I noticed that Haydn was not alone. Zoltán stood gazing into a crackling fire that looked to have been newly laid. He and Haydn both wore serious expressions. I stopped in my tracks and curtsied.

"Sit down, Theresa," Haydn said. "We must talk a little before we get to work."

It passed through my mind that he was not happy with what I had done so far. But he would hardly have asked Zoltán to stay to witness my dismissal as his scribe—he was not so unkind.

"Zoltán tells me that you have visited the Romany, and that you know something about our cause."

Their cause? "I really know very little, except that you are sympathetic to the difficulties the Gypsies face, and that you admire their music. I also know that my father had some dealings with them, but I have not yet been able to discover exactly what they were."

The two men exchanged looks. I thought I saw Zoltán nod very slightly.

"It's all related to the publishing contract I told you about yesterday."

Now my head began to spin. What could Haydn's publishing have to do with Zoltán's family, the serfs in Hungary, and the Gypsies who roamed the countryside everywhere?

"Prince Nicholas is a very powerful man," my godfather said. "He is liberal in most respects, treats his serfs with kindness and consideration, and values his servants—especially his musicians, even his Gypsy musicians. But he fears—as do most Hungarian nobles—the consequences of giving serfs their freedom. He also knows that where he leads, others will follow.

"He guards his family's traditions very closely," Haydn continued, beginning to pace slowly about the room, as if it helped him organize his thoughts. "I have long wanted to lay my music before a broader public than the prince's invited guests, but he feared that I would be lured away to some other court, and so has not permitted it. Not until I gave him my word that I would never leave his service so long as he lived would he finally agree to let me publish my compositions. Hence my recent contract with Artaria."

This still wasn't making any sense. I looked to Zoltán.

"What the maestro is not telling you is that he also agreed to give all the proceeds from this contract to a fund that is being used to argue the legal position of the serfs in the Austrian and Hungarian courts, a fund that your father helped to establish. The prince does not know this, and we thought Artaria did not either. But it seems that someone has discovered it and started to make trouble for the maestro. This same person may have substituted several clauses in the contract so that it appeared that the maestro agreed to terms he never even imagined."

"That's an outrage!" I said, rising from my seat and placing my hand on my godfather's arm. He patted it and nodded.

"In short," Haydn continued, "if I do not hold to the contract, its terms and my intended use of the money will be laid before the prince. Not only will I lose my position, but he will ensure that no one else ever hires me again. And the cause will be lost for lack of money."

I no longer wondered that my godfather was so distressed about his poor eyesight, and that the loss of parts from the previous day had put him into such a state. I did feel a little appeased to know that the money had not actually gone to buy gowns for his unfaithful wife. "But what about my father? You believe his death has something to do with this, don't you?"

"In order to build a case and put it before the empress, we have had to amass more than money. It was necessary to gather information about the lords who were mistreating their serfs, who have been selling them like slaves and . . . taking the virginity of their daughters." Zoltán paused is if the mere mention of such atrocities took away his breath. "The Gypsies have helped, reporting what instances they have witnessed. But their word is not admitted to carry any weight. Your father had a keen ear, as you know. He possessed the ability to hear what people were saying from very far away. He acted as a spy for the cause, and when he could, he wrote down conversations he heard and also copied out any documents the Gypsies managed to find. Then he hid them in the case of his violin so that he could get them from Esterhaza or the Gypsy camp to Vienna, where they could be transferred to those who were assembling evidence."

"So perhaps it was not the violin that was stolen for itself, but the case." The pieces of this bizarre puzzle began to fall together for me.

"It was more complicated than that," said Zoltán. "Your father would take the documents to Danior, who would then put them inside his violin, and that way get them into the hands of the right people, through the good offices of my sister, Alida. The final transfer of some very important documents containing irrefutable evidence was to take place at a ball this evening, where a high-ranking official in the empress's court was to receive them under cover. I had convinced Prince Nicholas that it would be to his glory to lend out his orchestra to play."

"Where is this ball?" I asked, not daring to make the connection that seemed all too obvious at that moment.

"It's at the assembly rooms. A councilor by the name of Theobald Wolkenstein is the host. He has been the most outspoken defender of the rights of the nobles, and has enriched himself with the bribes they paid him to put their cause before the empress."

My uncle? In the pay of the Hungarian nobles against a cause my father embraced? And yet . . . I smiled. "Why, that's perfect! Don't you see? I am going to this ball."

Both my godfather and Zoltán looked at me with skeptical expressions on their faces.

"But it's true! Councilor Wolkenstein is my uncle, my mother's brother, and he has agreed to take me to the ball and begin the process of finding me a rich husband." I could not look at Zoltán as I spoke, but the flicker of sadness in the maestro's eyes was painful enough to see. "I don't want him to find me a husband," I said hurriedly, stealing a glance at Zoltán, "but I promised my mother I would see him. He is a horrible man. He bought me clothes, and has asked me to be nice to a particular gentleman. I don't trust him, though, which is why I've brought Toby."

Zoltán strode over to the writing desk and helped himself to a piece of paper and a quill. He scratched out something quickly, then folded and sealed it. "Do you have a servant who could deliver this to my sister at the Hofburg?" he asked Haydn.

Without answering, my godfather rang a little bell. The maid entered, and he instructed her to ask one of the stable boys to take the note, giving her a Pfennig to pay him.

"I believe Alida can also arrange to be at the ball," Zoltán said. He still had not looked at me. "I have asked her in this note to keep a close watch on you. I shall be in the orchestra. You are walking into a very dangerous situation, Rezia. I was not aware of your kinship to the councilor."

But I wondered if my uncle, far from being ignorant of my family's activities in recent years, actually knew a great deal and had deliberately set up this evening's events to entrap the others who were trying to help the serfs. So far all I had seen made me believe him capable of it. And now that I knew he had taken the opposite position from my father with regard to the serfs, it seemed too likely to be coincidence.

"Now I must ask you to help me once again with my music, Theresa," Haydn said. "Zoltán will let you know later what to do at the ball to preserve yourself from harm."

Zoltán bowed to Haydn, then approached me and took my hand. He bowed over it and brushed it with his lips. No one had ever kissed my hand before. His gesture made me gasp a little and he at last looked into my eyes. "Mind you take care, Rezia," he said, and increased the pressure on my hand just a little before he released it. He left quickly, practically running from the room, I thought. I, on the other hand, hardly dared move.

When I finally recalled where I was, I cleared my throat. "Shall we continue?" I asked, but not before noticing the little smile on my godfather's face. For the next hour, I had trouble concentrating on the notes my godfather sang, and had to ask him to repeat himself several times.

CHAPTER 16

After I finished my work with godfather Haydn, he took Toby and me in his carriage to the Esterhazy Palace. While I was in the palace watching the prince's servants scurry around, I was suddenly struck with an idea, a way to take Toby with me to my uncle's and then to the ball: he could act as my page, carrying my fan and lifting my train when necessary. Mama had told me the wealthy families sometimes had little boys serve such a function. When I asked my godfather about it, he agreed, and also managed to secure a page's uniform from the prince's household.

We arrived home with it wrapped up in a bundle just in time for me to bathe and have my hair dressed by a friend of my mother's, a talkative widow who earned a living by recreating fashionable coiffures for the wives and daughters of merchants. "This is the very latest style, you understand," she said, as she made my hair puff out by cleverly concealing tangled lumps of horsehair beneath it, and then pinned false curls stiffened with sugar water at the nape of my neck. They scratched abominably.

My mother at first did not want Toby to accompany me, but I pointed out to her that it would be an opportunity for him to see the kind of setting where the violins and violas he would make might be used, and to understand the true place of music in high society. "Besides, if I have a page, it will make up a little for my not having a maid," I said, "and we will not seem quite so poor." I neglected to mention there was every likelihood I would never attend another ball, and I certainly made no reference to the disturbing facts the maestro and Zoltán had told me earlier in the day. She agreed, but insisted on sending word ahead of time to my uncle.

When the hour came to make my way to the mansion on the Graben, I was very happy to be clinging to Toby's hand. And he stayed close by me, too, as if he could sense something of the air of menace that hung over the evening. I was fearful of what might happen, more fearful than I had been of going to the Gypsy camp. My uncle possessed power far beyond that of the wandering Romany. Although they could do away with me if they chose with the slash of a knife, my uncle might have me confined in a convent, or even a prison, to live out my days in withering solitude. I thought I would prefer almost anything to that, even a quick death.

Mama had given me her pearl earbobs to wear. There were tears of joy in her eyes when she beheld me with my hair all piled up and powdered, my cheeks and lips rouged.

"*Du bist sehr schön.* Your papa would be so proud!" she said, although I knew he cared little for the fripperies and refinements of ladies. In fact, I thought he might rather have been disappointed to see me got up like that. For one moment I imagined flinging my arms around and tossing my head just as Maya had done during her dance in the Gypsy camp, and all the bits of horsehair flying out in every direction, powder dousing those nearest to me. I had to bite my lip to keep from laughing.

I soon contained myself, however. I hoped that the evening would prove to offer only dancing and gaiety, that my uncle would be too busy with his friends to bother about me, and that whatever Zoltán wished to accomplish would occur without fanfare or difficulty. I hoped.

⁂

Everything started off well when the valet informed me that my uncle had been called to an emergency council session and would meet me at the ball. "Your gown has arrived, and the carriage will be called to take you to the assembly rooms at nine of the clock," he informed me, then snapped his fingers at the snobbish maid who had treated me so disdainfully the first two times I visited my uncle's house. "Hildegard will do for you."

So, her name was Hildegard. I was secretly delighted that she was now called upon to help me dress, although I restrained myself from saying anything unkind to her.

She, on the other hand, expressed her annoyance in a thousand little ways, the most irritating of which was yanking so hard on the laces of my stays that I thought she would squeeze the breath out of me.

"Is that quite necessary?" I gasped.

"The councilor said to do my best with you," she said, giving another fierce tug. "And that will take some effort."

I was relieved when the doorbell jangled somewhere deep in the house and she let go of my laces. "Now who could that be?" Hildegard muttered. "I'd better see."

She left me standing in the middle of the room in front of a large cheval glass. My face was red and my head had already started to pound. I reached behind and tried to loosen my laces but I couldn't manage it.

A few moments later I heard excited chatter approach from the vestibule, make its way up the stairs, and crescendo toward my room. Hildegard sounded flustered. "Herr Wolkenstein said nothing about a maid! I'm sure I'm not to let you in."

"Ach, *Gott im Himmel,* he must simply have forgotten. I always attend Mademoiselle Schurman when she steps out."

Mirela! How on earth had she discovered where I was, and what had made her come? I prepared myself for the unlikely sight of the wild Gypsy girl in my uncle's sedate house, but when the door flew open, I had another surprise. Instead of her bright costume and the rings in her ears, Mirela wore a plain black dress with a simple cape and bonnet over it.

"Why didn't you say you had a maid coming?" Hildegard snapped at me.

"I . . . I . . . sent her on an errand and wasn't certain she would complete it before I needed her," I answered, doing my best to recover from my own shock. "Mirela can take over now. You are dismissed." I lifted my nose into the air and flicked my hand at Hildegard. I knew it was very rude of me, but I couldn't help feeling a small glow of pleasure as she sulked off.

"Please, can you loosen my stays," I begged Mirela as soon as the door shut behind Hildegard.

She got right to work, and in a few moments I could breathe easily again. While she continued to help me into my elaborate dress, Mirela whispered into my ear, "I'm sorry, Rezia, to surprise you like this. But Danior spoke to Zoltán, and—I don't really know how to make it right, but you see, I thought . . ."

She stopped speaking. I looked at her face in the mirror. She had gone red, and there was such a tightening around the corners of her mouth that for a moment I thought she might be about to cry. She finished lacing up the dress in the back, then put her hand in her pocket and drew out a brightly colored handkerchief, covered in patterns that resembled those on the rugs in Maya's hut. Without looking at me, she held it out in my direction. Was she giving me a gift? I already had a lace-edged *Handtaschen* to take with me to the ball.

I didn't understand her action until I realized that the kerchief was only a covering for something else: my gold medallion—well, the medallion my father had been wearing, at least. "Did you—," I began.

She put her finger to my lips. "I do not have time to explain now. You mustn't be cross. But Danior says you are to wear it this evening."

I was too surprised to be angry, and glad to have the medallion back. "Will you come with me to the ball?" I asked.

She smiled. "No, I must go back to the camp. Maids like me are not welcome at an assembly ball!" She stepped back, cocked her head to one side, and surveyed me from head to foot. "You look beautiful! Such a lady."

Her compliment made me glow from the inside. I don't quite know why, but I wanted to embrace Mirela, to hold her close to me like a sister. Her theft of the medallion seemed suddenly not to matter. Although I knew next to nothing about this Gypsy girl, I felt a kinship with her that I had never felt for another friend before, not even Toby. But there wasn't time to think about it much. I simply smiled as she dipped a quick curtsy to me and opened the door so that I could pass through. I held my head high and maneuvered my voluminous skirts out into the hallway and down the stairs.

∻

Toby was showing signs of boredom as he waited for me by the door, picking at a thread that dangled from the ruffle of his shirtsleeve. My little brother appeared very handsome in Prince Nicholas's livery—handsome, but small, I thought. One of the steps creaked as I descended, and he quickly jumped up from his seat and put his hands behind his back, as I had taught him on the way over. I think my appearance was so altered that he was struck dumb. It seemed likely his jaw would drop all the way to the floor. *"Bei alle Engeln!"* he said. I didn't know whether he was merely surprised or meant to compare me with an angel. I laughed.

Mirela saw us into the carriage, then stood and waved as we drew away from my uncle's door. I regretted that she would not be with us, and felt distinctly more anxious about the coming evening without her.

The carriage had an elegant, wooden body suspended on springs attached to large, delicate wheels. Inside, the walls were lined with satin, and we sat upon velvet cushions. Four beautiful bay horses pulled us along the icy streets, a liveried coachman drove, and two footmen stood on platforms at the back holding torches up high. A postilion sat on one of the horses at the front, calling out, "Make way for Councilor Wolkenstein's carriage!" I could not resist looking out to see the common folk—people no lower in status than we were—staring at us as we passed.

I could have ridden around Vienna all evening and enjoyed myself quite well, but we had only a short distance to go before arriving at the public assembly rooms. They were in a large, modern building behind the ancient Rathaus, the place where all the business of the city was transacted—licenses issued, criminals charged, heroes honored. We had to wait in a line of carriages before it was our turn to descend, but even before we turned the corner, I could see the glow from the assembly rooms' brightly lit windows. As we approached the entrance, the footmen hopped off their perches. One of them opened the carriage door while the other helped me climb down the steps. I had told Toby his job was to keep my train from trailing in the snow—which had now turned to mud and manure because of all the horse and carriage traffic that had preceded us.

Even though I felt as elegant as the most distinguished woman I had ever seen, I realized as soon as we entered the main ballroom that compared with the truly wealthy, I still appeared humble. I wore no diamonds in my hair or around my neck, buckled to my waist or wrapped around my wrist. Nonetheless, many heads turned to look at me when my name was announced despite the fact that all I had on in the way of jewelry was the gold medallion, which hung right at the level of my breasts and drew many eyes directly to that part of my body. I quickly tucked it inside my bodice.

To my dismay, as soon as I took a step forward my uncle rushed up to me and claimed my arm.

"You look very pretty," he whispered, smiling and nodding to his acquaintances as we passed. Toby had let go of my train. I looked back and saw him being ushered over to the side by a footman to stand in a group with the other pages. At least there were some boys his age present. Perhaps the evening would not be too dull for him.

"I am sorry I could not have escorted you here myself," my uncle said. "Some—developments, you know."

My uncle cut quite a different figure from the one I had met previously at his ease in his everyday garb. I wondered where he had gone to change into his purple satin evening coat, gold waistcoat, black breeches, and red high-heeled shoes with gold buckles. There was so much lace clustered at his throat that as he walked it caught a slight breeze and flipped up into his face. He blew it down quickly each time, but our step *poof* step *poof* progress struck me as so funny I could hardly contain my laughter.

I soon realized that we were aiming toward a group of old men standing off to the side. As we approached, I noted several diamond and emerald rings on their fingers, and one or two wore military medals and ribbons on their breasts. "Gentlemen, my niece, Fräulein Theresa Maria Schurman," my uncle said when we reached them. I curtsied low. Whoever they were, there was no question in my mind that they were all either noble or at least wealthy, and so required the deepest reverence. When I rose from my curtsy, I could not help noticing the expressions in their eyes, which were variations of the hungry look my uncle had when he watched me at the dressmaker's.

"Might I request the pleasure of the first dance with your niece?" said the one who looked the oldest and most decrepit.

"Of course, General Steinhammer," my uncle said, his smile stretching and pushing the folds of fat on his cheeks to the edges of his face. He didn't give me a chance to answer for myself.

But as the general reached for my hand, I felt a gentle touch on my shoulder.

"Ah, there you are my dearest!"

Everyone, including my uncle, bowed deeply to the lady whom I knew before I saw her would be Alida Varga. I turned and flooded her with a grateful look. She linked her arm in mine. "I know you will forgive me, gentlemen, but I wish to present my cousin to Her Highness the Archduchess."

Six pairs of astounded eyes shifted back and forth between Alida and myself. We looked nothing at all alike—she had golden-blond hair, round blue eyes, and clear, even skin with a warm glow, whereas I had light-brown hair and gray eyes that drew to points at their outsides, and I tended to freckle—making her claim to kinship rather unbelievable. I curtsied to the gentlemen and let her lead me away, knowing that my uncle would be utterly furious with me, and rapidly trying to figure out how I would avoid him for the remainder of the evening.

We took a leisurely stroll around the room. Alida's pleasant expression never varied. It seemed that every other person nodded or bowed to her as we passed. One or two elderly ladies stopped her and asked to be presented to me. She made the introductions with no excuses for my humble name, and we continued until we came quite close to the orchestra, which was arranged on a dais at one end of the ballroom. I noticed Zoltán, of course, who followed us with his eyes as we passed by.

"There is a certain plan for the evening," Alida said. "And we would very much like your help in executing it. I was meant to complete the task, but I would have put myself at great risk of discovery and jeopardized everything we have been working toward. And so now I shall ask you."

I was conscious of the light pressure of her skin against my arm.

"The general you were about to dance with was responsible for a terrible massacre near our estate in Hungary about five years ago," Alida continued, still smiling sweetly. "We believe he is one of the people named in the report your father was carrying the night he was killed."

I began to tremble. Somehow, until that moment, everything had seemed very remote and unreal. How could bits of paper, and secrets about people far from our cozy apartment in Vienna, have anything at all to do with me? Yet it was these bits of paper that had led my father to risk so much. And it was this general who had almost touched my hand who might have been involved in his murder.

Alida took two glasses of wine from a footman's tray and gave one to me. "You must be strong. You look beautiful. Tonight, if you are willing, you will learn how to use that beauty without giving up your virtue." She steered me casually into an empty anteroom. "Let me fix your train, my dear," she said loudly so that anyone nearby would assume that was our reason for entering the deserted space.

Alida leaned in close and whispered instructions to me, at the same time tucking a small, folded piece of paper into the top of my bodice, where it caught on the medallion and chain. I intervened, pulling out the medallion so that I could better hide the note.

"Ah, so you found the pendant," Alida said, taking the medallion in her fingers and turning it over.

"Yes. It was the most extraordinary thing," I began to explain to her, but she put her finger to her lips.

"You may tell me later. After I finish explaining what you are to do, you will return to the ballroom and let the general claim you for his partner. Wait until the musicians perform the Ländler. He will hold you close for part of the dance and you should lean forward—so." She demonstrated a coquettish pose that allowed me to see into the top of her gown so that I blushed beneath my rouge. "Then let the general know you have something important to show him."

"What do I do then?" I noticed that she hadn't really given me an opportunity to refuse, but I wouldn't have anyway. I was too much under her spell.

"Lead him off the dance floor to this room."

"Suppose he does not follow me?"

Alida smiled. "I have no doubt that he will do precisely as you wish."

"And once I am here? What then?"

She was about to tell me, but the sound of laughter

approached, and a young girl with a rather drunk-looking gentleman following her slipped into the room. "Oh! I do beg your pardon," she said.

"We were just leaving." Alida turned to me. "There, you are all fixed. Shall we return to the dance?"

CHAPTER 17

When we emerged from the anteroom, the ballroom was much more crowded than it had been before. Now it was difficult to get from one place to another, and Alida had to let go of my arm just to avoid bumping into people. Every other word I heard was "Pardon," or *"Entschuldigen-Sie."* Soon I lost sight of Alida completely. I remembered to hide the medallion away again. The attention it seemed to receive when it was in view made me even more uncomfortable than the stares that followed me. I did my best to appear as if such public gatherings were as natural to me as breathing, and listened to the music to calm myself. The small orchestra—more a band, really—was playing something quiet that was meant as a backdrop since the dancing hadn't started yet. I recognized a popular aria from one of Salieri's operas.

"Theresa Maria!"

My uncle's voice startled me into whirling around. He

reached out and grasped my arm with so much force that I thought someone might notice.

"How do you come to be *related* to a maid of honor?" he hissed into my ear. "Especially one who is known to have Reformist sympathies?"

I was spared the need to answer him by General Steinhammer, who bowed to me and restated his intention to claim my first dance. The orchestra struck up a leisurely triple time, and I decided I had better not put off the task Alida had given me. I saw her joining the dance with a handsome young officer. But they were down at the other end of the room.

To my dismay, however, rather than a country dance, which would have made conversation difficult, the movement changed to a Polonaise. The reason soon became clear: the archduchess had risen to take the floor, her partner none other than my uncle. Now we would have to promenade around the room, and I would be forced to talk to the general. What I had recently learned about him from Alida made my flesh crawl as he lifted my hand to lead me into the dance. I couldn't help watching my uncle smile and lean in to whisper to the archduchess, who more than once fluttered her fan in front of her face to hide a giggle.

ONE, two, three, ONE, two, three, I counted to myself, getting into the rhythm of the dance and trying not to forget to sink into one knee and point out the other toe on the strong first beat, then rise up on my toes to step for the weak beats two and three. I noticed that most dancers simply walked in time to the music, but a few stalwarts among us actually tried to dance. That made it a little easier not to talk, since it was also necessary to angle one's head out prettily in the direction of the extended foot every three beats. So I looked first toward the general, then away.

"I daresay you are a fine dancer, but I had something particular I was hoping to say to you, Mademoiselle." The general had gripped me closer to him so he could speak into my ear when I turned away, and now I could ignore him no longer.

"Yes, Your Excellency?" I said, lowering my eyes modestly and bending just a little from the waist as Alida had shown me. His eyes found my cleavage as if a magnet had drawn them there. I felt faintly nauseated. I could see the entire train of events before me and would have no power to avert them once they commenced. Once I did as Alida had instructed me, I would have crossed a threshold. I knew that such actions would initiate me into a world of deceit, and I could no longer claim to be entirely innocent.

At that moment we passed by the end of the ballroom where the orchestra sat. Zoltán was in the last chair of the first violins. I looked at him just in time to catch him watching me before he focused on the music in front of him again. I could not see his expression. What must he think of me? I wished I could clap my hands and make time stand still for a moment so that I could run and talk to him, explain that I was about to flirt shamelessly with this old general on the instructions of Alida, that my actions had nothing to do with what I really wanted or how I really felt.

But the moment flew by, and soon we were approaching the door to the anteroom where Alida had told me to bring the general.

Now was the time to act. On the next strong beat in his direction I puffed out my chest and leaned forward so that he could get a good look. "Perhaps if you have something particular to say we could find a private room, so that I may hear it the better." I drew him quickly out of the line and threaded us through the crowd. *What if they're all looking at me and they think I'm doing this because I want to?* I thought, suddenly conscious of other eyes upon us and one or two knowing smiles.

All at once, a disturbance at the opposite end of the room drew everyone's attention away. I thought I saw a flash of Alida's golden blond hair, followed by whispers all around of "She fainted," and "One of the maids of honor has swooned." I did not know whether Alida had timed the diversion on purpose, but I thanked her nonetheless as the general and I slipped into the anteroom.

⁂

The door closed behind us, and suddenly I was alone with a man I had been told was a heartless butcher. I did not know what to do next, because Alida's instructions had been cut short by the interruption. I said the first thing that came into my head. "What was it you wanted to tell me, General?" I batted my eyelashes in an attempt to act coquettish.

He moved toward me, eyes not on my face but on the

flesh just above my low bodice. I resisted the impulse to turn away or cover myself with my hands, instead puffing out my chest again.

"I wanted to tell you what a pretty thing you are, and suggest that we come to some mutually acceptable arrangement that would satisfy both our needs."

I had no needs that he could satisfy and I didn't want to ask myself exactly what he meant. I turned and walked a little away from him. "Sir, I do not know what you suggest. You cannot be speaking of marriage!"

"Marriage! I should say not. My wife, God bless her, is in excellent health. I speak of something much more entertaining." He walked forward, hands reaching out to grasp me.

I stepped quickly to the side to avoid him. "My uncle, sir, has undertaken to find me a suitable match."

The general's chuckle made me blush. "It was your uncle, my dear, who thought of this arrangement in the first place, knowing that I am willing to pay him well—and you, of course—for certain compensations."

It took all my powers of self-control not to spit in his face and storm out of the room. I had to remind myself that Alida and Zoltán would not have placed me in this position if there had been any other way to accomplish their goal, and that what was at stake was important enough that my father had possibly sacrificed his life for it. Yet however distasteful the general was, the thought of my uncle was worse. How could he do it? He had as much as agreed to sell me to the general! I hoped that perhaps in some twisted way he thought of it as advancing my position in society. Was it possible that other girls of my station—girls who had not been brought up to believe in honor and humility and saw it only as an opportunity to enrich themselves—would not think twice before agreeing to the arrangement the general presented?

Recalling Alida's instructions, I did my best to make it appear as if my hesitation were an act of flirtation. "Well, if my uncle has sanctioned it, then I have a message for you." I leaned over a little at the waist again, and reached into my bodice for the note that Alida had given me. I drew out the piece of paper, and in the process pulled out the medallion as well.

The general clasped my hand hard and took the note from it, opening it with one hand and keeping me gripped with his other. I watched his smile fade as he read, and then his eye rested on the medallion. A look of horror mixed with fury came into his eyes. "Do you know what you're playing at, *verdammte Tusse*?" the general snarled at me, yanking me toward him. I tried to wrench free, but he wrapped his other arm around my waist and pulled me into him, squeezing me so that I could hardly breathe. His breath smelled foul, like wine and rotten food. "I don't know where you found that bauble, and whoever gave you this note will find himself regretting it."

At first I thought he was going to bite me like a mad dog. But just as I realized he intended instead to give me a fierce kiss on the mouth, I heard a noise from behind me. Before I had a chance even to wonder what it was, two men with masks approached, laid hold of the general, and pulled him away, at the same time stuffing a gag into his mouth. I was suddenly at liberty. I opened my mouth to scream out of sheer surprise, but one of the men who had grabbed the general put his finger to his lips to shush me. The general struggled against them in vain. He was old and overpowered.

By now I had recovered enough to recognize Danior's eyes behind one of the masks. He smiled his even smile at me before whispering, "Well done, *Kushti.*"

CHAPTER 18

My heart would not stop thumping in my chest as I watched Danior and the other man drag the general through a door hidden in the paneling of the anteroom, its real purpose doubtless to permit servants to come and go discreetly. In an instant, I was alone, feeling how close I had come to being soiled by that despicable man's lewd proposition and still feeling the pressure of his clammy hands on my waist. I took a few deep breaths to calm myself and patted my coiffure, pushing a bit of horsehair back into its place and pinning my hat down more securely. I pulled up my bodice and tucked the medallion back in its hiding place. Now I had no doubt at all that there was some deep significance to the pendant. My father could not have possessed it by chance. I paused a moment longer to calm myself before opening the door to the ballroom again. I should rejoin the festivities as if nothing had happened.

As I was about to leave the anteroom, something on the floor caught my eye. In the scuffle, the general must have dropped the note I gave him. Although I told myself I must pick it up so that it would not fall into someone else's hands, my real reason was simple curiosity. The thought crossed my mind that I ought perhaps to let the message to the general remain a secret to me, that I might learn more than I wished to if I knew what it said. But that was only for a second: I had a right—and a duty, I told myself—to know what it contained. After all, I had risked both my reputation and my safety to deliver it. I smoothed it out with trembling hands.

The emperor will be informed.

That was all. Five words. For the general to have responded so violently to it only confirmed that he had something to hide. I still didn't know exactly what, or even how much it had to do with my father's secret activities. Or perhaps I was mistaken. The general may have assumed that someone planned to tell the emperor that he had tried to seduce me. The imperial family was notoriously virtuous and very religious. Yet who would really care? Didn't things like this happen all the time? And there was the medallion, too, and the general's response to seeing it.

My mind was spinning as I continued into the ballroom. Couples had formed for a contredanse, and almost everyone—except the older ladies and gentlemen with canes—was stepping through the complicated figures. I looked for Alida, spotting her once again with the handsome captain who had led her out in the Polonaise. On the opposite side of the room, the pages still huddled together, a bouquet of young boys in livery whispering to each other and playing what games they could without leaving their posts. I looked for Toby among them.

He was not there.

I quickened my pace toward the pages, at the same time scanning the room for my uncle, who had also vanished. *Perhaps they returned home,* I thought, but then dismissed that as impossible. They would not go without me—unless, it occurred to me, my uncle assumed I would be departing with the general. Over in another corner stood two or three of the men I had been introduced to by my uncle, deep in serious conversation. Uncle Theobald was not among them. Perhaps they would know where he and Toby had gone.

On my way to them I paused and asked one of the pages, "Did you see a young fellow named Tobias Schurman, in blue-and-gold livery? Prince Nicholas Esterhazy's livery?" He shrugged.

Then the fellow next to him said, "Oh, he was here, I remember, but Councilor Wolkenstein came and took him away. Seemed angry about something."

I thanked him for the information. *At least he was with my uncle,* I thought. My angry uncle, apparently. What had provoked my uncle Theobald? Had he seen my behavior toward the general? It was exactly as he had asked me. That should rather have pleased him.

Unless, I thought with growing unease, he had somehow discovered that the general had been abducted.

I tried to get Alida's attention, but she was caught up in the dance and gazing steadily into her partner's eyes.

Perhaps it would be easier to make my way to Zoltán, find some way to tell him what had happened, and see if he had noticed anything or knew why Toby and my uncle had vanished.

But as I started to move through the crowd, the music came to a stop and the entire assembly began to surge against me. I might as well try to fight the currents in the Danube as push against a ballroom full of dancers intent upon reaching the banquet hall next door.

I scanned the sea of faces for anyone I knew. All the ladies with their powder and rouge looked like puppets, and the men, faces red now from drinking and exercise, all blended into variations on the face of the general, which I could not banish from my mind.

I must get out into the air, I thought. The smell of food nauseated me. I did not know where the cloaks had been placed, nor whom to ask. I was so overheated that I wanted to run out without even bothering to retrieve my wrap.

"Theresa, what is wrong?"

I whirled around at the sound of Alida's voice. Her hand upon my arm felt cool. It stilled the rapid beating of my heart, and I felt calmer very quickly. "Toby is gone," I whispered, "and so is my uncle. I don't know what happened."

A flicker of alarm passed through her eyes. "Had you said anything to your uncle?"

"No!" I exclaimed, then lowered my voice again. "As far as I know he just saw me dancing with the general and then entering the anteroom, an event I believe he wished for as much as you did." I blushed.

"*Sei mutig*, Theresa. Have courage. Perhaps your brother stepped outside. It is very warm in here."

The dashing captain Alida had been dancing with joined us at that moment. "Might I fetch you some refreshments?" he asked, smiling into her eyes and hardly noticing me.

"Captain Berenger, allow me to present my cousin, Fräulein Theresa Schurman," Alida said. I curtsied and he bowed. "Theresa has lost her page, and wishes to return home. He was dressed in blue-and-gold livery. I don't suppose you have seen him?"

"No," he said, "but I am certain we could find someone to retrieve the lady's wrap and see her to her lodgings, if that is her wish."

"Excuse me," I said, and curtsied to Alida, giving her a look that I hoped conveyed the extent of my fear. I had to find Toby, and I intended to start at my uncle's house.

I asked the first footman I encountered to bring my wrap. I paced up and down in front of the doors while I waited what seemed a long time for him to return with it. I did not let him help me put it on, but threw it over my shoulders and ran out into the cold. I knew my elegant skirts were dragging in the mud, and I felt the satin of my slippers catch on the jutting edges of cobbles and tear. Somewhere along the way my hat flew off. I did not care. If I could have, I would have instantly transformed my finery into a plain, woolen dress, taken down my absurd coiffure, and covered my head with a simple cap. Anxious tears flowed down my cheeks, no doubt making the powder that coated them gather into unsightly clumps. I did not care.

⁘

In very little time I arrived at the door of my uncle's house in the Graben. It was dark and shut up, as if even the servants had retired for the night. I flew up the steps to the front door and began pounding on it and calling out. I knew it would create a disturbance, but I had to rouse my uncle and figure out where Toby was.

I noticed a few candles appear in neighboring windows by the time the bolt was drawn and the door opened to me. I found myself confronted not by the maid but by the icy valet. He smiled a humorless smile. "The councilor said I should expect you. Would you care to wait in the parlor?"

"No, I would not care to wait. Where is Toby? My brother?"

"I fear you must speak to your uncle, and he has gone out briefly. I expect his return at any moment."

The valet was tall, but he looked frail. He was also old. I had no doubt that I could outrun him. His only advantage would be in knowing the house well.

"Toby!" I screamed as I tore up the stairs two at a time, my petticoats bunched in my fists so that I would not trip. "Where are you?! Toby!"

Somewhat to my relief, the valet did not follow me, but remained in the vestibule holding the lamp. I soon wished I had thought to grab it from his hands, though. The rest of the house was darker than night, and I bumped into several small items of furniture and sent one or two fragile knick-knacks crashing to the floor. As I ran up and down stairs, opened doors, and peered into musty rooms that I could tell even in the dark were devoid of life, I became increasingly convinced that I was alone in the house with the valet. Even the rooms in the attic where the servants slept revealed nothing by the soft light from the street-lamps outside but neatly made cots and a crucifix on the wall. With the exception of the valet, the staff had obviously been given the night off.

I had been over the entire house except for the cellars. I gradually slowed my frantic pace as I returned to the vestibule to confront the dour face of my uncle's lackey.

"I would like you to show me below stairs," I said, mustering my most commanding tone of voice. I had no wish to descend to the cellars alone without a light to frighten away the rats. This fellow was so still and quiet I thought for a moment he might be a simpleton. In any case, I no longer feared him for himself, without my uncle to give him power. He was just a servant in a grand house.

"Follow me," he said, agreeing perhaps a little too readily when I thought about it afterward.

He led me through the kitchens, also empty except for a cat that stirred from its sleep on the hearth just long enough to hiss at me as we passed. He unlocked the door to the most lavishly stocked pantry I had ever seen—with more food stored on its shelves and hanging from its hooks than our entire family would eat in a year, I thought. We passed through this to a door so small I had to crouch to get through it, and the valet nearly had to bend in half. We descended a curved flight of stone steps and ended up in a vaulted underground space. The first room contained racks and racks of wine bottles. It seemed remarkably clean for a cellar. Several other rooms led off that one, the first of which contained stacks of firewood, another with barrels of something that might have been ale, and mounds of turnips and onions. Nothing seemed even the slightest bit out of the ordinary, and my brother was not hidden anywhere in this perfectly orderly space.

It was all as it should be, I thought, until I passed through to the last, large room, which I decided had to be beneath the grand dining room. This area was completely empty. Not in the way of an unused space, but as though it had been scrubbed clean in the recent past. At its end was yet another door, dark and ancient with a pointed top. I rushed to it, grasped the iron ring that served as its handle, and tried to open it. It was locked. The valet had followed me in and lit the way—by now I thought him quite accommodating—and approached with an iron key.

"I presume you would like to see this room as well?" he said.

Thinking back to that moment, I should have been more cautious. I should have paid attention to my first instincts, which were not to trust this servant, who was clearly devoted to my uncle. But instead I stood back and let him open the door. And once it was open, I stepped through it and found myself at the top of a flight of stairs. I could hear water dripping somewhere, and realized I was at the entrance to the new sewers that meandered beneath the city streets and took the waste from thousands of water closets and chamber pots away to the Danube. I turned to escape the stench and saw the smiling face of the valet as he closed the door between us, leaving me alone in the cold, dark space.

CHAPTER 19

There was nothing else to do for the moment but try to accustom my eyes to the dark. Somewhere in the distance I heard a splash. I didn't want to think what it could be. I was glad it was not morning, when practically all of Vienna would be emptying foul-smelling garbage into the sewers.

Yet if I did not find a way out, I would quite possibly still be there by morning. I turned and tried the door. Better to face my uncle than the sewers. It was locked. Perhaps the valet did not know it was locked and had just meant to frighten me? I pounded and yelled, "Let me out! I'm stuck in here!" But there was no response.

My uncle would never leave me here, I thought. Whatever he had done, I could not believe he would abandon his niece. But what about the valet? I did not even know his name, so how could I plead with him? He was the only one who knew where I was. What if he never told anyone?

Although it was not as cold below ground as it was in the winter air, the damp of the water and the night chill soon entered my bones, and I began to shiver violently. I had been cold before, but this chill was different. It wasn't like the cold of a snowy winter's day in the countryside, riding a sled to a cabin where a warm fire awaited, as we sometimes did during the holidays. Papa and several of his friends from the orchestra would bring their instruments, and they'd play and play while we drank hot chocolate and tea. Then we'd all bundle up and pile into the sleds and return to Vienna. Even Mama came along, and she was always so gay and happy.

My mother. I thought of her then, doubtless waiting up for our return so that she could hear about all the young men I had danced with at the ball. Would she ever suspect that something like this could have happened? And what of Toby? I prayed that despite what was happening to me he had simply been taken home. At first, I was mostly angry at having been treated like this. I realized that the valet would never have locked me in the cellar on his own initiative, that my uncle must have instructed him to do it if I came. But why? Unless he knew about the general. And why take Toby away?

This wouldn't be the first time I had been entrusted with Toby and lost sight of him, I thought with a guilty stab. I had begged to be allowed to take him to a puppet show when he was about four and I was eleven. Once we were there, I became so caught up in the action, the excitement of the puppet knights riding their wooden horses into battle, with the sparks and smoke and other tricks of the puppeteers, that I completely forgot where I was. When it was over, I looked down and Toby had vanished. My first thought had been that I would get a beating, but I soon realized I should be concerned more about my brother than myself. I found him quickly, though, huddled in a corner because he was frightened. By the time we returned home, I had managed to dry his tears and persuade him to say that he had had a wonderful time, and not tell anyone that I had nearly lost him. My final, desperate hope was that he was playing a joke on me now, getting back at me for that time years ago, and was safe at home.

As time passed and I remained where I was, my hopes for release faded. My anger began to give way to fear. If my uncle was capable of locking me in an empty cellar, what else might he do? He had been so angry when Alida had taken me away in the ballroom, and perhaps he suspected that I had been involved in the general's abduction. Whatever it was, I soon realized that simply waiting for him to come back and let me out of the cellar might be the most dangerous thing to do.

I forced myself to think and focus on saving myself. The dark had become less obscure to my vision by then, and I could see that the flight of stone steps led right down into the filthy water. I could also see that at the base of the steps a small skiff was tied up and ready to use. I had heard that servants were sometimes called upon to navigate the sewers looking for some lost item—a ring or a letter tossed away in haste—and that thieves occasionally used them to escape capture.

That skiff was my only hope. I would have to take my chances and paddle around the sewer until I found another way out. It would mean braving the rats, a small price to pay for losing Toby. What if he had been abducted to be sold to the Turks as a slave—the fate with which mothers threatened their wandering children sometimes? What irony that would be. Toby was the least adventuring boy I knew, the most cautious. He had never questioned the life my parents planned for him, always did his chores, and since my father died had followed me around willingly wherever I chose to lead him.

And now, whatever had happened to him would be my fault and no one else's. I did not deserve to be alive. And I did not deserve to sit like a spoiled child myself and expect someone to rescue me from a situation I had created through my own actions, whatever other forces had led me to it.

Stifling the urge to cry like a baby, I lifted my petticoats and tucked them into my belt so they would not trail in the mucky water when I reached the bottom, then picked my way down the stairs.

The damp had coated the lower steps with a thin film of ice, and I nearly slipped off and dunked myself in the sewer water. Once I'd regained my balance by sheer force of will, I pulled the skiff close to the stairs—it seemed dry and sound, from what I could tell of it in the dark. Although it was no doubt full of spiders and beetles, I stepped into it quickly, rocking it back and forth and sending a ripple splashing against distant walls and steps. A paddle had been secured beneath the seats. I pulled it out, then untied the rope that held the skiff to the stairs.

After using the paddle against the stairs to push myself out into the middle of the sewer, I had to decide exactly where to go. Which way would take me to an opening? I did not care where I emerged. The most dangerous neighborhood of Vienna would be preferable to remaining where I was. I sat for a time and thought, listening intently for any sound that would lead me to the surface again.

I don't know how long I sat, but it was long enough to notice that I had drifted a considerable distance. There was a current in the sewers, and it must, I reasoned, lead to the place where the water and muck spilled out. I knew that to be the Danube, a river known for its own dangerous currents, but the idea of release from this maze of underground drains overcame any fears I had for my safety in this tiny boat on the roiling river. Once there, I could yell and shout and call out, and someone would be certain to help me.

I was right about the current. All I had to do was keep the boat in the middle of the stream and it drew me quite quickly along. Once or twice I reached places I feared would not be wide enough to fit through and where the arch of the sewer came so close to my head that I had to crouch low in my vessel, but clearly the boat itself had been designed for the purpose of getting out of the sewers.

Unfortunately, I was also right about what to expect

from the river. I could hear it long before I noticed the light—not daylight yet, certainly, but perhaps the light of the moon reflecting off the snow on the riverbanks. I heard a rushing sound. I crossed myself and prayed to St. Christopher to preserve me as a traveler of sorts, and to St. Cecilia to keep me alive so that I could make music again. I confess I did not spare a thought for my brother at that time. What good was worrying about him if I was to die soon anyway? At least I hadn't done anything evil enough to send me to hell, I thought, and I had been to confession on Christmas Eve. It was not yet Epiphany. So much had happened to change me in so short a space of time. Would my father even recognize me if we met in heaven?

As I approached the mouth of the sewer, I saw that the water flowed down a gentle slope into the river, becoming a small waterfall at the end. Through the mouth of the tunnel the wide river looked like a huge, living snake, undulating in the moonlight, floats of ice dotting it like widely spaced scales. I saw no boats upon it. Dawn was still many hours off.

I placed the paddle beneath the seats and gripped the gunwales of the skiff with both hands, steadying myself in between. Thankfully, the small craft had indeed proved sound. Not a drop of water leaked up from beneath my feet. I began to think I had a chance of surviving, of not being tumbled into the icy Danube to drown and become a Lorelei to lure sailors to their deaths.

As I picked up speed and approached the frothing,

dirty water that would shoot me into the river, I closed my eyes and muttered "*Ave Marias*" and "*Pater nosters*" as fast as I could.

The sensation of whooshing that last stretch and emerging into the air was terrifying but exhilarating. Water splashed up and soaked me. It was so icy I gasped. But I did not overturn. I took some deep gulps of the clear air, still faintly tinged with the odor of human waste, and waited for my little boat to stop rocking. The strong river current began to pull me downstream. I reclaimed my paddle to try to steer toward what looked like a pier ahead. *I was out!* I would survive.

Now, though, the enormity of all that still lay ahead engulfed me. I had solved only one tiny part of my difficulty. I still had no idea where Toby might be found.

There was no time to reflect at that moment. The pier, which gave onto a sandy, sloped bank, approached me very quickly. If I could grab onto it, I could pull the skiff in and easily climb out there.

I caught hold of the first jutting pile. It was cold and slimy, and I yelped as a large splinter pierced my left hand—my playing hand—but I did not let go. I fought against the current, pulling myself from one leg of the rotting structure to another, until the bottom of the boat caught on the sandy bottom of the river. I stood and leapt out of the skiff onto the shore. Over to one side, stone steps were set into the bank so that I could climb up.

Stone steps. A rotted pier. Could it be?

When I clambered exhausted over the edge of the bank,

I found myself in a sleepy encampment of Gypsies, very like the one I had visited the other afternoon. I prayed that Mirela, or Maya, or Danior would come and find me. Surely it must be the same place. I knew of no other Gypsy camp near the city at this time of year. The huts were not arranged in the same way, but they had had to break them all down and reassemble them, so that needn't signify anything. I could hardly move. I lay stretched on the ground, heedless of the rough surface and the cold, and closed my eyes.

The sound of crunching snow made me open them again. A pair of men's boots stopped just by my nose.

"I—I beg your pardon," I chattered.

Without saying a word, the man leaned down, lifted me by the shoulders, and set me on my feet. He started walking away, a glance back toward me the only hint that I should follow him.

He led me into a large hut—not Maya's—where a woman nudged and fed a fire to life. Someone had already placed a pot of something that looked like gruel over it. The woman stared at me in silence for a moment, then poured some tea out of a samovar and gave the cup to me. As I sat there, one by one five small children uncurled from sleeping mats scattered around the room and came to stare at me with their round, brown eyes.

The family's quiet courtesy, their calm acceptance that a young girl could wash up on their shore wearing a tattered ball gown and smelling of a sewer, made me vow that I would never judge anyone by my assumptions again. This was the second time I had been generously treated by people my mother had told me to fear, while my uncle, the one person upon whom she had pinned all her hopes for our family's prosperity, was turning out not to deserve our trust.

"Thank you," I murmured, once the hot liquid had washed down my throat and I felt that I could speak again. "I need to get back to Vienna. I'm trying to find my brother. Is anyone going that way this morning?"

"Stefan," the man said. He said nothing more. I assumed that when the time came, he would take me to the fellow.

They shared their gruel with me, and the woman would not let me depart without wrapping me in a warm wool shawl. I had no money in my pocket and had dropped my reticule somewhere the previous night, but I told them that I would find a way to return their kindness.

I was glad of the wrap when I emerged into the pale dawn light.

"Theresa!" I heard Mirela call my name as I was about to climb into the back of Stefan's cart. She approached me so fast I barely had time to turn before she had flung her arms around me and started covering my face with kisses.

"You look terrible! What has happened?" Mirela asked, smoothing my hair away from my face and shaking her head.

"I was stuck in a sewer," I said.

"I thought you were going to the assembly rooms last evening!"

I could not help laughing. "It seems my uncle may have had his own plans for me."

"Tell me."

"I can't say right now. But I'll explain everything sometime, I promise. In the meantime, I have to find Toby."

"Thank the gods you are safe. But who is Toby?"

"My brother. He's only eight, and he disappeared from the ball last night." By now we had made our way to Stefan's wagon. "I must leave."

"I shall go with you."

Without giving me a chance to protest, Mirela took my hand, and soon we were both huddled in the back of the wagon. Apparently Stefan delivered his obliging nanny goat's milk to some of the grand houses in Vienna every morning just after dawn. As we rattled through the woods and onto the sleepy roads that would lead us to the city, Mirela kept up a more or less constant stream of chatter. I didn't mind. Her voice had a melodious quality that reminded me of church bells pealing on Easter morning.

"Danior has been teaching me to play the fiddle. You are a musician, too, no? Like your poor papa. Everyone has been talking about it. So sad that he is gone." Her round, brown eyes softened with sympathy.

"What do you know about what happened to him?" I asked.

She sighed. "No more than you, I imagine. Danior said they found him by the river. He was a very kind man, of course. When I was very small he made me a wooden whistle."

It struck me as odd to have this girl I barely knew tell me things about my own father. Papa had been well-liked among the Gypsies, apparently. Yet none of them had been able to tell me anything. And here was Mirela, clearly implying that my father's visits to the camp had been going on for several years. There was so much I wanted to ask, but suddenly I was afraid. What if I found out things about Papa that made him seem different from the way I remembered him? What if I found that he cared for people I had never known, spread his affections out far and wide so that there hadn't been so much for us? Once I started thinking, I found I had too many questions, and so I settled on only one small thing.

I grasped the chain around my neck to pull the medallion out from its hiding place. "You have to tell me," I said, "what does this mean?"

CHAPTER 20

Mirela took the medallion in her hand and gazed at it as if she were trying to read the future in her palm. "It is a curious thing," she murmured at last, "to touch history. Looking into the past is very much like seeing the ages to come." She looked up, keeping hold of the medallion. "Your papa said it belonged to a great Hungarian general who had protected the poor people on an estate from an evil lord, more than a hundred years ago."

"How did my father come to possess it?"

"He said it was given to him," Mirela answered, "in thanks for something he had done. He never said what. He has so many good deeds in his Book of Life."

"Book of Life?"

"The Book of Life is very important. At least, to me it is. Every time something big happens, or I make a decision to do something that I know will change who I am from that time on, it is written in a book that the angels keep. At the end of my life, I will be made to read my book before I am allowed to rest forever. Of course, I can't really read it now, but when I die, it will be a miracle and the words will speak to me. Depending on what I have done while I lived, my book will make me happy or sad."

"What about the ending?" I asked, my mind up in the clouds somewhere, imagining St. Cecilia holding my book, which when I thought about it was probably full of instances where I had acted in my own interest. Until now, perhaps.

"You see, that is the most frightening part! When I come to the end of the book, I will find out if I shall spend eternity in heaven with the gods, or in hell with all the evil people who have ever lived."

We sat in silence for a while. The milk buckets clanged together with every bump. The thin ice that had sealed yesterday's puddles cracked beneath the wagon's wheels. Somewhere a cock cleared its throat into the cold morning, and crows cawed bitterly.

Mirela let go of the medallion and placed her hand over mine. Her fingers were very delicate, which surprised me since I imagined she had to work hard around the camp. "I am afraid that when I stole the necklace from you, a bad mark was written in my book. But it was only a little one. Danior had spoken of the medallion and said he longed to have it returned to our people, so that it would not fall into unfriendly hands. We thought it was in Zoltán's possession, not knowing that he had given it into your father's keeping. When I saw you wearing it, I thought I was doing a great favor to my people to take it from you. You see, it became a symbol for all those who are oppressed, the serfs and the Gypsies. It's only a small disc of gold, not of great value—Maya wears more gold on her wrists when she dances—but it gives hope, so long as we have it to remind ourselves that we have powerful friends."

"I forgive you," I said. "I knew nothing about it, except that my father had it when he died."

"Then we are friends?" she said, her face lit up by a broad smile.

I nodded. She threw her arms around my neck. By now we had reached the farms on the edge of the city, and a few laborers were trudging through the snow to cowsheds for the milking. They looked up at us curiously as we passed. Mirela's passionate gestures were a little embarrassing to me, but despite our differences, I truly liked her. She released my neck and held my hand from then on, pointing out silly things along the way. She saw signs in everything: the shape of the clouds, the timing of a bird's cry, how often the horse that drew the wagon shook his head, and where the bits of foam from his mouth landed. She made me feel as if I went through life not noticing anything at all. She taught me a simple Gypsy song, a lullaby, in that strange language I had heard the Romany people speaking. She said she knew hundreds of songs and would teach them all to me if I wanted.

"I don't sing very well, but when I have a violin or a viola again, I would like to play your songs," I said.

"Ah, that is what your papa did. And sometimes he brought that older man, the one who works for the prince."

"My godfather? Kapellmeister Haydn?"

"Yes, that is him. I liked him."

I noticed that we had reached the Marienhilferstrasse. Suddenly the thought of Toby and of the danger I had faced the night before broke afresh into my mind. Mirela's stories had lulled me, but now it was time to act again. "I must leave you here," I said, turning to ask the milkman to stop his horse.

"Take care, Theresa," Mirela said, her face clouding over. "Do not take so many risks. We are friends forever, and forever can be a long time—or a short one."

I kissed her on the cheek before hopping down from the wagon, and watched her waving at me as the Gypsy milkman drove on toward his deliveries in the city center.

⁂

Although I would have preferred to speak with Zoltán and get his help in finding Toby, it was probably for the best that the cart's path took me to Haydn's apartment on Marienhilferstrasse. The maid almost shut the door in my face thinking I was a beggar, until I spoke and assured her that I was Theresa Schurman, the maestro's goddaughter.

Haydn took one look at me and ordered me to go to his wife's dressing room to bathe. "She's not there anyway. Stayed the night with her cousin."

I knew—and I could tell by his expression he knew that I knew—that she had very likely spent the night with a lover, not her "cousin."

"Please, Godfather, I must speak with you. Toby is gone, and I don't know where he is." I told him quickly about my adventure in my uncle's cellar, and my trip through the sewers.

"Perhaps he is safe at home. You go and freshen up then join me for some breakfast, and I will send someone to your house to see if he is there. He could have walked back from the assembly rooms. The distance is not far."

I knew what he said was possible, but after everything else that had befallen me, I hardly dared hope the explanation was so simple.

The use of Madame Haydn's scented dressing room, a hot bath in a copper tub, and a clean shift and simple dress did much to soothe me after my adventurous night. The maid also removed the splinter from my hand—which turned out not to be so very bad—and bound up the wound. Once I had refreshed myself, I joined my godfather for a simple meal. Between mouthfuls of fresh sausage and warm bread I tried to answer his questions as best I could.

"If Toby is not there, my mother will be worried," I said, imagining what bad effect such a concern might have on her in her delicate state.

"Do not be alarmed," my godfather said, "I sent for Zoltán. He will know just what to say."

For a moment I was lost in thought, thinking back over the scenes of the night before and wondering if I missed some clue that would solve the mystery of my brother's disappearance. I didn't notice that Haydn had gone quiet and cleared his throat politely.

"I hesitate to add to your worries," he began, once I had finished my breakfast, "but I find myself in more urgent need than ever of your help. Perhaps if you are not too tired you could spend an extra hour with me today?"

"Of course, Godfather," I said. "But have you not thought about seeing a doctor who might be able to fix your eyes? There is an operation now, I have heard. Mama and Greta were talking about it a few months ago. They can uncloud your vision."

The maestro grimaced. "And what if they fail?"

I could not answer him. And I also knew the surgery would be very painful, from everything my mother had said. The idea of someone cutting into one's eye—I didn't know if I could persuade myself to do it. But there was so much at stake.

"I must deliver three symphonies and four string quartets to Artaria by the day after tomorrow if I am to honor the contract I signed, as well as creating new works every day for the prince. You have already helped me with a quartet and a symphony, but as you see, it's not quite enough. And next week he expects an opera, which will mean assembling it from scattered bits, and replacing the substitute arias with something original."

I knew about the practice of taking popular arias with only the words changed and inserting them into a new opera, so the audience could have something familiar to hum and the diva could show off with something she knew well. But I saw that in this instance it made it more difficult for Haydn to furnish an entirely original opera.

Indeed, I did not see how we could finish half that amount without spending most of the next two days working—and he had rehearsals and performances, and I had to find Toby and put a stop to my uncle's activities—with only a vague grasp of exactly what they were.

We got immediately to work. I did my best to concentrate despite the worries that threatened to overwhelm me at every moment, reminding myself that there was nothing more I could do until Zoltán was made acquainted with everything that had passed the night before. Zoltán had previously said my uncle bribed the other members of the council so that things would go the way the nobles in Hungary wished. Where did the councilor get his money? Were the nobles themselves so wealthy? I became convinced that there was more concealed behind my uncle's remarkable affluence that I did not know about. He was a clever businessman, so my mother had told me, a merchant who traded in goods that everyone needed—wheat for flour and oil for lamps. But would cleverness be enough to account for his rise to such heights of influence, without a hereditary title and lands?

⁂

When the doorbell tinkled around noon, my mind had wandered so far from my surroundings that I jumped and sent a blot of ink from the tip of my pen over the page, spoiling the last quarter-hour's work. "I'll copy it out again. It won't take a moment!" I said.

I started scribbling quickly. Within a short time, I

heard Zoltán's solid, determined footsteps approaching. He entered the room without knocking.

"Your brother is not at home," he said, mercifully dispensing with formalities.

I felt a peculiar sensation of something flowing through my veins. I could not tell if it was scorching heat or ice. Toby was not at home. My worst fears were confirmed. "What did you say to my mother?" I asked, barely able to speak above a whisper.

"I told her you had both spent the night at your uncle's. She appeared content with that explanation."

I wondered how much longer we could keep her ignorant of what was passing outside her bedroom, in a world where she thought her children were safe. "Do you have any idea where Toby . . . he's so young . . ." I could not form the words.

Zoltán passed his hand across his eyes. "My sister received this letter. Unfortunately we cannot say exactly where it came from, although we have our ideas."

He took a folded piece of paper from inside his waistcoat and handed it to me.

The release of the general will secure the release of the girl and her brother. We will contact you with details.

"They think I am still in the sewer," I said.

"In the sewer!?"

Zoltán's astonishment nearly made me laugh, despite my distress. I explained to him as quickly as I could exactly what had happened.

"I think we had better make them believe we have not

found you," he said. "You must remain here until I send word that you can leave."

"Remain here!" I exclaimed. "I shall do no such thing."

"You will be in danger, and you will endanger your brother."

"Not if I am in disguise. Haven't I earned your trust? I cannot just sit by and do nothing."

Zoltán did not speak at first. "I won't—it wouldn't be—" He gave up and just shook his head.

I felt a little sorry for him. It crossed my mind briefly that I should do as he said and spare him any more worry. But I knew that if I did not persuade him to include me in whatever they planned to do, I would continue to search without them. I would never forgive myself if something happened to my brother. He was too small and timid to get himself out of difficulties as I was able to. "If you do not let me come with you, I will try to find Toby by myself."

"You are hurt already," he said, pointing to my bandaged hand. "It will be difficult to play the viola, and you might be injured much more seriously if you do as you threaten."

"It will be difficult to play in any case. I have no instrument. My mother sold it." I hadn't meant my words to sound so peevish and complaining.

"Why did you not say so, my dear?" Haydn's voice was kind, but I couldn't take kindness just then. It made everything too complicated.

"Just tell me what you need me to do," I said, not looking at either of them.

"We've persuaded the general to inform us where he

thinks you both were taken," Zoltán said. "He says the most likely place is in the house of your uncle."

"That's impossible—I don't just mean for me, of course—but I went through my uncle's house last night before I was trapped and did not find anyone."

"But there is nowhere else," Zoltán said. "We have people inside all the other houses of those Austrians who are in the councilor's pay, and the Hungarians who make Vienna their winter home."

Every time Zoltán told me something more about their cause, I saw its ripples widening far beyond the small world we inhabited, a world full of music and the tribulations and pettiness of court life.

The maestro interrupted him. "You have not hurt the general, have you?"

Zoltán paused before answering, leaving me wondering when he finally spoke whether he told the truth. "No, he is not harmed. Nor will he be—at least, not in any material way."

"Provided this is so, I shall do this evening as you have asked me," the maestro said. "I presume the concert is still to take place?"

Zoltán nodded. "Wolkenstein has not canceled. He is too sure of himself to consider the general's misadventure more than a temporary setback. After all, he has almost as much power behind him as the emperor."

Zoltán came to me and took hold of my shoulders, fixing me with his disturbing gaze. "You say you went all over his house. Do you think you can tell us exactly what you found in each room? Down to the tiniest details?"

"In truth, I had no light, so I cannot describe more than which rooms lead into which, and where the staircases are located. The only place I remember clearly is the cellar."

"If you are willing to help, I have been authorized to ask you for one final favor." Zoltán had let go of my shoulders and looked down at the floor. I waited for him to continue, but something held him back.

"Do you still doubt me?" I asked.

"Not doubt," he said, looking into my eyes again. "I simply hoped you would see sense and protect yourself. However, as you are determined . . . We want you to go back to your uncle's house. But this time you will not be alone. And you will be armed."

"Armed—how?"

Zoltán reached under his cloak and removed a pistol. It was not an elegant, pearl-handled dueling pistol such as gentlemen sometimes carry, but an ugly, black monster. I wondered when it had last been used, and for what. "It's mainly just to frighten," he said.

"So I wouldn't have to fire it, then?"

"I hope not," he said. "But one of us will have to make some noise, and we need to ensure that we have the greatest possible opportunity to do so."

"Noise?" I asked.

"The plan is to summon the guards to the councilor's house at the moment when we have found what we are looking for. Since the guards are controlled by the military and the military is currently under the illusion that Wolkenstein is on their side, they will need some compelling reason to enter, especially during a party. A pistol fired inside the councilor's residence would be something they could not ignore." He placed the pistol in my hands. "Think carefully, Rezia. You may be called upon to act in a way that would distress you."

The pistol was heavy and cold. For one tiny instant I pictured myself aiming it at my uncle's heart and pulling the trigger. The image in my mind frightened me. "I've never held a firearm before," I murmured. "Must I truly?"

"If you want to come, this is the condition," Zoltán said. "It is too dangerous otherwise. And you will be in disguise. You will appear to be an innocent young fellow newly part of the orchestra. That way you are less likely to attract notice or be singled out to search. Besides, we dare not involve anyone who doesn't already know what we are about."

"What if I am recognized? My uncle may be looking for me."

"We have thought about that," Zoltán said with a smile. "I will tell you the rest later when we meet at my apartment."

My godfather rested his gentle hands on my shoulders. "You do not have to go, Theresa."

I turned, stood on my tiptoes, and kissed him on both cheeks. "I trust Zoltán. I shall be all right, Godfather. I've already managed to survive the sewers." His smile at my pleasantry was halfhearted at best.

"Come. Danior is waiting for us. We'll show you what to do."

Haydn loaned me a warm cloak with a hood that was big enough to shadow my face against curious passersby, and Zoltán had come prepared with a mask in case I needed it. I turned to my godfather. "We must finish your scores. I shall come tomorrow and stay as long as you need me."

He nodded. I saw a hint of moistness in his clouded eyes just before I turned to go.

CHAPTER 21

We all met at Zoltán's lodgings—Danior, Maya, Zoltán, and I—to discuss the plan. The first things I learned were the details of my disguise as a young man of the orchestra.

"I think that in boy's clothing, and with your hair hidden away beneath a wig, you'd pass well enough," Zoltán said. I wasn't exactly happy that he thought I could so easily hide my sex. I know I blushed, and I could not look at him as Danior continued explaining what we were all to do.

Although I had nothing on which to base my impression, the plan sounded as if it would be dangerous to everyone involved. It would all take place at my uncle's house. He had invited some important guests to a concert to celebrate his victory over those who wanted to extend the reforms to Hungary. The council was supposed to vote against it that very day.

"It should never have come to this," said Danior. "Your father should have brought the documents to Haydn, who would have shown them to the prince. Then the vote would have been postponed until after the additional evidence could be placed before the emperor. I have some of the documents your father obtained safely hidden, but not the most important ones, the eyewitness accounts of atrocities."

"Someone must have known he had them," I said, as much to myself as to anyone else.

"We have the general, which will prevent the other side from winning their vote," said Zoltán. The vote was close enough so that one man would make a difference, apparently. Although my uncle had managed to secure a lot of support, he couldn't corrupt everyone.

Zoltán had drawn a crude map of the ground floor and cellars of my uncle's house, based upon my description. We clustered around his table as he moved hazelnuts around, explaining which one was who, and how we were to go about finding our way to the cellars in the midst of a party with hundreds of guests.

"Why is my uncle still having his celebration when the measure will not have passed?" I asked.

Maya, who had been sitting a little behind the others, now leaned forward. "The Hungarian ambassador is in Vienna. There are rumors that he intends to side with the reformists. Your uncle has apparently discovered that he has a certain weakness for the company of young boys, and intends to facilitate this for him. After that, simple blackmail is all that will be needed to ensure his cooperation."

Toby! I thought with horror. Surely my uncle would not do something so horrible to his own nephew. And yet, he had treated me as if I were so much currency to purchase the favors of General Steinhammer, and then had me locked up in the sewers, even if he did intend to let me out eventually.

Zoltán continued. "Maya will be among the kitchen help, and she will ensure that the pantry is unlocked. The four of you—Danior, two of his men, and you, Rezia—will look for Toby in the cellar. When you have found him and secured his safety, wait for a lull in the music from the dining room above and then one of you—whoever can manage it—fire off a pistol to summon the guards."

"Why so much noise? Why not just take Toby away?" I felt a little troublesome asking, but I wanted to be sure I was doing the right thing and not putting Toby in any more danger by my actions.

"Because we need official witnesses. No one will believe you and Toby, I'm afraid."

I had not thought of that. Of course my uncle's word would carry more weight than mine. There was still one other part of the plan that disturbed me, though. No doubt Uncle Theobald had discovered by now that I had escaped from the sewer and would be looking for me. By walking right back into his house, I would be giving him every chance to apprehend me again. Zoltán had not really answered my question before, so I asked again. "What if," I started, hardly daring to utter the possibility, "what if my uncle recognizes me, despite my disguise? What would I be doing there?"

"You will be doing precisely what he would least take notice of," Zoltán said. "You will be performing music, and therefore number among the menial servants he has hired to entertain his guests."

"I—performing music?"

"The third desk in the violas. The maestro has composed a work that requires an extra viola player."

Despite the seriousness of the conversation, Zoltán smiled. I knew that I, too, should be feeling only fear about what was ahead and disgust at my uncle's illegal activities, but my heart leapt at Zoltán's words. It had been only a few days since I had last played, yet so much had happened in that time that it felt like an eternity. I longed not only to hear music, but to feel an instrument come alive at the touch of my bow, feel the vibration flow like the river's current down my arm, through my shoulder, and into my heart. And I would—that very evening. What was still more wonderful was that I would do so among the musicians of the most skilled orchestra in the empire. I realized that perhaps I would play only a little, but even a moment was more than I had ever dreamed possible. Ladies did not play in the orchestra. Ladies sometimes performed harpsichord solos, or sang in the operas. But they did not sit among the men like equals and play under the maestro's direction.

". . . if you are nervous about it, you don't need to make any sound at all, you can just pretend," Zoltán continued.

I nodded. He probably expected that I couldn't really play. Of course. What else would he think?

"I must go now and start working in the councilor's kitchen," Maya said.

"Rezia, you stay here and rest. Here is your musician's uniform. I'll return to fetch you at six of the clock."

Danior and Zoltán departed with Maya, leaving me alone in Zoltán's apartment. It was very plain, I noticed. Without him actually in it, I would hardly have known he lived there. Except, of course, for the violin and viola cases on the table. Although I was tempted to do it, he had not given me leave to try out the viola, and in truth, I was very tired. It was hours until the evening. For once I decided to do exactly as I was told and climbed the two steps into the curtained bed to lie down.

⁂

I think I must have fallen asleep almost immediately. When I awoke, I found myself in the dark except for the glow of the fire in the stove. I was still tired, but the thought of what I had to do that evening soon made me leap out of bed. If all went according to plan, we would find Toby, expose my uncle's treachery, and vindicate my father's death. Soon after I finished dressing in the simple uniform of a musician, a plain black coat, black satin breeches, and white hose, I heard steps on the stairs to the apartment, and then the grinding of a key in a lock. Zoltán came in, accompanied by Alida carrying a wig box.

She took my presence there as a matter of course. I was heartily glad to see her, I must say. She had an air of serenity about her that was very reassuring. Perhaps it was her practical side that gave that impression. She always seemed to know what to do, no matter the circumstances.

"We must get your lovely hair out of the way," Alida said. She had made me sit on a chair and stood behind me, brushing my hair and sweeping it back into a knot. But I was blessed with a long, thick mane, and no matter how she tried, she could not hide it beneath the bob wig she had brought with her. Eventually she had to send Zoltán out for a bag wig. It solved our difficulty, my hair tamed into a thick braid fitting neatly into the black taffeta bag that hung down at the back.

Before we left the apartment, Zoltán loaded and primed the pistol I was to carry and showed me how to aim it and fire. It was heavy. I was afraid I would not be able to manage it.

"Use two hands," he said. He stood behind me and wrapped his arms around mine, his hands clasped over my fingers, completely covering them. I felt his breath on my ear as he explained how to look through the two prongs of the sight. The sensation of his closeness made my own breath quicken a little. I wished that if I ever had to fire the pistol, it could be like this, with Zoltán supporting me and holding me steady. "Aim for the middle of your target, and at least you'll have a chance of hitting some part of it," he said. "Although you will probably hardly be aiming at all, just away from us." I noticed that he avoided referring to a "target" as a person. I didn't really want to think about the remote possibility that I might have to use the pistol for something other than making noise, that it might just as easily be a means of defending myself from some unforeseen harm.

The concert was to start at seven of the clock. Musicians were therefore expected to arrive shortly after the vesper bells tolled from St. Stephen's. I was glad of the early darkness as I strode along next to Zoltán toward the Graben, my hand gripping the brass handle on the top of the viola case. I felt naked without the weight of petticoats anchoring me to the earth, but it was an exhilarating nakedness, full of freedom and danger. *Papa, forgive me,* I thought, wondering if he could watch the coming events unfold from his vantage point in heaven. I tried not to think about what was to come, instead concentrating on the sight of Zoltán walking slightly ahead of me, admiring the way his confident step and upright bearing cut a path through the evening crowds in the center of the city.

My stomach was doing battle with itself by the time we reached my uncle's house. I couldn't find it in me to enjoy the spectacle of the guests arriving in their elegant carriages and being handed out by footmen, and then ushered in through the door by the same valet who had blithely shut me up in the sewer. Zoltán and I followed the other musicians around to the back of the house, to a door that led in through the kitchen. I wondered if Haydn would have to take that same route, or whether he would be accorded the respect due to him as an officer in the prince's household and be allowed to mingle with the guests before taking his position with the orchestra.

We didn't say a thing as we shed our coats and cloaks and lifted our instruments out of their cases. I wasn't sure what everyone knew, or how many of the orchestra members would be familiar to me. I was acquainted with just about everyone in Prince Nicholas's orchestra by sight, and friendly with many of them. I knew I had to be careful not to let them recognize me. Not only my boy's clothing, but the press of the cold, hard pistol tucked into my waist beneath my coat made me feel especially conscious of myself. I thought all eyes must be staring at me as I followed the general movement of the players through to the dining room. A few of the musicians had already taken their places. Among these I noticed Schnabl, and turned my face away immediately. Seeing him reminded me that I had said nothing to my godfather or Zoltán about his unexplained presence near this same house two days before, carrying a folio of music.

The spacious chamber had been cleared of its table, a low platform erected on which we all took our places, and the remaining area filled with several rows of delicate wooden chairs for the audience. Some seats were already occupied by elderly ladies and gentlemen, whispering quietly to each other or sitting in silence with their eyes closed. The murmur of more lively guests reached me from another room.

When I finally worked up the courage to look around at the other members of the orchestra, I was surprised to find how few faces I recognized, apart from Zoltán and Schnabl. Many of them nonetheless seemed a bit familiar, but in that manner of people one knows from somewhere else appearing where you don't expect them. A few smiled in my direction. I quickly looked at the music in front of me and pretended to be finding my cues. They must not suspect who I was.

It wasn't until Haydn took his place at the harpsichord to direct us that I suddenly realized why the faces around me struck chords of recognition. Most of them had been in the Gypsy camp on the two occasions I had visited it. Yet there they had mainly dark hair and wore bright-colored clothes. Here all of them had on white bob wigs or bag wigs and wore simple, dark clothing. None of their gold jewelry was in evidence, either, although I noticed a hole in one fellow's earlobe that had clearly been stretched out by a heavy hoop. Scattered among the Gypsy musicians were only one or two of the prince's regular musicians. No one I knew well—except for Schnabl.

I was brought back to the present when Zoltán gave the A, there being no wind players engaged for the evening. I put the viola to my shoulder. Its shape was comfortingly familiar. I cradled the neck in the V of my thumb and first finger, stretching my hand farther along so I could reach the tuning pins. It was a lovely instrument, I thought perhaps Italian. And the bow I drew across to test the pitch of each string was well balanced. I winced every now and again as I accidentally hit the tender spot on my hand where the splinter had been.

A short serenade began the concert. I played the simple viola part quietly, not daring to open up the sound in case I made a mistake. But despite my anxiety I was able to enjoy the sensation of sitting amid the players for once, not outside of them. The music sounded so different here. From my position, the cello parts sang out loudly, and I realized how carefully everything must be balanced to make the music blend into a harmonious wash of sound for the enjoyment of those who sat out in front. I had never really thought about it before, and wished I could be in two places at once: where I was in the orchestra and out in the audience, just to hear the difference.

There were three violists, and we all shared one score. I tried hard not to look at my deskmates, instead concentrating on the notes. I smiled to myself as I recognized what we were playing—only a few days ago I had heard Haydn sing that very line to me so that I could write it down. And then my smile broadened when I realized it was similar to something I had heard Danior play in the Gypsy camp. Here was evidence of how music could find its own way through the world.

The audience applauded without much enthusiasm after the serenade. They were not the usual collection of music lovers who attended the gatherings at the prince's palace. Haydn stood and bowed to them, but rather than seat himself at the harpsichord again for the next selection, he remained standing until the applause died away—which wasn't long.

"Ladies, gentlemen, Your Excellency, distinguished guests," he began.

I looked up toward the audience when he said "Your Excellency." I assumed he must be referring to the Hungarian ambassador. I saw a gentleman in a gold lace-trimmed coat wearing many honors and sashes. Perhaps that was him. If so, he did not respond to the greeting in a very gallant manner, only nodding and then turning back to the lady he was conversing with. I still saw no sign of my uncle, dreading that he would appear at any moment and see me in the orchestra. I hoped Zoltán was right, that he would never think to notice the musicians.

"We have several unique compositions to perform for you this evening," the maestro said once the crowd settled. "The next requires only a small number of the players, as do the selections to follow, so please bear with us while certain of our performers are dismissed. They will return to take their places for the final work, a symphony whose extraordinary form will, I believe, prove surprising to you."

I caught Zoltán's eye. He raised one eyebrow and I stood up, laying the viola carefully on the floor by my stool before following about eight other players out through the door that had admitted us to the dining room. Among them were Danior and two other violinists, the percussionist, and the second cellist. I knew that Zoltán would not come with us. He had explained that he could not risk jeopardizing his sister's position. *Trust Danior,* he had said. I hoped he was right. So far, everything was going smoothly.

I made the mistake of glancing around me just before I disappeared into the anteroom with the others. Out of the corner of my eye I saw the obnoxious maid, Hildegard. Her eyes met mine and opened wide. I saw her nearly stumble as she presented an elderly lady with a cordial. *What should I do?* I thought. It was too late to change anything. The plan was already under way. Perhaps I had mistaken her expression. But no. I knew that at any moment, Hildegard would seek out my uncle, and that he would send someone back to get me. The only thing to do was to accomplish our task as quickly as possible.

"This crowd just wants to get in to dinner," grumbled the cellist who had left the orchestra with us, a new fellow whose name I didn't know. He flopped onto the only chair in the anteroom. The percussionist—a man I recognized from the Gypsy camp—sat on the floor.

I'd better warn Danior, I thought, trying to catch his eye. But he refused to look up at me, only lounging against the wall nonchalantly with the others, who I guessed were all Gypsies. I did my best to behave as they did despite my pounding heart and the certainty that soon we would be stopped from doing what we had come here to do.

I heard the beginning of a divertimento from the other room.

"I must excuse myself," Danior said.

"Breath of air," said another of the Roma, signaling to a violinist who sauntered after him.

They passed through into the kitchen. Danior gave a quick jerk of his head as he walked by me. Altogether four of us entered my uncle's large, busy kitchen, where the cook and her helpers scurried around through clouds of steam, orders flying from one end to another. No sign of Hildegard or my uncle there. A scullery maid nearly crashed into me with a bucket of boiling water in her hands, which I could see were so chapped and cracked they bled. "Get out of the way!" she hissed.

We huddled toward the pantry end of the kitchen. A prayer circled through my mind over and over: *Please, God, don't let her find my uncle; please, God, don't let her find my uncle . . .* Then I noticed Maya, her arms deep in a vat of dough. She hardly looked up, only subtly turning her head in the direction of the pantry. I saw that the door stood slightly ajar. The cook yelled at us, "Don't think you'll get any food by standing there!" But soon all the kitchen staff were once again so absorbed getting the many dishes prepared to serve when the concert ended that I think they forgot us.

We made our way to the pantry door. Without actually looking at him, only noticing from the corner of my eye, I saw Danior reach out his hand and grasp the latch. At the moment of greatest confusion, he opened it and slipped inside. The next violinist did the same. The third fellow elbowed me over toward the door, and I waited for my chance to follow the other two. Before long all four of us were in the cool darkness of the pantry.

"The door to the cellar is at that end," I whispered. One of the men fumbled around for a candle and a match bottle. I heard him strike the flint, and the tiny flame pooled over his hands as he touched the match to the candle's wick. Without a word, he took the light to the low door, which had been somewhat disguised by the clever placement of a shelf above it. The door was not locked. He pushed it open, illuminating the stairs so we could descend.

The first rooms of the cellar were much as I remembered them from my frenzied exploration the night before. Some of the wine bottles had been taken out of their racks and placed on a simple table, ready to be served to the guests.

"How did you get out?" Danior whispered to me.

"Through here," I answered.

I led them through the room where the beer and root vegetables were stored and was about to make my way toward the door to the last, long chamber, when Danior grabbed hold of me and pulled me back.

Ahead of us a guard sat slumped on the floor, his musket loosely cradled in his arms. His head lolled forward and nodded rhythmically in time to his breathy snores.

"There was no guard the other night," I whispered into Danior's ear.

I wanted to tell him about Hildegard then, to warn

him that we had no time, but his hand tightened on my arm. "We'll need to take care of him. You must not look."

What would they do? The fellow seemed as innocent as the greengrocer, his face all slack and his body limp. But if he gave the alarm, it would be impossible for us to continue. And now it was clear that someone—or something—was being kept hidden in that cellar room, the one that had been so unaccountably empty before. I could still see the valet's smug smile as he showed me the space and then let me walk unsuspectingly into the sewer.

I turned my eyes away obediently. Danior and the other violinist crept toward the sleeping sentry. I wondered what they could do that would be silent and still ensure our safety. I peeked and saw the other fellow slip a long, thin dagger out of a sheath. Danior reached into his sleeve and pulled out a length of rope. Would they stab him, as someone had stabbed my father? Or would they wrap the rope around his neck and squeeze the life out of him? I could not move. My eyes were drawn to them.

They acted so quickly and smoothly I hardly understood what happened. The guard opened his eyes wide in sleepy surprise just as Danior landed a punch in the center of his face that knocked him over and sent blood gushing from his nose. Quickly, they used the dagger to cut the rope into two lengths, one to bind his hands and one his feet. Then they wadded a rag and stuffed it into his mouth.

They moved the trussed-up guard away from the door

that led to the long room beneath the dining room. We entered that chamber in the same order we had entered the pantry and the cellar. Danior's and the other violinists' eyes were already as round as dark chocolate bon-bons by the time I was able to look around the room at the sight illuminated by our single candle.

CHAPTER 22

Lined up with their backs against the wall and their legs out straight, hands tied behind them, feet bound together, and mouths gagged so tightly the skin was stretched over their cheeks, were about a dozen young boys. The oldest looked to be a year or two younger than I was, the youngest about five or six. Some looked as though they had been beaten. All of them were frightened.

And right in the middle, one side of his face swollen as though he had been hit with a hard object, was Toby, still in the Esterhazy livery, which was now dirty and torn.

I ran to him as if in a dream, feeling as though my legs would not push against the ground fast enough to close the distance between us. When I reached him, I fumbled with the ropes tied around his ankles. Making no progress, I tried to untie his gag, but I had no strength in my fingers. All the while the faint strains of a string quartet, the beautiful adagio I had written down for my godfather only days before, filtered through the ceiling of the room.

I hardly noticed that Danior had come over and crouched beside me, using his thin dagger to slice through the ropes and the gag in an instant. Toby fell into my arms, weeping.

"I'm so sorry, Toby! He won't get away with it," I murmured into his matted and dirty hair.

Danior gripped my arm again. I looked around in annoyance, but he put his finger to his lips and glared at me. I held my breath, and heard what he had heard. The crunch of boots on stone. Someone was coming.

As quietly as the wild cats that slunk around the alleys at night, the three men withdrew into positions in the dark corners of the room. Danior motioned me to do the same, but I did not want to let go of Toby. I tried to get him to stand up. Either they had hurt his legs, or fear and fatigue had made him weak, because he could not support his own weight. "Come, Toby, lean on me!" I whispered. The violinist doused his candle with the palm of his hand, and we were instantly wrapped in darkness. I felt Toby's quiet tears soak into my shoulder.

The next moments went by so fast, yet I have relived them many times since then as though they had happened under deep water, all movements slowed by the effort of struggling through liquid. First, I heard expressions of surprise and anger outside the door. They had found the unconscious guard.

"Must have been ten of them at least! I could not

hold out." Even as the guard spoke, the door was being opened.

Torchlight flooded into the room, fanning out from the door. A musket barrel advanced into the space, followed by three men in the black-and-white uniforms of the imperial guard, all of them with muskets out. The music from above flowed in with them—they had obviously left the doors to the pantry and the cellar open behind them. I heard the end of the string quartet followed by polite applause. The sound of my heart beating filled the silence in my ears, and I was certain they could all hear it.

I remember finding it almost comical that they would creep in slowly, as though certain an army of cutthroats lurked in the hidden corners of the room. But their posture became more relaxed and they stood more upright as the torch illuminated empty space around them and caught the gleam of the first young prisoners' eyes, still staring in silent fearfulness, hands and feet still bound and mouths still gagged. I noticed all this as the pool of light shed by the torch crept closer to where Toby and I stood. *Danior, where have you gone!* I thought, willing the Gypsy men to leap out and surprise the guards.

I tried to shrink back, but the wall was in my way. I pulled Toby against my body, and felt the hard lump of the pistol in my belt. I had almost forgotten I had it. Without a moment's hesitation I slipped my hand down to where I could grasp the hilt of the gun and eased it out. "Stay still, Toby," I breathed into his ear, trying to quiet his trembling. I gripped him around his middle with my left arm, and aimed the pistol out from behind him with my right. By the time the light revealed us, I thought I would be prepared to pull the trigger.

The illumination of the torch felt warm and harsh. I blinked against it. The guard who saw us first registered surprise, then smiled slowly. "So these are the *ten men* who attacked you, Hugo!"

The others laughed, lowering their muskets to rest their stocks on the ground.

"I'll kill you if you come closer!" I yelled. I wanted my voice to carry to the floor above, but the music had started again. It was a lively symphony, and the tympani rolled. The noise would obscure just about any sounds from down here, as had been part of the plan.

"You won't be able to fire that thing when it's not cocked, lad," the main guard said, provoking more laughter from the others. His smile faded. "Tie them up," he barked.

At that very moment, I caught a gleam of Danior's eyes from the dark corner behind the intruders and saw the faint flash of his dagger. *Thank God,* I thought. He looked prepared to leap forward and surprise them from behind, but just as he tensed for action, a voice from the doorway stopped him.

"Is there some difficulty, gentlemen?"

It was my uncle. Hildegard must have found him and told him, and no doubt he could guess the rest. He came into view, his eyes taking everything in, and I saw that my disguise did not fool him for more than a moment.

"My dear Theresa, really. I thought the gown I purchased for you at great expense was much more flattering."

I might have found the guards' perplexed expressions funny if I had not feared for my life—and my brother's.

"Quite enterprising of you, my dear," Uncle Theobald said.

I wanted to spit in his face.

"Your father would have been proud of you, no doubt. He was just a bit too smart for his own good, and it seems he's passed that dubious quality on to you." He turned to the commander of the guards. "Secure her!" Then he addressed me again. "Your poor mother will be informed that, like so many children in this wicked city, you and your brother were abducted by Gypsies and sold into slavery in Turkey. She will weep, but with another on the way, I daresay she'll get over it."

I don't really know how I found the strength or even knew what to do, but I released my brother from my arm, gripped the pistol with two hands, pulled back the firing pin, and squeezed the trigger.

The flash nearly blinded me, and the force of the shot threw me back into the wall. I hit my head and collapsed.

CHAPTER 23

I came to my senses again in a familiar position, and with a familiar stink surrounding me. I was slung over someone's shoulder, my head pounding so hard I wanted to shriek with pain. The powerful smell of the sewer made me retch.

"Good, you are alive!" Danior's voice held relief in it. "Hold on, we're going to get out of here."

I could not tell where we were in the pitch blackness, but I heard Danior's steps sloshing through muck, followed by other similar steps behind us. He shifted me around and soon began climbing an iron ladder. I felt myself slipping, so I wrapped my arms around his waist.

"Good girl," he said, and climbed faster. Soon we stopped just long enough for him to lift a wooden hatch above our heads. We squeezed through the opening, and he set my feet on the floor so that I could take my own weight. I stood up quickly. The blood that had gathered in my head when I was hanging upside down rushed out, and I felt in danger of fainting.

"Slowly!" he said, and pressed my shoulders forward, releasing me gradually until I could remain both upright and conscious. After that we stood to the side while the other two Gypsies followed us. I was more than relieved to see that the second violinist had Toby slung over his shoulder. He laid him down gently on the floor. My brother's eyes were open wide with fear.

"It's all right, Toby," I said, crouching down beside him. "These men are our friends."

He whispered, "Gypsies!" through his cracked lips.

"He needs water," I said to Danior, then turned back to Toby. "They play for Kapellmeister Haydn. Papa knew them, and was helping them."

I wanted to tell him enough to ease his fear, but not to confuse him. "Where are we?" I asked, rubbing the back of my head as I turned to look at Danior and the others. I felt a bump there and a little blood matted my hair, which was uncovered and fell in unruly curls over my shoulders. The bag wig must have fallen off at some point. I wondered if the cushioning of its lamb's-wool curls had protected me from a worse injury.

"We are somewhere safe," Danior replied.

Only then did I notice that all three of the musicians had been wounded in some way. The worst was the one who had not been carrying either of us. He clutched a bleeding arm to his chest, and his face was pale. "I want to know what happened," I said.

"I'll tell you once we take care of your brother and Brishen, who is badly hurt."

Danior continued to lead the way through a door and up a winding staircase. Our pace was slow, to accommodate Brishen's weakness, and the fact that Durril—the other violinist's name, I later discovered—had to carry Toby.

We were obviously in a very grand building of some sort. We climbed and climbed and walked through corridor after dimly lit corridor until we emerged in an attic space. Although the ceilings sloped, and it was clear from the modest, narrow beds that servants or artisans lived there, it was spotlessly clean. The linens that covered the beds looked almost new. Durril placed Toby on one of them. Danior went to another door of the room and cracked it open, then whistled low and musically, making a sound like the call of a distant nightingale.

To my surprise, a moment later Alida bustled through carrying bandages, followed by a chambermaid with a bucket of water and an armload of clean clothes, mostly in the colors of the imperial servants. *We must be inside the Hofburg itself,* I thought. The maid handed Danior the clothes before going to clean off Toby's face and check him for injuries. I noticed that her skin was of a darker cast than was usual among the Viennese, and wondered if perhaps she was a Gypsy, too. All of us changed out of our filthy, blood-stained garments. I turned away, keeping my shirt on and hoping that no one stared at my scrawny girl's legs before I could cover them with the ill-fitting breeches and hose the maid had brought. I tucked my hair down into the coat, since she had not brought any wigs, then stuffed a soft felt hat down on my head to cover as much of it as I could.

Without saying a word, Alida began dressing Brishen's wound, cleaning it out and wrapping it carefully. Brishen did not make even the smallest sound, although he must have been in terrible pain. I stole a look at his injury. He had a deep gash running from his shoulder to his elbow, a gash that looked to have been made by a sword.

"Now, tell me," I said to Danior, knowing there must have been a fierce fight after I fired the pistol and hit my head.

Alida looked up. Her eyes locked with Danior's, and in that instant I understood that they were in love. That was why Zoltán told me I could trust this Roma man who would have no reason I could think of to put himself in such peril for the sake of me and my brother.

"Your bullet hit the councilor," Danior said, turning away from Alida and looking at me.

I gulped. Had I killed my own uncle? Whatever it was he had done, now that we were safe at least for the moment, I did not want to have murdered him.

"We left him alive," he continued.

I let my breath out, hardly realizing I had been holding it.

"We surprised the guards, but they were well armed. It was quite a fight. In the end we tied them all together, the guards and your uncle. Good that you had told us about the door to the sewers before you knocked yourself out."

He did not say, but I assumed they had done some

damage to the men who had been protecting my uncle. If they were indeed imperial guards, as their uniforms suggested, it would mean death to Danior, Brishen, and Durril if they were caught. As for myself—I had no doubt my uncle would exact the worst punishment possible. "Did they see you?" I asked.

"We did our best to hide our faces. But I cannot be sure."

Alida, who had continued staring steadfastly at Danior while he spoke, turned her eyes away to concentrate on wrapping the bandages around Brishen's arm. I saw the sparkle of tears on her lashes.

"What happens now?" I could not imagine how we would be able to get away. Anywhere we went might send us into the path of palace guards. I wanted to ask as well whether Alida knew what had passed at the concert, whether Zoltán had spoken to her. Had the party continued as if life and death were not being held in the balance in the chamber below the music room? I feared for my godfather, who had clearly already placed himself in a difficult position for the sake of the persecuted Gypsies. Someone would not have to look far to unearth his dealings with the Roma. In fact, someone apparently already knew enough to blackmail him over his publishing contract.

"Brishen and the boy can stay here. The rest of you will have to disperse." Alida spoke calmly, as if this were an event she had prepared for well in advance.

Danior nodded. "I'll lead them out," he said.

So, he was enough in the habit of visiting Alida in her

quarters at the palace to know all the secret passages and servants' nooks. There was something thrilling about a forbidden love. I wondered how Alida felt, desiring someone she could not be with. I knew from everything Zoltán had told me that she would be cast out if she married a Gypsy. I wondered if it would also destroy Zoltán's efforts to have their lands restored. And then, how would they live? I could not picture the elegant Alida as a humble musician's wife like my mother, much less a Gypsy herself, camping in a wagon and wandering over the countryside.

"Have you managed to get us an audience yet?" Danior asked her just before leading Durril and me out of the room.

"I have approached the archduchess," Alida said, tying off the bandage on Brishen's arm and standing up to face us. Her eyes were full and sad. "She says she could arrange something, but there are conditions."

Danior nodded. He seemed to know what the conditions might be, and did not ask her to explain. I wanted to rush over to Alida and say, *What conditions? Tell me!* but it was not my place to do so. We left quickly.

The secret exit let us out into an alley behind the palace. The sky was paling in the east. Soon it would be dawn. Danior and Durril looked left and then right, then each started to hurry away in opposite directions. "I don't know where to go!" I called out in a loud whisper to Danior. He stopped and turned. "Find Zoltán!" he said, then ran off.

Find Zoltán. Of course, I knew where he lived. But I was

tired to my bones, and now that I knew Toby was safe and there was no immediate danger to myself, I wanted more than anything just to return to my own bed. I wanted the comforting sound of my mother's voice. Greta's commands. The curfew bell ringing as my eyes drooped over a book. I wanted to sit at Mama's bedside and hear her prattle on about my marriage and suitors, about the matchmaker, and affording elegant gowns. Poor Mama. She still thought, I imagined as I dragged myself through the early morning city streets, that her brother was going to solve all our problems by giving me a handsome dowry. She no doubt also thought Toby and I were safely cradled in luxury, discovering how the wealthy lived, eating sweets and sleeping between soft sheets.

My fatigue and the half light of approaching dawn made the deserted lanes appear unreal. It had remained cold, and yesterday's snow still clung to rooftops and windowsills. A day's carriage and foot traffic had turned the streets to mud, however, and now the frigid night had frozen them into deep ruts. I had to look down at my feet to make sure I didn't trip. As a result, I walked on without thinking and didn't realize how close I was to Zoltán's apartment until I looked up and saw the two guards standing by the door of his building. They didn't see me—or didn't notice me, I was pretty sure. I turned and walked down the first alleyway I came to as though that had been my intention all along.

The presence of the guards suggested that someone must have made a connection between Zoltán and what happened at my uncle's the night before. But how? He had not been with us when we ventured into the cellar. Someone close to the Gypsies, or Haydn, or Zoltán, or my father—someone with ties or associations with all of them—must be a spy. I could think of no other way to explain it. That would be one more complication to add to everything else, but I could spare no time wondering who it might be at that particular moment. I assumed that the presence of the guards outside Zoltán's home meant that he had not been apprehended as yet, and they were waiting for him to return. I hoped that also meant that he had left my uncle's house unharmed and gone somewhere else. Not to the Hofburg, though, because Alida would have said.

I was beginning to feel frozen through. My own apartment was not far away, but I didn't dare go there. With Toby removed from the cellar, I had no doubt that our home was being watched, too, and my uncle had seen me and would have his spies searching for me. What had happened, I wondered, to the other boys who were tied up along with Toby and looked so frightened? I wished we could have taken them all away, but that would have been impossible. Why were they there? Who were they? How could we save them from whatever it was my uncle intended to do to them?

I couldn't wander the streets forever. I had to go somewhere. I could think of only one place that might be comparatively safe. Cold and tired as I was, I realized I must make the long walk to the house on the Marienhilferstrasse to see my godfather. It was light enough to be morning, so the sentries at the city gate would not challenge me.

And my godfather was in a high enough position that to arrest or abduct him would cause an uproar and require more explanation than my uncle might be willing to supply, so I was fairly confident that he would still be at liberty. I would tell him about the boys, and also about my suspicions concerning Schnabl. The old man had turned up in too many places for me to ignore the probability that he was involved in some way. Yet I could not imagine why Schnabl—the oldest of the Esterhazy musicians—would steal music from Haydn and take it to my uncle. It just didn't make sense.

Unless . . . No. It couldn't be. Schnabl was beyond the age where ambition or passion might push him to get involved in anything illegal. He would receive his musician's pension soon and live out his days quite comfortably. Why would he risk that? No, Schnabl could not be the missing piece of the puzzle. Clearly I was exhausted and letting my imagination run away with me.

⁂

By the time I reached Haydn's apartment, I couldn't feel my hands and feet, and my lips felt numb, too. I was so hungry my stomach hurt. I knew I would cry if anyone said the slightest unkind word to me. I knocked loudly on the door despite the hour, knowing that I would probably wake up the entire household, and not really caring.

To my surprise, the door opened almost instantly, and I was faced not with the maid but with my godfather himself. He looked haggard and tired. He wore a dressing gown and no wig, revealing his own sparse, gray hair. His eyes filled with tears, and he pulled me into a warm embrace as soon as he saw me.

"If I had known all of what they were about, I would never have permitted it," he said, his arm still around my shoulders as he led me into the parlor.

"Tell me what you do know," I said. "What happened upstairs while we were in the cellar? Was it that horrid maid?"

The maestro rang for a servant to bring me some breakfast before answering. "I only know that Zoltán had told me the order of compositions to play, and that I was to dismiss those who weren't in the quartets and the divertimentos—including you, of course. He did not tell me the rest, saying only that you could lead them to where they needed to go to find Toby. I waited to hear the pistol shot and to cry out for the guards, but it never came.

"When none of you returned for the symphony, I began to suspect there was a problem. But I continued, at that point deciding that I had better direct the tympani to be as loud as they possibly could."

"Did you notice my uncle? Did he do anything strange or act odd?" I asked.

"Well, he was there for a while, but it was quite extraordinary. I think it has to do with old Schnabl. I was going to tell him—he has a bit of a weakness for drink, and he's not really been in top form lately—I was going to tell Schnabl not to bother with this engagement, that I would make up the money to him later, but he insisted on coming. When not everyone returned for the symphony, I saw Schnabl get up from his desk at the back of the cellos and say something to the valet, that tall, skeletal fellow.

"Then the valet walked around and said something to Wolkenstein, who after that bowed to the Hungarian ambassador and left the room. I did see the maid approach him on his way out, but he didn't stop for her. That was the last I saw of him. When the concert ended, the valet returned to say that his master had had a bad turn and must beg his pardon to be excused from the company. No one seemed to mind, and the party went on. I expect they were a little relieved. They certainly seemed to be enjoying the food and drink. I stayed for only a short while after that. Zoltán left with the others immediately after the concert, as far as I knew then.

"It wasn't until I got back here and Zoltán intercepted me before I reached my door that I realized things hadn't quite gone to plan. Although when I never heard the shot, I should have known something had gone wrong."

I did not want to tell him that I had, in fact, fired the pistol as planned, but not with the hoped-for result. Instead I said, "I have something else to tell you about Herr Schnabl, but right now, I need to find Zoltán. Do you know where he is?"

"He left early this morning as soon as he realized you were not here. He was going to join Danior and his men."

I prayed Zoltán had not decided to return to his own apartment first, where he would most certainly have been apprehended by the guards. No point in worrying my godfather about that, though. "The important thing is that Toby is now safe. We found him, in my uncle's cellar, with eight or ten other boys. I still do not know what they were doing there. Toby couldn't say much. We got him out through the sewers. The other boys—I'm afraid for them. We could not bring them all."

At that moment my breakfast arrived, and I had to stop talking and eat. Never had plain, warm bread, butter, and eggs tasted so good. I drank an entire cup of chocolate while my godfather sat in silence opposite, gazing off into space.

After a time, he spoke. "I fear that, to add to everything, I have no hope of being able to complete the work for Artaria. This will mean ruin for the cause. One cannot fight the nobles without money."

"Oh! I nearly forgot! That's what I wanted to say about Schnabl. He may have been the one who took your portfolio." I described how I had met the old musician on my way out of my uncle's house a few days ago.

"How very odd. I simply can't imagine why he would do such a thing—if indeed he did. He's been here for so long. He's quite devoted to the prince."

"To the prince," I said, "but what about to you?"

Haydn rubbed his hand over his head, then took off his spectacles and cleaned them on a large handkerchief, frowning all the while. "I have always treated him kindly. There are those who say he felt that he should have been given the job of Kapellmeister instead of me, but he certainly seemed content enough to remain in the orchestra. Perhaps

I should have spoken to him more, done something for him . . ." His voice trailed off.

"Could he have discovered what you intended to tell the prince about the Hungarian serfs?"

"No. No, I do not believe so. I do not *want* to believe so. He is too loyal to create such difficulties."

"Perhaps he thought he was being loyal—to the prince." I could see that my godfather was not prepared to hear anything bad about one of his musicians, and did my best to cast the matter in a light that would give Schnabl some honorable motive—if he were in fact involved. In any case, what Haydn said about him confirmed my suspicions. Now I needed to alert someone to Schnabl's potential treachery, making it even more important that I find Zoltán and tell him about everything that had happened, especially about Toby and the other children in my uncle's cellar. I feared there was some connection between the boys and the efforts of Zoltán and his friends to lay the case for the Hungarian serfs before the emperor.

I was also convinced that we had very little time to accomplish our goals. I had no doubt that my uncle would be quick to use his influence to punish those who had injured him and the guards in his pay.

I stood and bowed to my godfather, my boy's clothing making a curtsy unsuitable. "Thank you for breakfast, but I must leave you and find Zoltán to inform him about Schnabl. I think I know where he is."

"Can I not persuade you to stay here in safety? I blame

myself for allowing you to be exposed to such danger. I would never forgive myself if anything happened to you."

I kissed his papery cheek. "No, Godfather. I must do this. It's important. For Papa's sake."

He nodded. Before I left, he gave me another cloak and some mitts. As I ran off away from the city and toward the Gypsy camp, I felt as if the maestro had his kind arms around me, keeping me warm and safe.

CHAPTER 24

I was surprised how quickly I reached the forest on the banks of the Danube near the Gypsy encampment. It had seemed longer in a closed carriage. It occurred to me that before, the horses would have had to travel at a walking pace because of the rough ground, and that now I was probably running faster than that, leaping over the deep ruts, fear pushing me on despite my fatigue.

By the time I approached the clearing, I was doubled over, gasping for breath, feeling as if the entire breakfast I had consumed at Haydn's house would soon be emptied from my stomach. I gulped some air and calmed my racing heart before crouching low to approach the camp. I thought it prudent to stay out of sight. I huddled behind a bush to watch and make sure it would be safe for me to enter.

Only a few sleepy women and children wandered around among the huts and wagons. A cauldron of gruel bubbled and steamed over an open fire. I was relieved to see Durril seated by it, wrapped in a thick blanket, head hanging.

Perhaps he was sleeping. As I watched, Maya came out of her tent and crouched down beside him to whisper something in his ear. Soon after that, two other men led an old fellow in a torn uniform out from a hut into the clearing. His hands were bound together and he was gagged, but I recognized him as the general who had tried to purchase my favors at the ball. His eyes were fearful, but he did not look otherwise harmed. After all that had occurred, I wondered how long that would remain the case. I was almost surprised at how strong an impulse I had to leap forward and scratch his eyes out. It wasn't like me to feel like harming someone. I restrained myself. He was valuable to Zoltán as he was. My one hope was that he would be punished for whatever part he had played in the entire wicked plot.

"Give him something to eat; then we must move him. It's too dangerous to keep him here now."

I heard Zoltán's voice before I saw him. I was so relieved to see his handsome face and tall body that I suddenly felt weak. I wanted to call out to him, to run into the clearing and fling my arms around him, sob into his shoulder and tell him all that had happened the night before. But something held me back. Maybe I just felt ugly in my ill-fitting boy's clothes, or maybe I didn't want to see him in front of all these other people. Perhaps, I thought, if I just waited, I could signal to him and no one would notice.

I watched Maya offer the general some gruel, but as soon as they removed his gag and held a bowl to his lips, he spat it out and started yelling. They stopped his mouth again immediately. Then Zoltán and the others got him onto the back of a horse, although he struggled against them. Once he was mounted, they tied his hands to the pommel of the saddle. Zoltán himself mounted another horse and took a lead line from the general's bridle, nodded a salute to the now bustling little community, and trotted away toward Vienna. *Why is he going that direction?* I thought. I wanted to run after him and yell out, "Wait!" But I knew that I should not do such a thing.

Still, watching Zoltán ride into the distance when I had just been so happy to see him again was almost more than I could bear. Something about the sight of my friend made me feel safe. I noticed how cold I had become only after he had passed out of my view around a bend in the path.

Now I didn't know what to do. I had found Zoltán, and he was gone again. There was no sign of Danior here, but I'd seen Durril, who no doubt told what had happened in the cellar. But still Zoltán did not know about Schnabl. I guessed that I might as well show myself to the Gypsies and stay with them. It would be safer than going home, and perhaps they had a new plan. There were only so many places to hide the general. Some action must occur soon to bring everything out in the open.

Just as I was on the point of standing up and walking out from behind the holly bush that had been sheltering me from sight, a commotion arose all around me. The thunder of hooves approaching fast sent me scurrying into a deeper thicket, scratching my face in the process. The Gypsies dropped whatever they were doing and started to rush around, trying to uproot themselves just as I had seen them do once before when I was in their midst. Only this time, they had no warning from their own men. Before even a single hut could be broken down, the camp was surrounded by guards on horseback, their swords pointed at the huddled community. I caught sight of Mirela, her deep brown eyes wide open and terrified. She wore only a shift and a skirt, obviously having still been asleep until she was awakened suddenly by the raid, and she stood shivering and vulnerable. I wished I could spirit her into my thicket and protect her from harm. As it was, I had to clamp my hand over my own mouth to prevent any involuntary exclamation from escaping. I watched one group of soldiers bind everyone—men, women, and children, including the proud Danior—and rope them together into a mass while another group ransacked the huts and wagons.

I had been concentrating so hard on watching this horrible spectacle that I had not noticed another smaller group of riders approach. I gasped when I saw my uncle among them, seated atop a large warmblood, holding the reins in one hand. His left arm was bandaged and hung down at his side.

"Do you see your assailants here, Councilor?" asked one of the guards.

My uncle scanned the Gypsies with his heavy-lidded eyes, his mouth turned down at the corners. "There's the ringleader!" he exclaimed, pointing so violently in Danior's direction that he nearly fell out of his saddle. "He shot me. He'll hang, on my word of honor!"

So, my uncle had, after all, seen Danior in the struggle down in the cellar. But why did he claim that Danior had been the one to pull the trigger, and not me? Alida was right to have been so distressed. My uncle knew that Danior had not fired at him, yet he claimed it, no doubt to ensure that he would be hanged. How could he get away with such a thing! It was Theobald Wolkenstein who was the villain, not the good Danior. I wanted to run out, pull my uncle to the ground, and hammer him with my fists. But I knew that I would pay with my own life if I did that. I stuffed my fingers into my mouth and swallowed my bitter tears. I would run immediately to Alida after this. Surely there would be something she could do. She always managed to do something.

In the meantime, the ransacking guards had made a pile of household effects, personal possessions, and a few rough weapons—mostly knives and clubs—to one side of the clearing. I watched with horror as a guard tossed Danior's fiddle on the top of the pile as if it were a cooking pot. Although not quite as beautiful as my father's Amati, it was a fine instrument, now no doubt damaged by its rough treatment. I saw Danior give it no more than a glance as the guards herded all the Roma in the direction of Vienna. Children had begun to cry, and the women started wailing and pulling on their hair. The commander of the small force removed a pistol from his sash and fired it into the air. This silenced everyone.

Somehow Mirela had ended up on the edge of the roped-up group. I saw her glance left and right and wait for a moment when everyone's attention was engaged elsewhere. Then, so quickly I hardly noticed it—and I was watching her—she slipped under the rope and slithered into the space beneath a wagon whose wheels had been removed. Once there, she was so still she could have been a mound of dirt.

In the meantime, the guards had herded the rest of the community along, all clinging to each other for warmth and comfort. As they shuffled away through the cold, the commander yelled out to one of the guards who had been pulling all the Gypsies' belongings out of their huts, "Did you find them?"

"No, there's nothing but rubbish here. Only a few pistols, and our men have them," he responded. "What shall I do with it all?"

"Burn it."

My God! I thought. Surely they couldn't intend to destroy the entire encampment. I wanted to stop them, most of all to yell to Mirela to get out of her hiding place and give herself up rather than risk being roasted alive. Yet I could do nothing. I watched as three of the guards yanked wooden supports from the huts and held them in the fire until they became huge torches, then touched them to each wagon and lean-to in turn, including the one that sheltered Mirela. Last of all, they ignited the pile of odds and ends, a mound of clothing, tools, even books—and Danior's violin.

As the heat rose from the fire, the soldiers withdrew, leapt on their horses, and followed the others. I was no longer cold. One of the burning huts was near enough to where I hid that it would put me in danger if I remained there. But that was not my main concern. First was to get Mirela to safety. I called to her, but the roaring fire drowned out my voice. The wagon she hid beneath was small and old, and the wood had caught quickly, but only on one side, the one whose opening was wide enough for her to slide under. She would never get out from the other side unaided. I took a deep breath and held it, clutched some snow in my hands to keep them cool, and ran as low to the ground as I could. The heat was intense. I reached the wagon, lay flat on the ground, and peered underneath. I saw Mirela rigid with fear, but still alive.

"The guards are gone! Give me your hand!" I yelled over the increasing roar of the fire. At that moment, the side of the wagon that was ablaze collapsed, and the space through which Mirela would have to crawl narrowed even further. I grabbed hold of her and pulled her as she inched snakelike along the ground. My eyes stung and I didn't know how long I could stay there, but I pulled as hard as I could. She was halfway out, and the wagon settled again.

"Argghhh!"

Her scream was unearthly. She was lodged there. I did the only thing I could. I started to dig with my hands beneath and around her. The heat of the fire had softened the ground, thank God, and I soon made enough extra space to free her body. She was near to fainting when I pulled her to her feet. She leaned on me heavily as we hobbled to the cover of the woods. We had gotten no more than five paces from the wagon when the flames engulfed it in a whoosh, and it crumbled into itself like a piece of paper in a stove.

Once we reached the cover of the woods, Mirela collapsed, gasping for air. "You . . . saved . . . my life," she said.

"Just be calm, and then we must get away from here."

But Mirela lifted her head and stared at the encampment. The look of horror on her face was painful to see. With great effort she pointed toward the pile of belongings. "The violin!" she whispered. "Get the violin!"

I followed her gesture. The mound crowned by Danior's beautiful violin was starting to burst into flame. Soon the heat would start to melt the varnish on the instrument. Then it might as well be destroyed, for it would never be the same again.

Not fully realizing how foolhardy my actions were, I ran to the pile of household goods, looking for a place around the edge where the flames had not yet started to lick up and catch. Smoke curled out from the middle of the heap, and I knew that I had only moments to act or it would be no use.

I found a spot and scrambled up, grabbed the neck of the violin, and leapt from the top to the icy ground beyond the flames. My ankle twisted when I landed, but not badly. The bottom of my cloak had caught a spark and started to smolder. I quickly scraped snow off the ground to douse it, then crawled into the forest on my knees and one hand, holding the fiddle out of harm's way with the other.

I made my way back to where Mirela lay, still wheezing from the smoke. I stopped to calm the beating of my heart and examine the violin. From what I saw, it appeared unharmed. I plucked a string, wanting to reassure myself with its rich sound.

Clunk. That's what I heard.

I plucked again. *Clunk.*

This fine instrument offered no resonance at all. What had happened to Danior's fiddle? I peered inside the F holes, angling the violin so the slanting sunlight illuminated the interior.

There I saw the cause. Wedged up inside and pressed against the body of the fiddle was a wad of papers. I could see that they were covered with writing. I could also see that I would not be able to remove them without taking the violin apart.

I crawled back to Mirela.

"You see," she said, her voice a little recovered now that she had been breathing the cold, winter air, "that's why the fiddle is so important. We must get those papers to the emperor somehow, now that everything has gone so badly wrong."

Mirela's shoulders began to shake and tears poured from her eyes, tracing paths through the soot on her face. She started to shiver. I removed my cloak and wrapped it around her.

Now I began to put all the pieces together. Zoltán had told me that my father had recently found documents that proved the atrocities against the Hungarian serfs and that he had hidden them in his fiddle case. He said that he was to give them to Danior on the night he died. Danior would have secreted them inside his violin until they could be safely taken to some other stronghold. It would have been the final transfer of papers, he told me. Danior must have kept the others somewhere in his hut, and decided—perhaps because of the increased danger, with the capture of the general and our failed excursion last night—that he should hide them for the moment inside his instrument again. But how could we know if the papers Papa had found were among these? Surely they were not. If Danior had them all along, why would he have said nothing to Zoltán?

I shuddered when I thought of how close complete disaster had been. If the fiddle had burned, we would have been left with no written evidence to lay before the emperor—assuming we might be granted the opportunity.

"How are you feeling now?" I asked Mirela. She had stopped crying and sat up.

"Better, I think. I can breathe."

"Are you hurt? Can you stand?"

The two of us leaned on each other for support and rose to our feet. Together we took a few steps. My ankle was a little sore, but I could bear it.

"My back hurts a bit. I think mainly I scraped it."

"Show me," I said.

Mirela turned and lifted the cloak. I saw that her shift had been sliced through at the back where the edge of the wagon had pressed down on her, and that she had a large, ugly bruise, but the skin was not broken. She must have been in considerable pain nonetheless. But I did not want to alarm her. "You have no cuts to speak of. Do you think you can walk far?"

"It will ease as we go. We cannot stay here. We have evidence that might save the others. We must give it to someone who can help."

By now Mirela had recovered a little of her spirit. I was glad, not only because I did not want her to be hurt, but because I needed her assistance. "We have to find Alida. She will know what to do."

"That is Zoltán's sister, no?" Mirela said. "Where is she?"

"In the Hofburg." I looked down at my dirty boy's clothes and at Mirela, who was very little better. No one would ever admit us to the Hofburg in such a state. I doubted we could even get into the kitchens looking as we did. "We must change into fine clothes, and I have an idea. Let us go."

I had only one hope. My uncle had given me unlimited credit for the period of one week at Mademoiselle Helene's. If Mirela and I boldly walked in and I demanded they furnish my personal maid and myself with elegant clothes at my uncle's expense, there was a chance they would not, and would simply toss us out into the gutter. There was also a chance they would. And right then, I could think of no other course to take.

I wrapped the violin in the folds of my cloak, linked my arm through Mirela's, and took the first steps on the long walk back to Vienna.

"Let's make up a story on the way," I said. "We have to have something to tell a girl at an elegant shop that will prevent her from slamming the door in our faces." I saw Mirela's impish expression, and I knew by the time we got to Mademoiselle Helene's, we would have at least a fighting chance of success.

CHAPTER 25

When the girl greeted us at Mademoiselle Helene's, Mirela and I were clutching our sides and laughing uproariously. That had been our plan: we decided we should appear to have come from an all-night revel, perhaps hint at some raucous games in which the girls dressed as boys and the maids pretended to be Gypsies.

To my immense surprise, our playacting worked.

They even let me bathe in a copper tub in a private room and poured me a restorative cordial while they took Mirela to the back, cleaned her up, and gave her a suitable, simple dress and cap for a lady's maid. My credit, I found, was excellent. I took great delight in requesting the most expensive fabrics, asking for an extra bit of lace, having the seamstresses trim the mantelet with miniver, and even choosing a jeweled comb to hold up my hair. By the end of two hours of frenzied work on their part and much-needed rest on ours, Mirela and I emerged from the *couturier* looking like a fashionable young lady with her maid in tow, ready to spend the morning shopping. So that they would not suspect there was anything at all important about the violin, we pretended at first to leave it behind.

"Oh, dear me! My uncle will be cross if I do not return that fiddle to his musician. Apparently he's rather fond of it. Can you wrap it in something soft for me, perhaps some velvet?" I asked, not quite believing I had the nerve to act a part so completely.

They did as I asked right away, and I sauntered out into a cloudy afternoon, Mirela behind me with the violin nestled in costly velvet and tied up with a silk ribbon. But I did not trust myself to keep up the pretense for long in the face of the real world, already feeling skeptical eyes following us as we walked. "Let's go this way," I whispered to Mirela. "It's shorter." I started to hasten my pace.

"Mind you don't ruin your clothes," Mirela said. I slowed down and went more cautiously, trying not to catch my skirts or muddy my slippers.

The streets were full of people rushing around on their daily business. A band played some songs and a group of children had gathered around them. I watched as a worried mother rushed up and took two of the smallest ones by the hands and dragged them away. As she passed me, I heard her scold them with, "They're Gypsies! You should know better. You'll end up sold as slaves in Turkey."

I couldn't help looking back at Mirela, who, although now clean and fresh looking and dressed respectably, had the telltale light almond-colored skin, dark eyes, and jet-black, curling hair of the Gypsies from the encampment. I don't know if she hadn't heard or just chose to pretend she hadn't, but she lifted her chin and assumed a haughty expression. I glanced at the faces of the musicians as we passed, and at least one of them seemed familiar. I thought he was looking at Mirela, too. I was too tired to worry, though. My mind was running fast and my imagination was on fire. I forced myself to think about the task at hand. The Hofburg. That's where we had to go, making our way as if we had every right to be walking freely in the street with everyone else, and no one had tried to capture either of us and prevent us from bringing terrible crimes to light.

I had never entered the royal palace except from the sewers the night before. Although I knew it was an enormous building, I hadn't really thought about it much when it formed no direct part of my life. The Hofburg was a landmark, a point of reference when I was going somewhere. Occasionally Toby and I stood to the side and watched processions of guards and gilded carriages when the emperor walked out into the city to greet the people, but that was as close as I had ever gotten to attaching any real significance to the place. And then it was just to peer into the carriage windows and see the ladies in their jewels. Once, I saw a young girl about my age and I wanted to be her. I still remember what she wore—her bodice, anyway. It was shot through with gold that caught the sunlight whenever a beam struck the window in the right way, so that it appeared as if the glow were coming from inside her carriage. She wore a string of large pearls around her neck, which was long and slender, and her skin was so white she looked like a porcelain doll. But as she passed very close by, I could also see that her big eyes were sad, and although she tried to smile, I could tell it was difficult. I remember thinking that I would not like to be forced to look really happy if I felt very unhappy. I rarely had to put on an expression for anyone, especially when I was younger. I laughed when I wanted. I cried when I wanted.

When Mirela and I reached the grand, curved front entrance of the emperor's winter palace and saw the ranks of sentries on horseback guarding it, we both stood and stared, not knowing what to do. It did not seem like a good idea to just walk up to one of the guards and ask to go in.

I turned to ask Mirela how she thought we should proceed, and was surprised to find she had vanished. I walked a little way back toward the park we had passed through to get there, and found her standing behind a tree, clutching the violin to her.

"What's wrong?" I asked. Her eyes were bright with fear.

"The guards!" she whispered.

Of course. The palace guards wore the same uniforms as those who had surrounded the camp and set fire to it. "These are not the same men. You must know that. We will be together. They will believe we are who we act like." I wasn't really sure of this, but Mirela's terror made me overly brave on behalf of both of us. "Look," I said, pointing to the crested carriages pulling up and disgorging their well-dressed cargoes. I watched the footmen open the doors and hand out the ladies, saw the fine folk walk right into the palace without being challenged. "All we have to do is look confident, and they will let us in."

"But the ladies don't have their maids with them."

She was right. I thought we might have to change our plan, but then I saw a footman follow his mistress in, bearing a gout stool. "I know. I need you to carry the gift that I have brought for Alida. The violin." It was our only hope. I did not want to go alone, for my own sake and Mirela's. Once inside the palace, she would be safe, too.

We waited until there was a queue of two or three carriages and a lot of bustling activity around the door, then marched forward as if we knew our business there. If the guards suspected anything, they didn't show it. We received a few curious stares from the people descending from the carriages, one or two lingering on Mirela's exotic face, but I answered them with smiles and a polite incline of my head. They could do nothing but smile in return.

Before I knew it we were in a large reception hall dotted with knots of visitors whispering among themselves. No one seemed to be in much of a hurry. The high ceilings and emptiness of the space created an odd, whispering echo. I caught words here and there that assembled themselves into accusations aimed at me. *She's a criminal,* and *No one should believe . . . a fake . . . condemned . . .* I wanted to reach for Mirela's hand, but that would have called attention to the fact that we weren't accustomed to the relationship of mistress and maid.

Through it all a large clock ticked. If I focused on the tick, it became deafeningly loud and drowned out the strange echo. I remember noticing that it was a little before two of the clock. As more and more people entered the large vestibule, I thought perhaps something would happen at that hour, and that everyone was waiting on purpose.

I wondered how long we could linger in that space alone without provoking comment. *We had better do something,* I thought. In addition to those who were clearly guests, a number of servants in the characteristic black satin imperial livery wandered through on their daily business.

"Mirela," I whispered, "find one of the servants who looks nice and ask if I may be presented to Alida. Say I've come to bring her a gift."

The hall continued to fill with people. While Mirela walked toward a footman, I wandered around slowly to disguise my growing sense that everyone was staring at me, and that soon a guard would approach me and escort me out to the street with Mirela. But the guards left us alone. Mademoiselle Helene and her seamstresses had obviously done their work quite well.

I happened to be standing quite near a long-case clock when it struck the hour with a very loud gong. I jumped and let out a shriek that drew all eyes to me. I know I blushed, but I was saved the embarrassment of continued attention by a fanfare that preceded the opening of a pair of tall doors. Everyone turned and started to walk through them, trying not to appear as if they were hurrying so that they would be first.

I supposed, although I did not know for certain, that someone was giving an audience. Through the open doors I saw a large, ornate chair on a dais. Perhaps it was a throne. I glanced around and did not immediately see Mirela. The last thing I wanted was to be ushered in with all the rest, because without Zoltán, Alida, or even Mirela and the violin to give me some purpose, I wasn't sure exactly what I was supposed to say or do. I doubted that it would be appropriate to make wild claims about children imprisoned in my uncle's cellar and Hungarian serfs being tortured and sold as slaves.

Yet for the moment, there was nothing else to do except follow the general movement of people. I kept sweeping my eyes around, looking for Mirela. Just before I was about to be nudged into the audience chamber, I spotted a girl with a bucket wearing the simple, muslin dress and apron of a chambermaid, with Mirela following behind her. I started to walk toward them, but the maid pressed a spot on a wall panel, a panel sprang open, and she and Mirela disappeared behind it.

I stopped where I was and pretended to examine a spot on my skirt until everyone had passed around me as if I were a boulder in a brook. Once the crowd had gone in, I found myself almost alone in the huge vestibule. The few stragglers were too intent on following the rest to bother much about me, so no one noticed me pressing that same spring on the hidden door and entering the secret spaces of the palace known only to the servants.

The corridors between the walls were well lit by

windows at regular intervals, but narrow enough so that my skirts brushed either side as I passed. I had no idea which way Mirela and the chambermaid had gone. I hoped I'd soon find someone I could ask.

The first soul I came upon was a young girl with only one tooth in her head. She scurried along with a basket of wood that was almost as big as she was, huffing and puffing through her open mouth.

"Excuse me," I called out to her.

When she saw me, she nearly dropped her entire load and was so flustered that I could barely understand her lisping speech. "Yes, mistress, what's the matter?"

"My maid came past here, I believe. I had asked her to seek a maid of honor to the Archduchess Maria Elizabeth, for whom I have brought a gift."

"*Himmel.* You're lost," she said.

"Yes, but can you direct me to Alida?"

"All the ladies-in-waiting is at the audience."

"Where might I wait for her when the audience ends?" I asked.

"Not here!" she cried. "Ladies is not allowed here!"

I wanted to tell her that I was no more a lady than she was, but I realized that in my present costume that would seem unlikely. "Then perhaps you could lead me to where I *am* allowed?" I said, trying not to let my irritation creep into my voice.

She dipped an ungainly curtsy to me. "This way," she said, and I followed her around and around. At any moment she looked as though she would drop her heavy load. I wanted to offer to help her with it, but I decided that if anyone saw us, she might get into trouble.

At last we left the servants' corridors and entered a comfortable sitting room through a panel next to a small fireplace. "Here's where the maids of honor sit," the girl said. She stood there shifting her weight from one foot to another. I saw by the ample supply of wood in the hopper next to the fire that her destination had not been this room, and wondered why she did not leave me quickly so she could continue with her chores.

"If it's all right, Madame," she said, "I'll get on with my work."

"Yes! Yes, of course you may go," I said, realizing with shame that she needed my permission to leave.

I hoped that Mirela would soon appear, but at least I was out of the way of general scrutiny there. I suppose I had not realized how exhausted I was, how the constant strain of the last few days had taken a toll on me, but it was not more than a few minutes after I sat in one of the upholstered chairs that I fell asleep so deeply I completely forgot where I was.

⁂

"Theresa," murmured a voice quite close to my ear. At first I thought it was my mother. But it didn't smell like my mother. There was no faint odor of wood smoke and medicine. Instead, I smelled lavender. "Theresa," the voice repeated.

I opened my eyes and saw two strange young women

dressed in the latest fashion peering down at me. I turned my head, and there was Alida, kneeling by the side of the chair. Beyond her, hovering in the background, stood Mirela, the velvet-wrapped violin still in her arms. I sat upright, then got to my feet quickly, staggering a little because I wasn't quite awake. "Oh! I beg your pardon!" I curtsied.

"I am so glad you came, my dear, as I asked you to, and sorry that you did not simply enter the audience chamber and await me there."

Alida could certainly think quickly, I thought. "I was quite comfortable here, thank you," I said.

"Apparently!" said one of the other two ladies—who I now saw were not much more than girls. Their fine gowns gave them the appearance of maturity. The one who had not spoken giggled.

"Is your maid carrying a package for me?" Alida said, gesturing toward Mirela, who came forward with the velvet-wrapped violin.

"Yes! It is a gift, from—" *From whom?* I thought. I hadn't planned for such a public encounter.

"From my dear brother! How kind of him." She took the violin from Mirela, who then stepped discreetly into the background. The two young maids of honor ignored Mirela as if she were just another invisible servant, but I saw Alida nod slightly in her direction before placing the wrapped package behind her chair. The other maids of honor looked very disappointed that Alida did not intend to open the mysteriously shaped package then and there.

"Shall I ring for some tea?" said the girl who had giggled. She looked to be about my age, perhaps a little older.

Alida nodded.

"Are you come to be a maid of honor?" the other one asked me. I noticed that we all remained standing, as if there were some confusion about who took precedence.

Alida solved the difficulty by introducing me—again—as her cousin, to Lady Liesl and Lady Rebekah, and then suggesting we all sit. Workboxes were opened, and all three of the maids of honor were soon occupied with embroidering tiny designs on squares of linen. I glanced at Mirela, then at Alida, willing her to look in my direction. We couldn't just let Mirela stand there like a fireplace ornament.

Without looking up, Alida said, "I expect your maid would like to see about the arrangements for your stay this evening. Rebekah, will you ring for someone to show her to our bedchamber?"

Rebekah did as Alida asked, and a footman arrived. After Alida explained matters, he led Mirela away. She glanced over her shoulder at me, and I tried to convey in my answering look how sorry I was that she was being treated like that. I think I would have felt more comfortable being considered of the servant class in that grand palace, so that Mirela and I could stay together.

Once Mirela left, I longed for a private moment to talk to Alida. I could tell she was curious not only about how I managed to find her—and look so respectable, considering my condition the last time she had seen me—but also to hear whether I had found Zoltán, why Mirela was with me, and what had happened to Danior since she had last seen him that morning. But she gave no hint that she was anything but entirely content simply to sit and sew.

Part of me, though, wanted to postpone forever telling her the news that her beloved Danior had been taken away by the guards and put in prison. I did not want it to be me that distressed her by reporting my uncle's accusation and threat. Worse, I would have to admit to her that he had been taken away under the falsest of pretenses. It had been me, not Danior, who had fired the shot that wounded my uncle.

No, I did not want to tell her any of this. Alida did not deserve such unhappiness. Yet I knew that soon I would have to find a way to say something, or all hope of justice would be gone.

"Liesl, Rebekah," Alida said to the two girls, "I believe it is time to take the archduchess her tonic. Would you care to do it, so that I may stay with my cousin?"

Clearly this was a great honor that Alida bestowed on her two charges. They stood up at once, nearly dropping their work on the floor, and could barely restrain themselves from running out of the room to accomplish this task.

As soon as we were alone, Alida turned to me. "Tell me quickly. We have very little time."

I gave her my information in as few words as possible, telling her about the raid on the camp and Danior's peril. But I could not tell her that final piece of information, about my own guilt. I simply couldn't.

"He could be in the dungeons below," she murmured,

already far away from where we were and thinking rapidly, I could see.

"The violin," I said, "Danior's violin. It contains documents." I pointed. I had also not told her about my climb to the top of the pyre of household effects, or my desperate rescue of Mirela. I thought it best to distress her as little as possible.

Her eyes opened wide. "You brought them? Here?"

I thought for a moment I had made some terrible mistake and was about to apologize.

She lifted her hand to stop me from speaking. "You cannot know what you have done!" she said, leaping from her chair and pacing across the room. "Now that we have them, I must think how best to bring our case." I had never seen Alida so agitated. She ran to me and crouched beside my chair, taking both my hands in hers. "Don't you see? If these are even half the documents we have been collecting, we have proof! I wanted to show them to the archduchess long ago, but my brother said we should wait until we had the final evidence. But this is enough, I am certain! The Gypsies will be freed, and we will regain our lands."

And then you and Danior could marry, I thought, more hoping than believing that would be so.

"Can we not take these to the emperor or the empress right away?" I asked.

Alida wilted visibly before my eyes. "The empress is always ill. The emperor has been running things, but as her son he still has little real power. Everything he decides has to be ratified by the councilors. Including your uncle."

"Then how—?"

"Tomorrow all prisoners who were captured today will be brought before a magistrate to be judged and sentenced," she said. "We must find a way to make an extraordinary appeal. This can occur only if someone is sentenced to death, and there is a strong possibility he has been wrongly accused."

"And if the appeal fails?" I hardly wanted to know. Alida did not answer.

I could tell that she warred with herself, trying to maintain control over her feelings. "I cannot go. It would cause a scandal and probably harm rather than help the cause. Can you perform this one final service for us? After this, we will either have won, or we will be completely lost."

I wondered exactly what she could ask of me that was more dangerous than anything I had already done. "Toby is still safe here?" I asked.

"Yes. You need not worry on his account."

I agreed to attempt whatever task she gave me. It was the least I could do, with Danior imprisoned for a crime that I had committed. In the few minutes we had left to ourselves before the other maids of honor returned, she explained everything to me.

When she finished, I asked, "Where is Zoltán now?" I longed to see him. To know he was safe. Even though Danior was in such great peril, I felt as if I would die if anything had happened to Zoltán.

"Don't worry, he is safe." Alida touched my cheek when she said this. *She knows how I feel,* I thought. "He has taken the general to a place where he will not be found. When I inform him of our next steps, he will bring our prisoner forward. It must all be done with the utmost precision. If the timing is not exactly right, they will be able to lock us all away forever."

I spent an agonizing, quiet evening with Alida and her young charges, my heart fluttering about what I would have to do the next day. They all seemed happy to have me as a guest, and the servants took my presence in stride. I was surprised to discover that ladies in the imperial palace slept in beds that were no softer than my own humble bed, and kept the same hours as a farmer, retiring soon after sunset and awakening before sunrise.

CHAPTER 26

Mirela had spent the night with the maids in an attic room of the Hofburg. She must have awakened very early to be up before we were, but she came in to "help me dress," she said. Fortunately, the younger maids had duties to attend to that took them away from us so we had a few moments where just the three of us could talk.

"I shall go with Theresa, of course," Mirela said, pacing up and back like a caged panther after we had finished listening to Alida explain everything I must do that morning.

"It's best if you stay out of the way." Alida grabbed hold of Mirela's wrist as she passed by her, gently but firmly making her stand in one place.

"But I want to help Danior! He is like my brother." Mirela's beseeching eyes filled with tears.

"You will not help him by getting yourself recognized as one of the band from the encampment. Besides, there may be something else we need you to do."

Alida gave Mirela a warm smile, and Mirela blinked her

tears away rapidly, doing her utmost to smile in return. "Well, that is different," she said, and sat on the edge of a chair while Alida finished giving me my instructions. We fixed it that I would part from Alida and the other ladies on the pretext that I was going to the shops to look for a ribbon of a particular color.

When we joined Liesl and Rebekah for breakfast, I wondered if they could see right through me and only out of politeness didn't say anything, or whether necessity had made me an excellent liar. Whatever the case, they accepted our explanation without question, and after eating only a few bites of bread and drinking half a glass of tea I departed from their presence on my grim business.

∴

Outside the magistrates' court the atmosphere was like a carnival. Common people jostled for positions that would get them seats inside, where they would be able to hear prisoners accused of foul crimes and hear people beg for their lives and their dignity. A juggler tossed flaming torches into the air, and elegant carriages lined up waiting for the doors to open so the wealthy could enjoy a day's entertainment hoping that someone would be condemned to hang.

Alida had provided me with clothing that was a little less fine than the gown I had procured from Mademoiselle Helene's the day before, and I had a long, warm cloak with a hood that covered my face almost completely. She had told me where to stand for the greatest likelihood of getting one of the few places reserved for the rabble, in the balcony, and had given me exact instructions about what I was to say and when to say it.

While I waited, I had a few moments to reflect. Somewhere between the day before and the morning of the trial, my entire world had been set on its ear. Events and people had pushed me beyond limits I thought were built of unyielding stone, starting on Christmas Eve, when Zoltán and the others brought my father's body to our apartment. But it was more than just the outside things, the world that was not under my control, that had changed. I had discovered that I had wits and, I supposed, courage—although looked at in another light it could be considered a sort of madness, and my courage had failed me when it came to admitting to Alida that Danior might hang for my offense. Yet provided I was able to keep my wits about me and focus all my thoughts on the matter at hand, I would be able to achieve something that was important not just to me, but to a whole group of people who were depending on me alone.

The doors of the Rathaus opened. I slipped through the crowd just as Alida had instructed me, rehearsing her soothing words as I went. "They will not want to let you pass," she had said, "but you are slender and agile and will get through before they even notice." Sheer necessity made me bold as I subtly elbowed my way past older men and women who cast hostile glances at me, squeezing through the door and up the stairs to the balcony, boldly stepping over the rows of benches to get a prime position near the front. I was well settled in my place when I heard the groan of disappointment after the guards closed the doors behind me. No more than seventy people had been admitted, whereas the crowd that was trying to enter had amounted easily to several hundred.

The nobles and other wealthy people had not had to push in among us common folk. They simply sauntered into the chairs below that had been specially reserved for them, although I could tell they were nonetheless eager for the spectacle to begin. From high and low I heard excited voices conjecture about the day's proceedings.

"They say there's a Gypsy murderer among the accused," said a man.

"What matter if anyone murder a Gypsy?" replied a woman next to him. "There're too many of them as it is."

Several people laughed at the misunderstanding. I felt my face burn.

"No, I mean a Gypsy has murdered someone. A noble or something."

"A councilor," said a third voice.

My ears tingled. Had my uncle died? He had looked alive enough when I saw him seated atop a horse the day before. Alive and kicking—hard. The conversation turned to other matters: a pickpocket who might have his hand chopped off, since he'd been caught already several times before, and a few whores who might be publicly flogged. "It's not like the old days, though," said one grizzled gentleman to my right. "Now that the emperor has his say, they never use the acid or the barbs on the ends of the whips."

My papa had taken me to a public execution once, a

little over a year before. "Look," he had told me. "Do not be tempted to glance away. That fellow there—the one who is being bound to those boards so that the executioner can break his bones into little pieces under the wheel—he was caught poaching rabbits to feed his starving family. And that woman, the one they've stripped half naked? A prostitute. She is guilty only of selling the use of her body to the same guards who keep public order. They will whip her until you can see the white bones of her ribs." I was already crying before a single blow was struck. My father took me away, relinquishing our good view to two young boys who were happy to have it. "Remember this well, Theresa," he had said. "There is injustice in this world. Never turn your back on it."

He told me, too, that the young emperor believed in justice, and wanted to better the lives of the poor as well as to allow all people to practice the religions they cherished. Today, I was counting on Joseph II's renowned clemency and his lack of tolerance for corruption. Although it was too late for my father, there was still time for Danior, and for Alida and Zoltán—and Haydn, who stood also to lose more than money if he could not fulfill his contract with Artaria. I wondered what he would do or where he would go if he were dismissed from the prince's service, or worse.

I don't know why I looked to my right, along the row of common folk waiting for everything to begin. Maybe it was because I felt someone staring at me. But I lifted my eyes just long enough to see Herr Schnabl seated at the far end of the balcony, and to know that he saw me. I stifled a gasp.

What is he doing here? I thought. *He should be on his way to the Esterhazy palace to rehearse.* I concentrated on staring straight ahead. I would not look at him again, although I could feel the blood washing into my face.

At last a fanfare announced the entrance of the magistrate. He arrived in state, wearing a full-bottomed wig and the insignia of the empress. For small matters, Alida had explained to me, he was the representative of the state, and, except in certain circumstances, had complete discretion to dispense justice as he chose.

The guards quieted the crowd. The first prisoners entered. People squirmed in their seats as the petty criminals were sentenced to floggings and to pay fines, or perform hard labor, or be banished from the empire. Lewd whistles followed the whores in and out of the court. By the sores on their faces and their red eyes, I judged they were sick with syphilis and wouldn't live much longer anyway.

"They always haul in those that are too old to give satisfaction anymore," complained one fellow in a loud voice.

"That's because the guards aren't through using the others yet!" said another, setting off a round of raucous laughter.

The room quieted, though, for the next prisoner. My eyes filmed over when I saw Danior led in at the end of a rope, like a stallion who'd just been broken to the bit. He stood tall, although I could see by the bruises on his bare arms and his face that he'd been beaten. He lifted his chin up and scanned the crowd. The defiance in his eyes made everyone shrink back a little. I leaned forward. I did not want to show my face yet. Danior probably had no idea that he had a friend in the room.

I thought the evidence would go much the same way as it had for the other criminals, where a tired-sounding official read out the charges in a monotone and the magistrate swiftly gave his verdict. But to my surprise, a door on the other side of the magistrate's chair opened and my uncle walked through it, his arm bandaged even more heavily than before and strapped across his chest for added effect. I gasped, my breath trapped in my lungs, afraid to breathe. He stopped several paces away from Danior, who had not flinched, or even flicked his eyes in my uncle's direction.

"Face your accuser, criminal!" snarled Uncle Theobald.

"It'll be death for sure!" whispered a lady behind me.

"I thought the councilor'd been killed," said a man.

"Silence!" roared the major domo, pounding his staff on the floor.

"This man," my uncle continued, "attacked me in my own home, with the purpose of murdering me and robbing my house of its valuables."

The silence was thick enough to slice with a knife.

"What say you to your accuser?" the magistrate asked.

Danior turned slowly until his steady gaze was trained on the councilor's smug face. He worked his mouth as though he were going to speak, but instead, spat at him with such force that a globule of saliva landed on my uncle's bandaged arm.

Immediately the crowd exclaimed and shouted, "Hang him! The blackguard!" The major domo pounded his staff on the floor again, and again yelled "Silence" until everyone quieted.

"As you have nothing to say in your own defense, and no friends to attest for you," the magistrate said, "and your crime is against a councilor of Vienna, I hereby sentence you to be hanged by the neck, then taken down while you are still alive to have your entrails cut from your body and burned before you. After that, your limbs and head are to be separated from your body and dispersed to the four corners of the empire. The execution will take place in St. Stephen's square, tomorrow at dawn."

That was my cue. I stood up suddenly. Although my mouth was completely dry, my voice rang out clear and loud. "I wish to challenge this sentence, and possess evidence to vindicate the accused."

If I thought the uproar was mighty after Danior spat at my uncle, it was nothing to the complete mayhem my pronouncement caused. When I stood, I had pulled back my hood to reveal my face. My uncle looked up at me with shock that soon turned to intense hatred. I knew that so long as both of us were free, I would never be safe. Danior looked up at me, too, with an expression of wonder I shall never forget. I realized only then that he had given up hope and assumed the outcome. His eyes held gratitude, but also fear. *He must be worrying about Alida,* I thought. Now, my actions had both created the possibility for his salvation and assured that all the evil deeds that had previously been hidden from sight would be revealed.

It took quite some time for the court to settle down. I

remained standing, waiting for the instructions that would set the hour when Danior and I would be permitted to go before the empress or her son with our petition.

"The woman who speaks so eloquently in this Gypsy's defense has clearly not studied the law," my uncle said, his eyes hard but his mouth twisting up into a grimace of a smile. "Which is hardly surprising, as she is an ignorant peasant. No appeal is granted when the accuser himself appears in court, if his rank is such to place him above suspicion."

Is this true? I thought. Murmurs rippled through the court. The magistrate himself called for a large book to be brought, and spent agonizing minutes tracing over the lines with his finger. After a time, he closed the volume with a resounding thud. "Apparently, the councilor is correct. The sentence stands as given."

I hardly noticed the room empty around me. I watched Danior be led away, his movement impeded by the chains that linked his ankles together. My uncle walked out with a swagger that made me wish I had the pistol now. How could I return to Alida and tell her what had happened? All our hope was lost. I pulled my hood back over my face, praying that no one would notice me when I left, and that I could lose myself in the crowd before my uncle sent someone after me. I especially tried not to look in the direction of where Schnabl had been sitting, but once I got into the open air and the crowd emptying out of the courtroom began to disperse around me, I felt a hand grasp my arm. Before I thought of jerking away and running off, I turned my head and saw not my uncle or a guard, but old Schnabl. I pulled my arm free of his grasp and continued walking rapidly.

"Wait! Fräulein Schurman!" he called after me.

I turned. He was rushing as much as he could, but he could not move quickly. I felt people staring at me and whispering around me and wanted desperately just to flee, but Schnabl did not look as though he wished to entrap me, only as if he wanted to tell me something urgently. I paused to let him catch up, then continued walking off at a speed he could match, ensuring that a few paces always remained between us. "What is it you want, Herr Schnabl?"

"Only that I need to say something to you, but not here. Please. You must give me a chance. It is about your father!"

At that moment I saw the crowd behind Schnabl scattering to permit four tall imperial guards to slice through them. They were heading directly for me. What if my uncle had sent them? I was in terrible danger if they caught me now. Thank God Toby was safe in the Hofburg. Quickly I threw my hood up and hurried away, doing my best to mix in and lose myself in the crowd, hoping no one else would notice me. Schnabl's voice calling after me to wait disappeared into the general mayhem.

But I had made far too public an appearance to slip away completely quietly. Cries and jeers followed me.

"There she is!"

"Must be his lover!"

"His sister!"

"A noblewoman in disguise!"

"A common whore!"

I hardly knew where I was going. Before long I stopped, winded, and decided I could lose no time in finding Alida again. She would have to be told about Danior and better she hear it from me than by insensitive gossip.

I now knew which door would gain me entrance to the private apartments of the Hofburg. I didn't believe the guards would think to look for me there in their very midst. The serving maids and lackeys had seen me leave earlier, and so did not question my return. I rushed to the sitting room where the maids of honor had taken their ease the day before, but it was empty. "Where is Alida—the Lady Alida?" I asked the same toothless char who had led me through the hidden passages yesterday.

"She's attending the archduchess," she said and punctuated it with a curtsy.

I could not follow Alida to the presence of royalty. That would be too brazen. Yet, if I did not, valuable time would be lost. "Take me to her," I commanded, deciding all at once to risk punishment, and knowing that only the appearance of confidence gave me a chance of success.

"Yes, Madame," the maid said, dusting her hands off on her apron and straightening her cap.

I followed her through many rooms, linked to one another by doors like a chain of opulent jewels. As I went, each room became grander and more ornate, until the maid stopped before a closed door and took a deep breath. She lifted her hand and knocked.

A footman in livery opened the door and let us in. There I saw a woman who was not young, but had been made up and dressed in the latest fashion, half reclining on a sofa. Seated on stools in a semicircle around her were Alida and the two young maids of honor. They were in turn surrounded by several older women, perhaps aristocrats or nobles, who fanned themselves languidly. No one spoke.

On seeing me, Alida stood and curtsied deeply to the archduchess. "I beg your pardon, Madame, but someone has come to see me on a matter of urgency."

The archduchess looked over in my direction. She let her eyes take in my appearance head to toe. "Who is this young person?" she asked.

I curtsied to the ground and stayed there.

"She is my cousin, Madame, newly come from Hungary. I had asked her for news of a matter that is of great importance to my family, and I see that she has brought it."

"What is this news?" the archduchess asked. "You can have no secrets from me."

"Why—I—yes, of course, Your Highness," Alida said.

I immediately realized what a mistake it had been to come into the presence of the archduchess. I would have to think of a way to give Alida the information without telling it all too obviously.

"Is he—safe?" Alida asked.

"I fear not, Cousin," I said, tears threatening to choke my voice. "Tomorrow, at dawn, he will meet his fate."

I had thought Alida the strongest person I'd ever met,

stronger even in her way than Zoltán and Danior. But she crumpled now before me like a leaf fallen from a tree. The archduchess lifted a tiny bell and rang it furiously. The two other maids of honor rushed to Alida, as did I. Soon a maid and a footman entered, and together we laid Alida on a divan. The older of the maids of honor, the one called Liesl, produced a bottle of smelling salts, which she waved under Alida's nose. The archduchess had risen from her seat. She scanned the faces of her visitors, who were all eyeing Alida and me with open curiosity.

"I am fatigued. Pray leave me until this evening," the archduchess said.

The visitors curtsied and left with obvious reluctance just as Alida regained consciousness, thanks to the ministrations of Rebekah and Liesl.

"Now," said the archduchess, "I think you had better explain everything to me. I mean everything."

CHAPTER 27

The archduchess remained standing and listened in silence to the long tale Alida told, starting with the persecution of the Gypsies, continuing through her father's disinheritance, and ending with Councilor Wolkenstein's underhanded attempts to ensure that the Hungarian nobles did not have to comply with the laws now imposed upon the Austrians, whereby the serfs were given their freedom and protected from severe taxation and abuse. She avoided talking directly about the night I had passed in my uncle's cellar, saying only that in the process of trying to rescue young children destined for lives of slavery on a Hungarian estate, Danior had wounded Wolkenstein. I was ashamed of myself for not correcting her, but I said nothing.

When the entire tale had been laid before her, with all my uncle's unscrupulous deeds and bribes detailed, the archduchess walked slowly around the room. "Is this what you wanted me to help you lay before their imperial majesties?" she asked. Alida nodded her response.

"These are heavy accusations," said the archduchess. "Councilor Wolkenstein is a very respected man. And the word of a Gypsy is worth nothing."

I drew my breath in sharply at the archduchess's remark. She turned and fixed me with a stare. I glanced at Alida, who shook her head to discourage me from speaking. But if I said nothing, what would happen to Danior? Still, I held my tongue.

"There is also the matter of General Steinhammer," the archduchess continued. "No matter how just a cause, one cannot go about abducting generals. It is a crime against the state, and punishable by death. He will have to be released before I consent to intervene in this affair."

"But you do consent?" Alida's voice betrayed doubt as well as hope.

"Against my better judgment."

Her Highness's expression did not change at all. Alida merely curtsied to her. No one otherwise moved a muscle, yet if we did not act quickly, Danior would face a horrific death tomorrow. I could not stay silent any longer. "We must do something! Immediately! Danior will die if we do not! He did not shoot my uncle!"

I didn't know which expression made me regret my words more: the shocked and saddened look on Alida's face, or the stern disapproval on the archduchess's.

"I sincerely beg your pardon," I said, blushing to the roots of my hair and curtsying as low as I could without touching my face to the floor. I prayed that I had not ruined everything.

"The child is right."

I lifted my eyes to gaze into the face of the archduchess. I noticed then that the powder she wore could not disguise the fine lines around her mouth. Her eyes were a little watery, and the skin of her neck was slack in the manner of women who have passed their prime. Yet she was beautiful, in her way. She did not look at me unkindly, but turned away as soon as I caught the softness in her eyes.

"Have the general brought before me," the archduchess said. "I would prefer it not to interfere with dinner."

Alida pulled me gently to my feet. "With your permission, Ma'am, I shall send word to my brother. I believe he can have General Steinhammer here in a very short time."

"Mirela can go!" I said.

"And who is Mirela?" the archduchess asked.

"She is my friend," I responded, enjoying the sensation of the word, and realizing how deeply I meant it. I would never have thought that someone whose life was so different from mine, and whom I had met only in recent days, could so thoroughly have worked her way into my heart.

"Your maid, surely you mean," said Liesl.

"No, she is no more a maid than I am a lady. I beg your pardon for deceiving you, but it was necessary."

"Perhaps your young cousin—if she is your cousin, or"—here the archduchess gave half a laugh—"even if she is not—would care for tea?" Her Highness turned to nod to Liesl, who rang the bell. "I give you permission to withdraw, Lady Alida."

I caught just the flip of Alida's skirt before the door had quite closed behind her as she started to run off through the palace rooms.

"Now, *Kindlein*," the archduchess said, indicating that I should sit on the stool nearest her sofa, "I think I had better hear what you have to say about the matter. You assert that the Gypsy did not injure the councilor?"

I tried to take my cue from Alida's manner with her royal employer and soften down everything I told the archduchess. I was a little afraid to reveal all the sordid facts I had discovered in the week or so since my father had died. But the first thing that slipped out was that I was not, in fact, related to Alida and her brother. She didn't flinch at that revelation, having guessed as much already, nor at my explanation of our connection, which meant revealing that I was the daughter of a humble violinist. I did not tell her about my role in abducting the general, deciding that it probably wasn't a suitable story to share with the other maids of honor, who for all their high station and advantages seemed much younger than I was. As it was their eyes practically popped out of their heads by the time I described the scene in front of the magistrate that had passed earlier that day. And I know they were shocked to discover that Mirela was a Gypsy. But there was one fact I had to tell the archduchess.

"In the cellar of my uncle's house, when the guards

were about to seize me and take Toby again, I fired a pistol at the councilor and wounded him. So you see, it is I, not Danior, who should have been on trial." I couldn't look into her eyes. I felt so unbearably wretched.

"No magistrate would have found you guilty of anything but defending yourself, given all the facts," Her Highness said. "I expect your uncle knew that, and also knew that he could falsely accuse a Gypsy and no one would doubt his word."

I'm not sure what I had expected her to say. I had half thought she'd summon the guards immediately and have me conveyed to prison. In my concern over the injustice of the accusation against Danior, I'd completely forgotten that I had fired the pistol to protect myself and my brother, and that it would be very difficult for Uncle Theobald to explain why his niece would have been in a position to have to defend herself in that manner. I sighed deeply. "Of course, you are right, Your Highness."

"Did it never occur to you to let the lady Alida's brother and the other gentlemen pursue their course while you remained by your mother's side as was your duty?" the archduchess asked, but not in an accusing or judging tone, just as someone who was genuinely curious about my actions.

Mother, I thought. I would never tell her all that had transpired that night. If she ever discovered even half of what had happened to Toby and me since we last saw her, I feared for her health and the baby's. "No, I am afraid I thought only of discovering the facts about my father's murder, and helping Alida and Zoltán and my godfather as much as I was able."

"And you nearly got yourself killed in the process!" exclaimed Rebekah, immediately covering her mouth and coloring.

"Lady Rebekah expresses my sentiments, perhaps not exactly as I would, but my sentiments nonetheless," said the archduchess. "I expect your mother would be deeply distressed to hear about everything you have been through."

"I know I should have been more careful, but I could not have done any differently. Mama will soon have a baby, you know, and was powerless to take any action herself, and I was afraid if I just let everything be, I would never know, and Papa's death would not be vindicated." The more I tried to justify my actions, the less justification there seemed to be. So I was very relieved when I heard the sound of several pairs of feet approaching the door.

A moment later the footman opened it to admit Alida, Zoltán, and General Steinhammer. I couldn't help gazing at Zoltán. He was unharmed, and looked more handsome and sure than ever. At first he didn't look at me, but when he did, I saw him smile. I looked down quickly, feeling myself blush. Then I noticed that behind the group of men stood Mirela, no longer wearing her false maid's clothes, but brightly clad in a swirling red skirt with black lace trim, a homespun blouse, and a shawl tied over one shoulder that had been pieced together from small bits of gorgeous silks and velvets. Alida and Mirela curtsied and the men bowed deeply. The general was no longer bound and had on a clean uniform, with all his military decorations polished and in order. I wondered where they could have been keeping him that would have made it possible for him to appear so quickly—and in such a clean state. I suspected that he had been tucked away in some remote corner of the Hofburg itself.

"What have you to say, General?" the archduchess asked.

He opened his mouth to speak before he actually noticed me. I cleared my throat and his eyes flicked in my direction. He paused in confusion before proceeding. "It's not what it appears, Gracious Madame," he said, a nervous smile spreading across his face. The hand he lifted to wipe his brow was trembling. "You see, Councilor Wolkenstein told me she was a lady of the night."

I wasn't sure which of us was more surprised by what he said. We all stared at him in shock.

"I see now that my actions toward this young girl were despicable. I did not know she had the protection of your good self, thinking only that she was the poor orphan of a musician who had decided to advance herself using her only talent—admittedly a considerable one. I humbly beg your pardon for my mistake. But forgive me if I am somewhat relieved! I thought perhaps Your Highness had taken leave of her senses to give even a moment's thought to a band of outlaw Gypsies and serfs who are the rightful property of their noble masters."

I watched for a reaction in the face of the archduchess. She was so practiced in betraying nothing by her demeanor that the general could have been telling her about a tea party. But a vein in her neck began to throb. I judged that she was becoming angry. When she spoke, her voice had a sharp edge to it. "For how long, General, has Councilor Wolkenstein been procuring for you?"

"Well, I, I . . ."

I bit the inside of my cheek. I wanted to exclaim aloud, to leap around for joy. The general, with his assumption that only his actions toward someone acquainted with the archduchess could be of concern to her, had turned her completely against him and made our point quite well.

"And what, pray, have you to say about Councilor Wolkenstein's practice of abducting young boys to serve as forced labor on Hungarian estates?"

"Or the fact that he sends the imperial guards out to attack an innocent camp of Gypsies who have done no one any harm!" The violence of Mirela's outburst startled me.

"I . . . I . . ."

The general had completely lost the power of speech.

The archduchess spoke in the same icy tone she had used throughout the interview. "I think, General, that you had better cooperate with these people or you may find yourself with more than your dignity wounded."

Words started to gush out of the general's mouth. He practically tripped over his own tongue in his haste to distance himself from my uncle's activities. As it became clear that he was willing to betray my uncle to save his own reputation, I stopped listening to what he said and let myself watch Zoltán. He, too, had changed into more respectable clothes. His blond hair was secured at the nape of his neck with a black ribbon. He stood tall and proud—perhaps even a little taller and prouder than usual. He did not look at me again, but his smile when he saw me at first told me more than I dared hope for. I longed to talk to him again about nothing—no, not about nothing; about music. Once this nightmare ended, we would be able to meet at my godfather's house, perhaps. And perhaps I might be allowed to sit among the musicians again, during a rehearsal, and share their music-making. It was not so much to ask.

I let out an involuntary sigh during a lull in the general's groveling confession. Everyone looked at me. "I was thinking of my godfather, and the difficulty with his eyes," I said, trying quickly to come up with some excuse for letting my mind wander so far from the important matters being discussed in that elegant reception room in the Hofburg. "I think the musician Schnabl has been working for my uncle." I told them about seeing the old man in several places, too often for it to be mere coincidence, and about his approach to me after the trial.

"He must have discovered what Kappellmeister Haydn intended to do with the money from the contract with Artaria," Zoltán said. "He has been jealous of Haydn for a long time. He felt he should have been given the position of Kapellmeister. Though I would wager he did not know the full extent of the deeds he had become entangled in."

When everything that Alida and I had revealed was confirmed by the general and Zoltán, the archduchess sat in silence for a short while.

"It is time to dress for dinner," she suddenly said, standing so that everyone else had to stand as well. "I believe that Councilor Wolkenstein must be approached with some caution. If he suspects he is about to be apprehended, he may disappear. It seems that he has powerful allies. I shall speak with my brother this evening. I cannot make any promises. Alida, you should prepare yourself for the worst."

What was she saying? Even after all this, might Danior still die? I looked from Alida to Zoltán and back again. This time I decided I had to heed her warning glance, especially now that the general was in the room.

"General, perhaps you would lead me in to dinner later? Fräulein Schurman and her friend—Mirela, is it?—may remain with you, Lady Liesl and Lady Rebekah. I give you permission, Lady Alida, to pass the evening in whatever manner you wish."

The general and the archduchess departed arm-in-arm like old friends. From thinking that we were close to victory and saving Danior's life, I found myself back in the depths of despair. Had all my efforts been for nothing?

Zoltán and Alida left. I didn't have the heart to say

anything. Mirela and I stayed and ate supper with the young maids of honor. I was too tired to do much more than listen to the stories Mirela told them, and unable to concentrate on the card games they tried to get us to play. I was relieved when the curfew bell rang and we all retired to bed.

CHAPTER 28

Alida caught up with me just before we reached the room where the maids of honor slept. Liesl and Rebekah had been discussing excitedly which of them would share her bed with me and which with Mirela that night, and I was afraid it would turn into an argument. I think we were the most fascinating thing ever to occur in their quiet lives.

"Come with me, Theresa," Alida said, and I thought my new friends' faces would drop through the floor, they were so disappointed.

"No matter," Mirela said, linking her arms through each of theirs. "I shall teach you a Gypsy lullaby, and Theresa already knows it, so she won't miss anything." This cheered them up quickly. I heard their giggles and chattering fade as they continued to their bedroom. I hoped for a moment that Mirela would not feel tempted to wheedle them out of a bit of jewelry, or show them a magic trick involving the convenient disappearance of coins. She had already won a tidy sum at cards, and I suspected she had used some sleight of hand to get it. Her movements were so quick, and her understanding easily leapt beyond everyone else's. Mirela's talents could be used to much better purpose, I was certain, although I couldn't at that moment imagine how. After coming to know her and seeing all that the Gypsies faced, I could easily comprehend what led her to scratch out an existence by use of her wits and guile—doubtless her only possessions and all she had to depend on for her future well-being. I just wished it didn't have to be that way.

Alida led me up to the servants' quarters of the palace. "There's someone who wishes to see you," she whispered.

I said nothing, but I hoped she meant Zoltán.

We went through a door to an attic room, and sitting up in a cot by a window was not Zoltán, but Toby. I ran to him, only for the tiniest instant disappointed.

"Theresa, they've been so nice to me here," he said. "I've had all the hot soup I want, and sweets after every meal."

"I see you're feeling better," I said, ruffling my fingers through his hair, which had been washed and combed and felt as fine as a baby's. He still had some bruising around his eyes, evidence of his harsh treatment at my uncle's hands.

"Toby," Alida said, "do you think you're strong enough to help us if we need you to?"

His eyes flitted back and forth between us. "I'm strong. Why wouldn't I be strong?"

"Would you be able to tell the emperor about your uncle's cellar?"

Toby's eyes clouded over. I thought for a moment he would cry. But he drew in a deep breath and lifted his chin. "Yes. I'm not afraid of my uncle. Not now."

As Alida prepared to leave us, telling me that I could sleep on the other cot, which had been made up with clean linens after Brishen had left that morning, I took her aside.

"What next?" I asked, not daring to ask too directly.

"We won't know until tomorrow."

Tomorrow? That would be too late. Perhaps after all, Danior would have to be sacrificed so that justice could be done.

"I'm rising before dawn," she said, not explaining. No point in distressing Toby.

"Wake me," I said.

Toby and I stayed up for a little while talking about violins and music. He asked about our mother, but I could only tell him that I believed she knew nothing at all of what had happened, and that I hoped she would remain ignorant of the entire episode forever.

⁂

Toby fell asleep quite quickly, but I could not shut my eyes. I wanted to stay awake, to sit a vigil for Danior, who did not deserve to be punished so gruesomely. But try as I might, as soon as I closed my eyes phantom visions danced in front of them. I saw Danior playing the fiddle; then he turned into my father. My uncle smashed a violin apart and birds flew out of it. I was on a boat in the middle of the Danube, and people were running along the banks calling out to me, but the current was too strong and I could not control the boat. The waves rocked me back and forth. I clung to the gunwales for safety.

"Wake up! Theresa! It's me, Alida!"

Alida was rocking me gently by my shoulder, trying to wake me without making any noise. As soon as I realized where I was, I sat up and rubbed the sleep out of my face. I had not undressed, so it was a quick matter to be ready to go. I took the cloak she gave me and followed her through the twisting corridors and out onto the predawn streets of Vienna.

Crowds were already gathering in Stephansplatz. The carpenters had been hard at work overnight constructing the gibbet, a rack, and a wheel. Alida clung to me and I to her. I thought if we had not been able to borrow strength from each other, both of us might have collapsed.

The faces that surrounded us were grim and tired. *What macabre entertainment to begin a day*, I thought.

As the cold air woke people out of their half-sleeping states, conversation began. "Think anyone will get the wheel?" one young boy not much older than Toby asked eagerly. Once he started, speculation about the horrible punishments that awaited the criminals on display that morning enlivened everyone. Would a thief be whipped to the point of flaying? Would a usurious moneylender be able to withstand the pain of thumb screws? I wanted to stop up my ears. The more I heard, the more impossible it was to keep from imagining Danior's dark eyes wracked with unspeakable pain.

I looked up at Alida and saw her gazing out over the heads of the crowd. She appeared neither to listen nor to care about what anyone said. She was still hoping. I knew it. Just as I was.

We heard the ominous beat of the drums before we saw the cart in which the prisoners stood, chained to one another. Several looked broken already. A woman had had her hair torn out of her head, and her scalp was partly scabbed over and partly still bleeding. Others had clearly been beaten or whipped. All were aware enough to be terrified, though, of what awaited them in the square.

The bells in St. Stephen's tolled seven. Dawn came late in midwinter, so it was still necessary for torches to illuminate the scene. Their light cast constantly shifting shadows on the icy ground. The stone buildings that surrounded the square loomed dark and massive against a flat, predawn sky. I gripped Alida's hand as the cart rolled near enough for us to see Danior. His face was set, eyes just dark, blank indentations not looking at anything.

The executioner and his assistants began readying the prisoners. I felt Alida tremble.

All at once confusion arose in the crowd. The attention shifted from the black-hooded executioners' activities to something behind us.

Horses.

A detachment of about two dozen mounted guards cut a path through the people. The executioner didn't stop strapping some poor woman to a rack until they were almost upon him. I wondered if perhaps he was a deaf-mute—convenient for him not to hear the screams of his victims.

The commander of the guards pulled a sealed document out of his saddlebag, opened and unfolded it without hurry, then read aloud to the crowd.

I couldn't understand it. It was in Latin! The executioner rubbed the top of his head. He didn't understand it, either. He pointed to his ears, confirming that he was deaf, shrugged and turned away to continue his work. The guard drew his sword out of its scabbard and poked it in the executioner's back. The crowd laughed. The executioner turned around, mouthing and gesturing that he hadn't any idea what the fellow had said.

I looked to Alida. "Did you understand?"

"Yes." She breathed. "Clemency. By order of the Holy Roman Emperor."

So it was Joseph II, not Maria Theresa, who had listened to their case. "But what if he cannot make the executioner understand?"

One of the guards had dismounted and showed the paper to the deaf fellow, but he only gestured that he could not read. Finally they pointed out the imperial seal, then went to the cart. "Release the prisoner Danior to me." One of the executioner's assistants took Danior by the shoulders. His expression had not changed, perhaps because he did not want to believe in his good fortune.

The crowd by now was laughing uproariously. This magnificent act of imperial power over the life of one individual became ridiculous before our eyes. But I didn't care. Just so long as Danior was safe.

Eventually they succeeded in extracting Danior from the others. His luck subdued the rest of them, who looked even more hopeless and defeated than they had before. I felt so sorry for them. I hoped they had done terrible things to deserve the fate that awaited them. But I suspected they were only caught in the act of trying to survive a cold winter by stealing firewood or selling their bodies.

Alida and I had already started toward Danior, whose chains were being removed one by one by an officer of the guard. When he saw us, his face washed over with joy. Alida ran forward. The guard raised a sword in her way and she stopped abruptly.

"He is granted a temporary stay only, and must now appear before the emperor," said the guard.

They hoisted Danior onto a horse and surrounded him. We followed along behind, all the way into the courtyard of the Hofburg where the guards and Danior dismounted, then through the corridors to a part of the palace I had not yet seen. It was grander and more austere than the archduchess's quarters.

No one stopped us. Alida was known to all. I felt as if I

were watching from a great height as events unfolded down below. The sensation of unreality was complete when we walked into the emperor's audience chamber and saw Zoltán, the general, Toby, the archduchess, the other maids of honor, my godfather—and my uncle.

CHAPTER 29

We had to wait some time before Joseph II entered the room and took his place at a large desk. He was dressed like a simple gentleman, in a black cutaway coat trimmed with deep scarlet and gold, perhaps with more decorations on his sash. He certainly did not look very imperial. Rather than a wig, his face was framed by nicely arranged hair, curled at the sides and drawn into a tail at the back. He left it his natural blond color; it was not powdered. And his profile—that long nose—was familiar to me from the coins that changed hands every day.

The advisers who followed him into the chamber were similarly plainly dressed, consisting of a group of three men and a monk. They stood respectfully behind him when he sat. Before he did or said anything, the emperor read a stack of papers in silence for about a quarter of an hour. When he had finished, he looked up at us, pinched the bridge of his nose with his fingers, then turned his head and nodded to the monk. This fellow whispered in the emperor's ear, causing him to nod every once in a while and look around at all of us, standing there silently, our eyes all boring into the emperor's face.

The monk finished whispering and stood back. The emperor swept his gaze over all of us and rested his eyes on my uncle. "Councilor Wolkenstein," he said, "I understand you have a grievance against the people gathered here. Perhaps you would explain."

My uncle with a grievance! I wanted to rush forward and start talking, give the emperor the real story. I knew Mirela would have done so if she had been there. I was suddenly disappointed that she was not there to lend her spirited voice.

Joseph II leaned his elbows on the table and cocked his head to one side. My uncle approached in what I can only describe as an advancing bow, never quite straightening up, but never actually achieving the position that would indicate the greatest degree of respect. He stopped only when a guard stepped forward and put his arm out in front of him to block his way.

"I was set upon and severely wounded, Your Imperial Majesty," my uncle said, "by that disgusting Gypsy!" He gestured toward Danior.

"Yes, I see your arm is bandaged. And where did this attack occur?"

My uncle straightened up and puffed out his large, paunchy body. "Under my own roof."

"Do you care to explain how this Gypsy managed to enter your home while—I see by these documents before me—you were giving a party?"

"He insinuated himself into the orchestra."

"He *insinuated* himself?"

I saw Zoltán press his lips together to stifle a laugh. It sounded as if the emperor was toying with my uncle—and enjoying himself. Could it be that this was a ploy to make him incriminate himself before we even presented our evidence?

"Maestro Haydn." Joseph II turned toward my godfather. "Perhaps you could shed some light on how a criminal managed to *insinuate* himself into your orchestra, so kindly lent by the esteemed Prince Nicholas Esterhazy for the occasion."

The Kapellmeister walked forward and bowed with natural grace when he reached the distance at which my uncle stood. I thought he looked more imperial than the emperor, in his blue-and-gold uniform. "Your Majesty, this fellow"—he indicated Danior—"is one of the finest violinists in Vienna. He plays with the prince's orchestra regularly. I can vouch for his character." *It was only a slight exaggeration,* I thought.

My uncle opened his mouth to speak. The emperor raised his hand to silence him. "You defend a common Gypsy?"

At that moment, Zoltán came forward, not waiting to be summoned. In his hands was Danior's violin. "With your permission," he said, "perhaps the accused will prove his ability?"

"I protest!" shouted my uncle. "What has music to do with any of this!"

My uncle's outburst brought a stiffening of the emperor's pose. "Well, if he is to die, I would like to hear him first."

The emperor was known to appreciate music, even play the cello himself. In recent years he had been promoting German over Italian opera in the Burgtheater, my father had told me. I had no idea how he felt about Gypsy music.

The guards let go of Danior. He strode forward proudly, bowed with precision, then took the violin and bow Zoltán presented to him. He brushed the strings with his fingertips and adjusted the tuning, then lifted the instrument to his shoulder and brought the bow down in a quadruple stop that resounded through the room, filling it with a thrilling sound.

I gasped. What had happened to the papers? When I had tried the violin, it would not make a noise worth hearing. And the papers were wedged up so high I didn't think anything would get them out. Yet here was Danior, executing some brilliant, fiery passages. He stopped abruptly in the middle of a phrase, his bow held high. "Your Majesty," he said. "This is not my violin."

To my surprise, he turned to look at me. His eyes were full of pride and sadness. I thought I saw the hint of a smile on his face, somehow glowing through the dirt and scrapes. He nodded to Zoltán, who signaled to a guard. The guard pressed a hidden spring to open a door in the paneling, just like the ones that were apparently to be found in all the grand rooms of the palace. Another guard came in, leading Herr Schnabl. Mirela followed him, carrying a wooden violin case. It was a plain one, made of birch and highly polished, with a brass handle on the top. With a leap of my heart, I knew right away that the case was my father's.

Herr Schnabl looked at me with deep shame in his eyes. Mirela smiled.

"This instrument belongs to the late father of that young lady over there," Danior said to the emperor.

Then boldly, with a quick gesture that was half bow, half curtsy, Mirela stepped forward to address the emperor. "I found it in Herr Schnabl's quarters."

Herr Schnabl with my father's violin? He was a cellist!

"It seems," Zoltán continued, "that professional jealousy was another of the weaknesses Councilor Wolkenstein found it easy to use to his advantage. Herr Schnabl sabotaged Haydn's contract with Artaria as instructed by Councilor Wolkenstein and spied on Antonius Schurman, whom the councilor suspected was engaging in activities that would undermine his plans. It was Schnabl who led Herr Schurman to the councilor's house the night of his murder. Herr Schnabl had been told to give Herr Schurman false information about boys locked in the cellar—perhaps not realizing that the information was, in fact, true. The trap was easily laid, and Herr Schurman did not stand a chance against the men hidden in the cellar. They murdered him and took his body to the Gypsy camp through the sewers in a small boat."

Zoltán turned to me. "We believe the boat you took, Rezia, was the same one used to take your father's body away from the house in the Graben. Without this, of course."

He gestured toward Danior, who held the violin out to me. I was hardly capable of thinking. I looked at the emperor. He nodded to me to approach. I just barely remembered to curtsy first before I took the violin. It was truly my father's Amati. I could see that, now that I held it. I could see the nuances in the grain of the wood. I had not laid eyes on that instrument since before my father's death. I felt as if in stroking my fingers over its perfect form I touched him, as if I could feel his warm arms again. I struggled against tears. I wasn't willing to believe that Schnabl could have done all that they said he did, for any reason at all. I forced myself to look at him. There were tears in his eyes.

"You must believe me, Theresa, that I did not know your father would come to any harm. I was supposed to bring the violin to the councilor, but when I heard of Antonius's death, I pretended that I had not found it." Schnabl spoke barely above a whisper, but the atmosphere in the chamber was so tense and quiet, everyone could hear him.

I didn't know what to think, and so I said nothing. Mirela brought the case over to me and stayed close by. She grasped my hand. I squeezed hers in return.

"This, Your Imperial Majesty, is the violin that belongs to the Gypsy," said Haydn, who produced from behind a chair the velvet-wrapped package Mirela and I had taken such risks to bring to Alida.

We all watched in expectant silence as Danior unwrapped the package. He peered into the F holes. "Yes, this is it," he said. But instead of starting to play again, he lifted the instrument up high and brought it crashing down to the floor. It splintered into hundreds of pieces. I cried out involuntarily.

There, amid the remains of the loveliest violin I had ever seen or heard, next to the one I now cradled in my arms, were the tattered documents for which my father had sacrificed his life.

I glanced at my uncle, who had already started backing away. He was stopped by a guard. The monk, who had remained standing just behind the emperor through all of this, came forward and collected the papers from the floor, laying them respectfully on the desk before Joseph II.

I watched as the emperor's face expressed shock.

Haydn cleared his throat. "There is more, Your Imperial Majesty. Theresa, open your father's fiddle case."

I exchanged the Amati for the case Mirela held and did as Haydn asked. There, tucked into the velvet that lined the wooden box, I found another sheaf of papers. I took them out. A quick glance revealed General Steinhammer's name and my uncle's.

My knees felt weak as I walked forward with the papers and gave them to the monk, who had stepped out again to receive them.

"In addition to these documents, Fräulein Schurman possesses the final proof that all of these items are genuine, and that I am who I claim to be," Zoltán said.

He approached me and reached his hand out to touch my neck. A shiver went through me as he gently took hold of the gold chain, pulled the medallion out from its hiding place inside my bodice, and lifted it over my head. With even steps, he approached the emperor and placed the gold medallion on the table. "It is decorated with our family's crest and was worn by the Hungarian general who defended the serfs from their oppressors over a hundred years ago."

The emperor gazed at all the evidence now spread out on the table before him. I think I was holding my breath. He placed his hands on the scattered papers and pushed himself up to a standing position before lifting his chin and fixing my uncle with a hard, angry stare. "Theobald Wolkenstein, you do not deserve the honor of holding the office of councilor of Vienna." He shifted his gaze to the guards. "Take him away."

The terror on my uncle's face almost made me feel sorry for him. I was afraid that he would start to scream and protest unbecomingly, but the door shut him out before he had recovered his wits enough to utter a sound.

"And this fellow should be brought before the magistrate at the earliest opportunity." He indicated Schnabl.

Haydn and I looked at each other. I think we both had the same idea at once. "Your Majesty," I said, curtsying and trying not to let my voice shake. "Herr Schnabl is elderly, and a fine musician. It is clear that he did not know precisely what evils he had become a party to. Although my father was murdered in part because of Herr Schnabl's treachery, I believe Herr Schnabl did not know that would be the outcome. I have my father's violin in my possession once again. Could the cellist not be allowed to return to the prince's service?"

The emperor stared into my eyes. I had never seen an expression that gave away less, even when it was so completely focused on me. I kept my gaze steady. I wanted him to know I was in earnest. If I thought about it the next day, I might want Herr Schnabl punished severely, but right now I was so relieved that things had turned out as they did that I felt I could be forgiving.

"What say you, Kapellmeister Haydn?" the emperor asked my godfather.

"I'd say the injury to this young lady is greater than any I have suffered at Schnabl's hands. And I could ill afford to lose one of my best cellists at this time of year."

"Very well. Deliver the man back to his abode. But he is warned never to involve himself in such plots again, or I will not listen to any entreaties on his behalf."

He turned his attention again to the guards, who had

laid hold of Danior after he finished his brief performance. "Please release the other prisoner."

The guard let go of Danior and stepped away, and Alida, against all protocol, ran forward and covered the Gypsy's dirty, bruised face with kisses. The emperor rose and left quietly. Those of us who noticed him go curtsied and bowed.

CHAPTER 30

I held onto Toby with one hand and the case that protected my father's violin with the other. We walked toward our home like two ordinary people who had nothing to fear. Shopkeepers and peasants went about their affairs and took no notice of us. The baker even waved and smiled, as if we had not just spent the last few days in a state of constant terror and confusion.

I was in a happy glow on one hand, and overwhelmed by a feeling of bittersweet sadness on the other. It seemed that one of my uncle's spies—we would probably never know which, but it had certainly not been Schnabl—had been sent to find my father in the cellar and caught him trying to free the prisoners. Papa was unarmed and did not have Gypsy comrades in the corners to leap out and come to his aid. It tore at my heart to think that the last thing he saw in his life was that horrible place. I hoped the guards reached my uncle's house in time to free the ones I had seen the other night. As to the rest, Alida had said they would do whatever they could to restore them to their families, but it would be very difficult to find them all.

Earlier, while we were still all gathered at the Hofburg, Schnabl had also confessed to changing several clauses in Haydn's contract with Artaria that would make it impossible for him to fulfill it. Word had been sent directly from the emperor himself to Artaria to explain the confusion, and to request that adequate time be given for Haydn to complete his work. And my godfather also agreed to see a doctor about his eyes.

All the Gypsies who had been rounded up with Danior were released, and given official leave by the emperor to establish a settlement on the banks of the Danube, never to be harassed by the guards to leave it. The archduchess offered Mirela a position as lady's maid in the Hofburg, but she refused. "I cannot stand the idea of stone walls around me all the time. I was born to be among my people. Besides," she said to me when I scolded her for not taking this wonderful opportunity to better herself, "as a Gypsy, I serve no one. We can be equals, and remain friends."

I tried to understand. I realized that someone who could do as Mirela had apparently done, followed Schnabl home and broken soundlessly into his house to take away my father's violin, would find it difficult to lead a sedate life as a lady's maid in a very proper imperial court. Still, it seemed a little foolhardy to me. Perhaps no less foolhardy, though, than my wanting to become a better musician rather than letting my mother arrange a suitable match for me.

But there were other revelations. In the hour after my uncle's humiliating exposure, while we were at Zoltán's apartment still rejoicing over Danior's deliverance from death, the archduchess sent word dismissing Alida from her service. She made her a very lovely present, and it was clear she regretted the necessity, but she also knew that Alida would not be permitted to marry Danior if she were a maid of honor at court.

This, though, was accompanied by news that their family's lands had been restored—yet their domain was far off in Hungary, and Zoltán would have to journey there immediately to start seeing what could be salvaged of the farmlands and if any of the ancient buildings upon them still stood. He was now Zoltán, Baron of Varga.

Everyone had turned away and pretended to be busy talking to each other when he came to thank me for my part in aiding their cause.

"Your father would have been proud of you," he said, and then kissed me on both cheeks. The kisses were not like the quick pecks he had given me in the past. I could feel the soft imprint of his lips, and they conveyed more than respect. Zoltán's kisses made me blush, and sent a tingling sensation down into my legs. He then raised my hand to his lips, taking time to squeeze it and stroke it a little before letting it go. I wanted to bury my face in the folds of his coat, to feel the grip of his arms, just as I felt them when he was showing me how to fire the pistol. His eyes burned into mine. I felt like crying, and I thought perhaps he did, too. But everyone was there, noticing us, even if they were looking in the other direction.

When he let go of my hand, I discovered that he had placed the gold medallion and chain in it. "But it's yours!" I whispered.

"Keep it, in honor of all your father—and you—have done for our family."

I could no longer see for the tears that had filmed across my eyes.

"Will you come and play with us at Esterhaza during the summer?" Haydn asked Zoltán when he turned to give his general farewell to the rest of those present.

"Of course I shall try, and I will return to Vienna as well. I am certain to have business here."

He said it for my ears, I knew.

"And Theresa," Haydn continued, "I still need your help with the music. Will you come to me tomorrow? I have spoken to Prince Nicholas, and he has agreed to make your father's stipend over to you, as court copyist, and completely forgiven me for my innocent falsehood before. If your family can spare you, I would like to take you to Esterhaza after Easter. You might also perform—in private, you understand—as a violinist in the last desk of the orchestra on occasion."

I was free to run to my godfather and give him the embrace he deserved for his kindness. Somehow, things had turned out almost as I'd hoped they would, with the exception that nothing would ever restore my father to me.

I had no right to be unhappy anymore. But even after we left Zoltán's apartment, that lump in my throat refused to go away, and I could not answer Toby's constant, chattering questions.

When we arrived at our apartment, I expected to go running in to greet my mother, having prepared a tale that would not upset her too much and would keep her in ignorance of the extent of her own brother's corruption. I would not tell her about Toby's ordeal, how close he had come to being one of the hundreds of boys who had been kidnapped. I would not tell her that it was my uncle's spies—including the poor, pathetic Schnabl—who had discovered the role our father was playing in exposing the abuses of the nobles and seeking to rein in those who persecuted and tormented the Gypsies.

I would tell her that my uncle had been sent off to represent the emperor abroad. I would spare her the truth, which was that he had been banished, sent off to the New World without so much as a servant, and with only a small amount of money and valuables. I did not feel sorry for him. It was nothing compared with the fate that Danior might have suffered, but Councilor Wolkenstein would never be brought to suffer such a cruel death in front of the people. He was neither poor, nor a Gypsy. At least all the wealth he had amassed by preying on the weaknesses of powerful men would be given to help restore the boys to their Austrian families, and to make amends for the losses so many had suffered.

I had practiced exactly what I would say to my mother

to make the whole affair palatable to her. But the sight of the apothecary's curricle at the door caught my heart in my throat. Mother was ill again! I let go of Toby's hand and raced up the two flights of stairs, burst into the parlor, and was assailed by my mother's screams of agony.

Frau Morgen, the apothecary's wife and the woman who had helped me prepare my father's body, sat by the fire, knitting. She looked up, her expression remarkably calm. "There you are at last, Theresa! It's about time you came back from your life of luxury at your uncle's. Your mother has been calling for you."

I laid Papa's violin on the table and started toward my mother's chamber, reaching for the door handle.

"Don't go in just now. You'll have to wait."

Before I could fling a biting response at Frau Morgen for imagining that I would not run to be at my mother's side if she were ill, the screams stopped. Then I heard another sound, a baby's raspy cry.

All at once I understood. It was our new brother—or sister. I ran to Frau Morgen and kissed her on the cheek. Toby stood in the middle of the room, confused. I was too happy to speak. I hugged myself, waiting for the signal that I could go in and see them both.

A few moments later, the apothecary and the midwife emerged. "Ah, the children. You may enter now."

Frau Morgen gathered her things and left with her husband. Toby and I went in. Our mother was propped up against her pillows, a bundle clutched in her arms, looking very pale, but well. Greta stood by with pride and love in her eyes. I wanted to embrace her, too, for being so loyal to Mama.

"Come, meet your sister, Anna," Mama said, smiling.

My sister, I thought. A sister.

Even though I realized baby Anna's arrival might prevent me from journeying to Esterhaza for that summer, and that her little mouth would soon gobble up a generous share of the modest income we had been granted through Haydn's good graces, I loved her the instant I saw her magically tiny fingers. Would she learn to play the violin? I could teach her!

And now I knew I did not have to marry right away. Mama would not want me to, now. She would need my help. And I could rely on my own wits and talent to survive. There was so much I could do.

My new life would start the very next day, when Toby would begin his apprenticeship as a luthier. I would take him to Herr Goldschmidt myself. His room would become the baby's when she was old enough.

And I—I would practice on my father's violin, absorbing his talent through the instrument he had held against his shoulder for all those years. I would prove my mother wrong about what girls should be able to do. At the very least, I knew that I would give lessons myself when I was able, and even perform whenever it was allowed.

So much has happened since then. As Alida promised, I have met Mozart and heard his incomparable music. Mirela and I have remained close, and have had more adventures together. I have become acquainted with the Weber sisters, and am now very friendly with Signore Salieri, too—but all that is part of another story. Suffice it to say, I think my father is smiling down upon me, knowing that my uncle has been punished for his crimes and that I have kept faith with everything he held dear: justice, fairness—and most of all, music.

AUTHOR'S NOTE

Historical novelists are always asked, "What's real and what's invented in your novel?" Some historical novels are fictionalized history, where the purpose is to bring to life an actual time or event as closely as possible to what is known to have happened.

The Musician's Daughter is not one of these books. Most of the characters—with the exception of Haydn, his wife, the emperor and empress, the princess, and other famous names mentioned in the course of the drama—are fictional. Theresa is what I imagine a talented young daughter of one of Haydn's musicians might have been like. There were indeed Gypsies and plenty of Hungarians in Vienna, but Zoltán and his sister are also fictional, as is the entire cast of Gypsies.

Having said that, the issues they all faced were real. In 1779, when we meet Theresa, the revolution in America had made the ruling families of Europe very nervous. Although the French revolution and its Reign of Terror was still some way off, many courts were seeking ways either to accommodate the demands of common people or to crack down on them. For instance: the slavelike treatment of the Hungarian serfs, the mistreatment and suspicion of the Gypsy population, the general inability for girls to fulfill any of their dreams unless they involved marriage and children.

And torture was still used, along with hideous public executions, as an example to keep the populace in check.

Haydn's words and actions in this novel are also fictional, although his setting and circumstances are not. He had been fortunate as a child, yet his childhood was bleak. He was sent away at the age of six to study music in his uncle's household, where he was mistreated and often hungry. He sang in the church choir and was talent-spotted by the music director of St. Stephen's Cathedral in Vienna. He was accepted, and moved to the glittering capital.

But even talent didn't save Haydn from difficulties. When his voice broke, he was tossed out on the streets to make his own way, ending up being taken in by a friend and freelancing in musical gigs and as a teacher.

Rather than making him bitter, though, it seems his struggles gave him a lot of sympathy for the musicians he later hired when he landed the position with Prince Esterhazy. He was also a practical jokester, and became a friend and confidant to many of his musicians, standing as godfather to their children. His nickname of Papa Haydn seems to have been well deserved, and I felt he was the perfect figure of authority and kindness for Theresa's difficult days.

As for Theresa herself: although she is entirely my creation, I am extremely fond of her. My life was nothing like hers (thank heavens), yet I know what it's like to want to disappear into music and hide yourself away from difficult truths. I started piano lessons when I was five and could read music fluently before I could read words. Something about the feeling of the keys under my fingers and the beautiful sounds made me feel safe and let me dream far beyond the suburban life I led with my three brothers and my parents.

My parents were very supportive of my musical ambitions, and they went out of their way to make sure I had access to the best musical training, for which I will always be grateful. Our lives were not difficult like Theresa's life, yet growing up in the fifties and sixties was tough, just as growing up in the twenty-first century is, but perhaps in a different way. All I know is that the combination of music and reading is what got me through youth and adolescence.

I pursued music in college and graduate school, eventually giving up on having a career as a performer to concentrate on music history. I was fascinated by the stories—the ones that were told and the ones that remained untold, most often to do with women and girls. When I turned to writing fiction, it was only natural that I would find my inspiration in the music and music history that has permeated my own life.

Although I have never been a violinist, I have picked up a violin from time to time and tried to play. I am privileged to know some superb artists: among them the amazing Peter Oundjian, former first violinist in the Tokyo string quartet, and Elizabeth Wallfisch, one of my dearest friends and perhaps the foremost Baroque violinist today. I listened to them both play in intimate surroundings, and lived through many of Libby's struggles with injuries and eventually her triumph in the musical world.

My Theresa is a combination of myself at her age, Libby's deep devotion to the violin, and my imagination.

Suggested listening

Haydn, The London Symphonies, Volumes 1 & 2; Colin Davis conducting the Royal Concertgebouw Orchestra (Philips)

Haydn, String Quartets Op. 76; the Kodaly Quartet (Naxos)

ACKNOWLEDGMENTS

Many thanks to my writer friends who read all or part of this book in manuscript, including Victoria Zackheim, Susan Willbanks, Susan O'Doherty, and Chloe Reynolds.

Extra special thanks to my two young readers, Ben Donnenberg and Daylon Orr, who were really helpful.

And the sisterhood of historical fiction authors who are so supportive and stimulating—what would I do without you? Especially Stephanie Cowell, Sandra Gulland, Barbara Quick, and Rita Charbonnier.

Thanks again to my indefatigable agent, Adam Chromy, and to Melanie Cecka and everyone at Bloomsbury Children's who helped make this book happen.

Not to forget my ever-inspiring family, whose encouragement keeps me going: Cassie, Chloe, and Charles. Mwah!